Fateful Days

Kate Vale

Published by North Cascades Press

Copyright 2019 - Kathleen Auerbach

All rights reserved

ISBN: 978-1-7321082-4-0

Cover Artist: LLPix Designs

Discover other titles by the author at: http://katevale.com

Other Titles by Kate Vale

Single Titles
Where This Goes
Gillian's Do-Over
Package Deal
Dream Chaser

On Geneva Shores
Safe Beside You
Choices
Just Friends
Granddad's House
Crossing Paths
Family Bonds

Cedar Island Tales
Secrets Revealed
Her Daughter's Father
Heartstrings
Concealed Attractions

The Lamberts of Pacific Knoll
Friends Forever
Only You
Chance Encounter

Short Stories
The Christmas Car

PUBLISHED BY PROMONTORY PRESS
Destiny's Second Chance

Dear Reader:

Every married couple experiences complications during their family life. Some derive from situations occurring at work: his or hers, maybe even both! Other complications are part of the parenting experience, whether they occur during a pregnancy, during the birth process, or after the child is born.

Eden has been a happy stay-at-home mom since the birth of her son, Kenyon. But now that little Ivory enters all-day kindergarten, she is eager to share the breadwinning duties with her husband, Hale. But finding a job that will mesh easily with her parenting duties isn't so easy, as she quickly discovers.

Then there's the unexpected complication of a third pregnancy. And to make matters worse, Hale's position at the Lambert-Knoll College finance office is threatened when scholarship monies disappear and he is thought to be the culprit.

These issues coalesce to threaten Eden's sense of security, particularly when she learns that her new baby may have an inherited and potentially fatal disease.

Hale is a glass-half-full person; Eden tends toward glass-half-empty thinking. I was fascinated when she and Hale reveal how they deal with the issues that plague them, as a married couple, as well as individually. As I watched them tackle the difficulties challenging them, I came to understand that the power of the marriage bond depends as much on their less visible strengths as on a couple's more obvious love of family and each other.

I hope you agree that the Brinker family is built on a foundation likely to see them through any future challenges they may face.

Special thanks go to Doctor John Raduege and Nurse Jeanne Brotherton as well as the people who shared their stories of health challenges, and those IT experts—who insisted on remaining anonymous.

I love to hear from readers and I hope you decide to follow these characters as their story continues through this series.
Enjoy!

One

Eden Brinker turned away from the kitchen table where her youngest sister, Elaine, was demolishing a dish of ice cream, to peek out the living room window. Her two children were on the swings, chattering happily. A nice change from their arguments during breakfast.

Only a week before the kids start school. Not just Kenny this year. Ivory, too.

Kenyon was dark-haired like his uncles, his green eyes as mesmerizing as his father's. Eden's son was looking forward to second grade. He'd already loaded his backpack with the supplies they'd purchased. Eden had hoped his casual enthusiasm would rub off on his sister, but Ivory's mood about school was mixed. Going to kindergarten wasn't something Eden's daughter was all that keen about.

Some days she declared she was a big girl now because she was going to school just like her brother. In the next breath she plaintively stated that Mommy should come, too, so she wouldn't be alone. At five years and two months, Ivory— called Ivy within the family—was constantly in motion. Eden recalled how shyly her daughter had approached life until sometime after she turned four. Last year, Ivory seemed to come into her own, no longer content to tag after her big brother. Instead, she'd started talking back to him, as well as the adults in her life.

Hale had taken in stride—proudly, in fact—Ivory's transformation into a miniature of Wonder Woman. He encouraged her, after telling Eden she ought to be proud that they were raising a daughter who would never become a pushover. Iona Lambert, Ivory's grandmother, didn't agree. She held decidedly old-school views of how a woman should act, what being a woman meant.

"I think Ivy pays close attention to Aretha when you put her albums in the tape deck, hon," Hale had said with a chuckle. "Ivory's going to be our 'natural woman,' insisting on inspiring R- E-S-P-E-C-T from everyone she meets."

Eden sighed. *Hale.* Her husband. *What's he going to say if...*

She glanced out the window again at an argument that seemed to have developed between her children. *The tree house? Again.* Eden sighed. Kenny was in the tree house his father and Uncle Chris had built. Ivy was determined to climb the ladder after him, in spite of Kenny's shouted declaration that girls weren't allowed. Eden watched as Ivy shouted back at her brother from her perch on the third step from the ground. Would she continue climbing, or give up, as she had the other day, and stomp into the house, complaining to her mother about mean boys, mean brothers?

Eden moved toward the door to interrupt, then hesitated. Hale had suggested, more than once, that she allow the kids work out their differences, that each would be stronger for it. More empathetic, too, he'd said, claiming Ivory needed that lesson more than Kenny. *Hale's probably right.*

Her gaze shifted to the calendar on the wall next to the back door. The children's first school day would be a first for her, too. She would come back from dropping them off, to a house empty of the sounds of her little girl as she rearranged the furniture in the doll house her father had made, or begged to watch a DVD, probably picking one where she knew all the words and music and happily sang along.

"Are you going to keep staring out the window at your kids or come back and listen to me? Better yet, if you're not going to finish your ice cream, can I have it?"

Eden glanced over her shoulder at Elaine, who'd come over to diss her ex-fiancé.

"You can have it." Deciding to let the kids work out their differences without her input, she returned to her seat at the kitchen table and pushed her ice cream dish closer to Elaine.

Elaine pulled the dish into range of her spoon and scooped up some of the chocolate mint ice cream. "Are you still worried about Ivy managing to stay awake without an after-lunch nap now that she's starting kindergarten?"

"No. I'm sure she'll do just fine." Eden took in her sister's work wardrobe, a pale pink blouse setting off a burgundy jacket and matching pencil skirt. "You know I've been looking forward to Ivory starting school."

"Then why don't you *sound* happy? Or is it that you have yet to get serious about looking for a job? Like you've been threatening for months? Do you want something part-time or full-time?" Elaine's brows rose with each question. "Or does Hale not want you to go back to work? Is that it?"

Hale. Her husband hadn't exactly discouraged her, but his enthusiasm for her job search had seemed less fulsome than Eden preferred. She recalled him running his long fingers through his sandy brown hair, leaving it sexily rumpled when he'd said she didn't *have* to go back to work if she'd changed her mind. All because she'd complained that finding the right job was more difficult than she'd expected.

"You know Hale isn't standing in my way. But I thought it would be easier to find the right one."

"Why don't you just go back to the college where you worked before? I'm sure Dad would put in a good word for you. Hale, too."

Elaine waved off Eden's stuttering objection.

"Okay, okay. So you don't want to go the nepotism route. But you have a history there, even if the only people who knew you back when are Hale's boss and the secretary. Arlene what's-her-name, right?"

"Helen. I doubt I'd like Mr. Randolph any more now than before, especially after he was promoted into the top job. If you ask me, Hale should have been given that position." Eden shook her head. "Going back to the finance office is one job I don't want. Besides, my previous position isn't available. Hale said the person who took my place left almost eighteen months ago when they reorganized the office. What I used to do is being handled in that new IT office. I've decided I need to think more broadly, consider positions that use my skills for other than straight finance work." She gazed at Elaine as she ate the last scoop of ice cream from Eden's bowl.

"You know it's been seven years since I set foot in an office. Hale's always talking about how much the work of the finance office has changed since he introduced all those new computer programs. He enjoys having the latest and greatest, newest gizmos and gadgets, the best possible programs to streamline the work. Besides, he's had his hands full lately trying to convince Andy to let him incorporate more security measures. If I worked there, all I'd hear from morning till night is how difficult Andy is. Get enough of that when Hale comes home these days. I'd rather find a job somewhere else, one where everyone's happy, or at least the problems are different." She nibbled on the last of the cookies she'd arranged on a plate to go with the ice cream. "Besides, I'm not sure I could jump right into another finance job like what I was doing before Kenny was born." She wiped her mouth, certain her lips showed evidence of the crumbly cookie.

Elaine nodded. "Maybe you're right. I'm sure you'll find something. With all Hale's contacts around town, not just on campus, he ought to know the offices that are hiring. Even though he's been supportive of you staying at home."

"I haven't asked for his help, Ellie. That would just be another form of nepotism, if you ask me." Eden shook her head. "I need to find a job myself." Eden pursed her lips, recalling her last conversation-qua-argument with Hale. "He doesn't care if I work part-time or full-time. In fact, his only suggestion the last time we talked was that maybe I should start with something I can do at home. Sort of like dipping my toe in the water instead of just jumping in the deep end with something full-time. But I miss not talking to adults all day. Or at least being around them. I'm not sure working at home would feel the same as actually getting dressed and going to an office, even if it's only for half a day."

"You're probably right." Elaine stood up, reached for the ice cream dishes and placed them in the sink.

As if to emphasize how much she'd been thinking about the job she had yet to land, Eden added, "Working in my pajamas isn't what I want—or even wearing a pair of jeans and my favorite sweatshirt. Why shouldn't I work with adults all day like he does, or you and Deb? I've been wondering about my vocabulary. I keep thinking I talk more like the preschoolers Ivy hangs out with than like adults."

Elaine shrugged, then grimaced. "As long as you practice adult talk with Hale, which I'm guessing you do, what does that matter? Or is something going on between you two? Is that why you've been so down in the dumps? I thought you'd be turning cartwheels now that you can go back to being a grown-up in an office."

Eden chose not the mention the subject of their latest spousal argument. "Do Fletch and Lexi still have date nights like when they first moved here? They used to drop Chance over when they went out, but they haven't asked to do that this summer."

Elaine shrugged. "Probably because they've asked me to watch him. Ever since Norm dumped me." She grimaced, then giggled. "That weekend you guys went camping, Lexi asked Chris and Teddy to watch Chance. Turns out Chris helped put together Chance's new train set and Teddy said it was like sitting with two kids, one age seven and the other one old enough to know better. Still can't believe Teddy finally tamed Chris. Wanna make a bet about when those two get married?"

Eden relaxed at the change of topic. "Good idea. I'll write down your guess and check in with Deb and Lexi, too. Whoever's guess is closest takes the rest of us out to dinner."

"We should invite Teddy to join us. Make it a sisters'-only party. So we can help her plan the ceremony."

"And make sure she understands that we'll protect her from whatever Mom might want her to do."

Elaine nodded. "Put me down for the last Saturday in November. Something tells me they'll pick a date when the construction business isn't all that busy."

Eden jotted down Elaine's selection along with her own, for mid-December, and shoved the papers into a jar, which she topped with a lid and placed on the middle shelf in the pantry.

Elaine wiped her hands on a towel and claimed the seat next to Eden. "Getting back to you and Hale. Are you guys having issues?"

"No, but we barely have time to talk these days. I can't even remember when we've had a date night. Just the two of us." She grinned ruefully at her sister. "I guess taking the kids to their favorite fast food place doesn't count, does it?"

"But weren't you the one who told Deb and Lexi how important it is, especially after babies?" Elaine smirked. "Speaking of, I think Deb and Todd are practicing to make little Miss or Mister Perfect these days, if you get my drift." Her cheeks pinked up.

"Their business, not ours, sis," Eden berated mildly.

"You're right. None of my business." Elaine reached for her purse. "Maybe you and Hale should reinstitute date nights now that both kids will be in school. If you need a sitter, call me. My nights are free. Or you could call Chris and Teddy. Give them practice with two kids instead of just one."

Eden snorted. "Kenny would love that. He thinks Chris hung the moon, ever since he helped Hale with the tree house. Which reminds me." She went to the window and saw that the children were both back on the swing set. Hale was right. Again. Kenny and Ivory must have resolved their previous argument about the tree house. Maybe girls were no longer banned.

Eden grinned at Elaine. "You feel better now that you've buried No-Good Norm with all that ice cream?" She huffed. "To think he wasted more than three years of your life."

Elaine nodded. "So much for long engagements being a good thing. Why did I ever think that?"

"It wasn't you, sis. Mom was the one who said it and you were too much in love to consider the consequences."

"Right."

Eden hugged her sister. "Deb and I have decided we need to find you a nice guy. Too bad Fletcher doesn't have a new associate at his firm. Like Todd. Maybe Teddy could help. I'll ask her if any of those buff and suntanned construction guys are single."

Elaine frowned. "No, don't. You know I've sworn off men. Totally."

"Seriously?" Eden smirked. "Doesn't sound like Miss Social Butterfly Lambert to me."

"Well, at least until I don't end up in tears again for being so stupid." Elaine's chin quivered ever so slightly.

"What about at the mall? Aren't there any new store managers—single ones—you'd consider?" Eden asked. "It's been ages since I've cruised the stores. About the only places I visit these days are the children's clothing and shoe stores, and the food court. And it's always a zoo. Too noisy, too crowded."

Elaine shook her head. "We're getting two new vendors, but not until closer to Halloween. And I only rarely handle that part of the business." She glanced around the room. "With all the new kiosks we're making room for during the holidays, in between the holidays, even *after* the holidays, I've got too much on my plate right now to worry about meeting a guy, going out on a date. I'm going to play spinster for a while. At least ten years." She paused and grimaced. "Or maybe five."

At Eden's groan, Elaine laughed.

"Too long? Okay. Then how about if I hold off until after the New Year? No men for me until at least January. I'll be your favorite always-available babysitter until after Chris and Teddy get married."

Eden turned on the dishwasher. "Offer accepted. You should have seen Ivy when she met her new teacher last week. Mr. Wyecliff has to be the tallest teacher for the younger grades, maybe even the whole school. She kept saying how much taller he was than Hale. Even asked him if he could touch the ceiling."

She walked with Elaine to the front door. "Tell you what I'm going to do, sis. While I make the rounds interviewing for a job, if I see a good candidate who looks like he might be right for you, I'll scope him out, ask the key questions. You know, if he's single, heterosexual, plans to make Pacific Knoll his forever home, that sort of thing. And get his name. You can take it from there. That way, all you have to do is dust off your social skills. I'm sure you'll find the right guy this time."

After her sister left, Eden wondered if Elaine was serious about avoiding the singles scene for months. She'd seemed more subdued than the last time they'd had a chance to share ice cream and a sisterly chat.

Eden looked up at the sound of the car entering the garage. She opened the kitchen door, and the children scampered in ahead of Hale. Eden plastered a smile on her face. *No sense giving Hale a reason to tell me I don't* have *to find a job.* Her husband was so good at reading her moods, especially when he suspected she felt less than 100 percent happy.

~ ~ ~

While Hale read to the children before shooing them into their rooms to prepare for bed, Eden retrieved her phone from her pocket. Deb's returning text included a wedding date guess for Chris and Teddy and mirrored what Eden had been thinking since Elaine had gone home. *Ellie swearing off men, even temporarily? Never imagined she'd do that.*

Lexi's smiley face emoji followed with her wedding date bet and a message Eden suspected Elaine might have suggested. *Will you and Hale go out with Fletch and me next Saturday? He wants to try out a new restaurant that just opened. Let me know.*

Hmm. A shared date night with her brother and sister-in-law? Maybe Hale would be willing, knowing he'd have a man to talk to, someone unlikely to want to discuss what Eden had been discussing with him for the past several weeks. Discussions about the problems he was facing at work usually ended in his saying there was no real solution except time and Anderson Randolph's retirement. Or the other topic that left her feeling less than gleeful, her thus far unsuccessful hunt for a job.

She'd been conducting the search in fits and starts, interrupted by children's questions and other parental concerns. *Work, going back to work, having an adult life again.* Eden feared she might never experience that elusive new job except in her dreams, if that *other* issue she had yet to mention to Hale happened to become yet another mutual concern.

~ ~ ~

Eden's stomach growled, a reminder that she'd skipped breakfast as she concentrated on helping Ivory and Kenyon get ready for school. Kenny had wakened, eager to leave for school, but Ivory was whiny and giggly by turns as she prepared for her first day at all-day kindergarten. Leaving later than planned wasn't helping Eden's mood.

"Kisses for the first day, kids," Hale said when he and Eden walked with the children to the front of the nearby elementary school. Kenyon brushed his face against his father's, looking momentarily embarrassed.

"Do we have to, Dad? In public?"

Hale ruffled his son's hair. "Gotcha," he said, and bumped Kenny's shoulder with a closed fist. "How about a high five and hug instead of a kiss now that you're a big second-grader?"

Kenny grinned and slapped his father's outstretched hand, then gave Eden a quick hug.

"Bye, Dad. Bye, Mom," Kenny called out. He spotted a friend, waved to him and trotted up the steps with the other boy.

Ivory clung to her father before reaching for Eden's hand.

"You're going to have so much fun, Ivy," Hale enthused. "I want you to tell me all about it tonight."

Ivory's curly white-blond ponytails bounced when she nodded. "Okay, Daddy. Will you take me to meet my teacher?"

"Can't today, babycakes. If I don't leave right now, I'll be late for work. Mommy will walk you in."

Eden gave Hale a look of barely disguised resentment that he was leaving Ivory's first day at the big-kids' school to her. Hadn't he walked Kenny in his first day? He'd declared it was a beautiful day, and that he'd walk to work. After all, Lambert-Knoll College was only ten blocks away, up and over the hill.

"Call me if you want me to pick you up tonight," she said, hoping Hale would come home with news of an opening somewhere in town. Even if it meant she was breaking her rule about getting tips from him.

"Will do, hon. You going to be okay?" He lifted a shoulder toward the elementary school, his nonverbal acknowledgement that Eden would be alone all day for the first time since Kenny's birth.

She nodded, kissed him good-bye, then forced a smile in her husband's direction as Hale stepped out of the way of a group of children running toward the school entrance.

Eden squeezed Ivory's hand. "Are you ready to see your new teacher and the other kids in your class, sweets?"

"Uh-huh," although the little girl hesitated to take a first step toward the building.

"Then let's do it. Didn't Kenny say how much he liked kindergarten?"

"But he had a lady teacher. I've got a *man* teacher."

"I'm sure Mr. Wyecliff is very nice. Remember when we met him at the New Teachers open house?"

"He's really big," Ivory declared. "Even bigger than Daddy."

"Yes, he is." Eden recalled thinking the lanky man was at least six feet, six inches tall, with the long arms of a basketball player. Hadn't middle sister Debra said she thought he'd played semipro ball before becoming a teacher?

Eden entered the building with Ivory and paused to catch her breath. The shouts and laughter of children greeting one another echoed down the long hall of the building. "Come on, Ivy. It's this way." She turned to the right and entered a shorter, quieter hall. At each door, a teacher stood, smiling as students entered their rooms.

"There he is," Ivory pointed. "He's so tall," she declared.

Eden nodded. Her impression at the late summer meeting had been of a man who looked like he could hold at least ten of his charges in his arms simultaneously. His bald head shone in the light from the ceiling fixtures and his laugh reminded her of her older brother, Fletcher. Deep and full-bodied, but kindly. And he looked eager to meet the children in his charge.

His deep voice contained a hint of laughter. "Hello, Ivory Brinker. I'm happy you're in my class this year. Can you find your desk? I put your name on it and a special gift, too." The man nodded at Ivory before smiling at Eden.

Ivory pulled her hand away. "I already know my name," she said. "Let me look." She trotted around the room between the clusters of desks, stopping at one with a tented piece of card stock that sported her name in large letters. Next to it sat a small stuffed kangaroo.

"Look, Mommy! A kangaroo! With its own little baby 'roo." She held up the stuffed animal, beaming.

Eden glanced up at the teacher, who murmured, "I remembered what she said about wanting to visit Australia. Excuse me for a moment." He turned back to the door and welcomed another child, a boy, whose tears streaked his cheeks, as he clung to his father's left leg.

Ivory pulled Eden into a crouch. "That boy over there looks like he's scared. Do you think he's afraid of my teacher, because he's so big?" Her blue eyes widened.

"Maybe you could tell him that everything will be fine," Eden suggested.

"Okay." Ivory left the kangaroo on her desk and approached the little boy. "Hi. I'm Ivy. What's your name? Teacher gave me a kangaroo. Want to see what he gave you?"

Mr. Wyecliff managed to shift the child's hand from around his father's leg and into his large paw. With Ivory on the other side of the boy, he walked him to a desk, on which sat a polar bear.

"Wow! You got a white bear!" Ivory exclaimed. "Did you know they live in Alaska? My daddy went there once and he brought me a picture. Of a mama bear and her two babies!"

Watching Ivory engaging with the little boy, Eden knew that her little girl was going to be fine. "I'll see you later, Ivy. Kenny's going to walk home with you. Don't forget to wait for him."

Ivory waved. "I won't. First-day kiss?" she asked.

"Of course." Eden bent down to give her a kiss.

"Bye, Mommy." Ivory turned back and began chattering to the other child, who was hiccupping quiet sobs.

At the door, Eden smiled at the teacher. "Will you remind her to wait for her brother? He's in second grade."

"Be happy to."

"Have a good first day."

He nodded. "I'm sure it will be."

Eden climbed into the car, her heart full, and aching only slightly less than when she'd entered the large building, determined not to cry now that Ivory was in school. All-day school seemed so final, a sure sign her daughter was growing up and away from her. So unlike the small neighborhood preschool Ivory had attended only two hours a day, three days a week. Missing a day or two there hadn't been a bad thing, not like now. The two car seats in the back of her years'-old SUV were reminders of how full Eden's life had been at home, and how empty it now felt with both children in school.

She pulled the papers she'd shoved into her purse and re-read the job descriptions she'd printed off the previous weekend. Full-time jobs, the kind on which to build a career. If only it wasn't so long since she'd worked outside the home.

She and Hale had agreed that she would be a stay-at-home mom until the children were in school. She'd loved being home, although this last year had been harder than the others as she'd looked forward to what she'd begun referring to as "becoming an adult again."

If only Hale hadn't acted hurt that she wanted to bring in another salary. She knew he was worried about their personal finances. He'd reminded her more than once that an unexpected emergency could decimate their meager savings. Her quiet statement that a second income would take some of the pressure off had not resulted in his encouragement that she go ahead with her plans to find a job. Instead, he'd continued to assure her that they could make it on what he earned.

She'd never doubted that he was doing well in his position in the finance office at Lambert-Knoll College. And he'd been promoted twice in the last six years. But the raise they'd expected with his last promotion had yet to materialize: one of the costs of staying at a small private college, whose endowments never seemed to match the changes required with a steadily increasing enrollment and the hiring of new faculty. Her question about why the administrators couldn't see that the people running the various offices deserved raises, too, just like the faculty, had resulted only in Hale shaking his head. He'd run his fingers through his hair, then slid them down to squeeze his nape, a gesture Eden thought of as purely Hale, whenever he felt stressed.

What if their car needed a new clutch? What if the house needed a new roof? It was twenty years old. And the renovations they'd planned when they moved in, right before Kenny's birth, had somehow never happened. Even though Chris, the builder in the family, had offered his expertise more than once.

Eden knew college costs were much higher now than when she and Hale had attended. A second income would assure a college fund for Kenny and Ivory. Hale had agreed that Eden's money going into a fund for their children was a wise plan. He seemed to find this use of her money more acceptable than using it to buy groceries.

She looked back at the elementary school. Two students ran up the steps and into the building just as a bell rang and the doors were pulled shut by the principal. She stood beside the car, about to slide behind the wheel just as nausea overtook her. She dove for some nearby bushes and dry-heaved, hoping no one saw her.

I should have eaten breakfast this morning. But she'd been too busy overseeing Kenny climbing into his clothes and then spending extra time with Ivory's hair. Thank goodness Hale had taken over in the kitchen, urging both kids to eat up so they could learn lots, his usual admonition to Kenny. But he'd looked askance at her when she ate only a single bite of her eggs and refused the mug of coffee Hale placed in front of her.

"Nerves," she'd said, anticipating his question. But his skeptical expression forced her to speculate on the other possible reason she felt so awful.

Eden left the school parking lot and headed out of town, determined to find out if she was right, even as she clung to the hope that she was wrong. Twenty minutes later, she pulled into the parking lot of an unfamiliar pharmacy. She slid out of the car, glanced to the right, then to the left. Pleased that the store didn't seem very busy, she spotted a man behind the counter toward the back of the store. He was filling prescriptions.

"Excuse me. Pregnancy tests?" Eden croaked, wishing her mouth didn't feel so dry, wishing her heart would stop racing.

The pharmacist pointed to her right. "About halfway down that aisle."

Eden snatched up a bottle of aspirin and paused to check out the different pregnancy tests, their boxes lined up like so many accusatory soldiers on the shelf. She selected two, paid for them and the analgesic, and trotted back to her car.

On her return to Pacific Knoll, she pulled into a fast food place, and ordered food and an extra-large glass of water. She slid the breakfast burrito back into its bag, unable to face it, and gulped down the water. When she felt certain she was ready, she headed for the women's room and opened both pregnancy tests, peed on the respective sticks and waited. And waited some more, her chin resting in her palms, her elbows pressed almost painfully into her thighs, determined to give the tests plenty of time. She wanted them to be accurate in their negativity, even as she feared the results would tell her something else.

When she concluded she'd waited long enough, she forced herself to check the results. The first stick showed a distinctive blue cross. The second stick spelled it out in letters she couldn't ignore. Pregnant. *Two for two.* She stifled a groan, tossed the evidence into the trash and adjusted her clothes.

As Eden approached the turnoff from the highway that would take her home, she debated calling Hale then concluded, *No. I'll wait until tonight to tell him.* She suspected he would be happy. Or would he focus on what another baby meant for the family expenses? Maybe she should take a page out of Lexi's pregnant-again playbook. Say nothing until she was past the three-month mark, because of the baby Lexi had lost last year. *Only Fletcher knew until after Lexi went to the hospital.*

She recalled Lexi's reaction, and Fletcher's, to their miscarriage the previous year. They had been devastated. Fletcher, even more than Lexi, probably because she had helped Fletcher to see that his love for his first family in no way took away from the love he had for Lexi and Chance. Eden liked to think it was a legacy from his first wife, Jacquie, and infant daughter, Raffie, who were killed by a drunk driver. They'd taught Fletcher how to love, and Lexi and her son were the beneficiaries of that lesson.

Deb, too, wanted a family, although she claimed she and Todd had nothing to report yet on their baby-making efforts.

Hale was her husband, the father of this baby. Didn't he deserve to know what she didn't want to tell him? What she didn't want to accept?

She'd never considered having an abortion. Was it even in the cards? But how could it not be, when another baby would totally interfere with what she'd been planning, looking forward to, yearning to do, for months? To say nothing of what another baby would do to their budget, which barely seemed to cope with two growing children. *I need a job, not just for my mental health.*

Had Iona questioned having a third baby when she became pregnant with Deb? Eden doubted it: her mother had always wanted a large family. But what would Deb say if she knew what Eden was contemplating? Would she question her? No, Deb would understand. She loved her job, but had never mentioned becoming a stay-at-home mom after having children. And the budget issues Eden worried about were a non-issue for her sister and Todd, a lawyer in Fletcher's firm.

Eden pulled into the driveway, walked into the house and stared at the wall calendar. When had it happened? She'd missed only one period, but endured two days of nausea, both of which she thought she'd hidden from Hale. He had asked why she'd only picked at her dinner earlier in the week and if she thought she was coming down with something when she'd spent so much time in the bathroom. And this morning, she couldn't face the eggs he'd made for her, even though he'd kept his questions to himself. He trusted she would tell him whatever was bothering her. Hale had always trusted her. One reason she loved him.

She flipped the calendar back to August. Nothing out of the ordinary that month. Back to July. No? She looked again at the family's August activities. The exclamations around their camping trip weekend seemed to fly out at her.

She recalled how much she and Hale had allowed their enjoyment of their last camping trip of the summer to extend late into the night. She recalled their peaceful walk along the shoreline of the lake under a starry night sky, the children so exhausted from swimming and hiking and racing around under the trees that they'd collapsed in their sleeping bags almost immediately after a hotdog dinner with s'mores singed over a campfire. Now she wondered if she'd just wanted to be swept away in her love for her husband, in the happiness her children had displayed while they tramped through the woods and played in the water of the lake shortly after they pitched their tents.

This pregnancy was her fault. She'd assured Hale she wasn't fertile when he'd asked after admitting he forgot to pack condoms. Obviously, she'd miscalculated. But *damn* his little swimmers!

Eden approached the breakfast dishes still in the sink. She scraped them, placed them in the dishwasher, and turned it on. Remembering the burrito in her purse, she threw it away, wrinkling her nose at the stomach-turning smell of sausage and egg, and rummaged in the refrigerator for an apple.

As she nibbled the fruit, she imagined herself on the job, answering questions of her boss, participating in a group meeting with the other employees, much as she'd done years before. She dropped the apple core into the trash, grabbed up a book and took a seat in the living room, in the chair that provided her a view of the front yard and the sidewalk down which her children would skip as they walked home from school.

After several minutes during which she found herself unable to concentrate on the words that swam on the page, she turned sideways in the chair and leaned her head back, the warmth from the sunlight coating one cheek and the side of her neck. She imagined where she might find that elusive job she'd been dreaming about, one she could do while pregnant, maybe even after a brief maternity leave.

Should she take the bus or drive to that downtown office that was seeking an experienced finance executive? Wasn't that how they'd described the job? She was sure if they selected her, she'd have a well-appointed office. She'd spend her days answering peoples' questions, participating in conference calls. Or should she apply at that realty office? It was a less prestigious venue, but one likely to need someone skilled in money matters. After all, buying and selling houses involved many thousands of dollars per transaction. She'd never paid much attention to realty offices, but work there might prove interesting, a challenge, different from what she'd done before.

Then there were those other jobs that she'd circled, even though she'd been less inclined to call them. Taking care of the books for a diner felt beneath her, less of a challenge. Nor was she interested in interviewing for that position a trucking company was offering. Why had she even sent them her resumé? She imagined herself surrounded by men with grimy hands and sweaty shirts. But was that fair? She knew nothing about the trucking company's employees. Besides, didn't women also drive trucks these days? Maybe the owner was a woman. There was no way to know when the information she'd gleaned from her internet search referred only to the person she was to reply to as B.J. Wagner. Those initials could as easily refer to Barbara Jean as Bubba Joe.

Now that she was pregnant, how would Hale feel about her taking a job, even one that was short-lived? He felt so strongly about babies and small children needing their mother. Would her income be large enough to cover childcare *and* the contribution she intended to make to the children's college fund?

Eden closed her eyes and allowed her mind to drift away from those questions, so vexing because the answers skittered out of reach, like so much dandelion fluff on a brisk breeze.

Nearly an hour after settling herself in the chair, Eden jerked and opened her eyes at a sudden buzzing sound. Temporarily confused, she glanced down at her watch, before realizing where the sound was coming from. *My phone?* But who was calling her at eleven in the morning? Was it about Ivory? Kenny? Something was wrong at their school? She lurched out of her chair, hurried into the kitchen, and grabbed her phone.

Caller ID showed Hale's name.

"Hi, hon. How'd it go?" he asked.

Eden's heart began a slow gallop. Had Hale guessed that she was pregnant? They'd joked for years that he was psychic when it came to her moods, to her worries.

Before she could ask, he clarified, "You know, with Ivy. First day at school with the giant killer. What's her teacher's name again?"

Eden closed her eyes for a moment, relieved, and took the time to breathe in and out slowly. *Oh. Ivy.*

"Mr. Wyecliff. Everything went fine. She got distracted by one of her classmates. Her teacher had little stuffed animals for each child. So cute. He remembered when she talked about Australia. Her gift was a kangaroo."

"That man knows how to get a kid's attention." Hale chuckled.

"Yes." Her heart slowed to a trot. "Um. Do you need a ride home? Is that why you called?"

"No need. But have you heard from Paige Landvik? At the bank?"

"No, why? I made sure we weren't late with our last mortgage payment." Her anxiety about that one-week-late August payment returned with a rush. A result of her last-minute preparations for their camping trip. Hale had wanted to leave as soon as he got off work that day. She'd forgotten to drop the bills in the mail slot when they passed the post office. Not that their late payment had generated a penalty. But Paige, long a friend of the Lambert family, had called to ask if there was a problem she should know about.

"Never crossed my mind, Edie. Did you know the bank's opening a new branch south of town? They're looking to hire people, according to Paige. Just thought I'd let you know, in case you want to follow up. After all, that's all we talked about all summer—you and your new job."

Was Hale goading her? She couldn't tell. Eden glanced out the window at the sound of a lawn mower starting up across the street. "Could we discuss it when you get home?"

"Of course." A pause told Eden her husband was wondering why she hadn't reacted with enthusiasm. "Or have you changed your mind about a job now that Ivy's in school?" he asked, his words coated with gentle concern.

"No, of course not." He was so caring. Tears threatened to prevent Eden from saying more. *I have to tell him. He deserves to know.* And doing so would give Hale hours to think about what another baby would mean for their family.

But before she could do so, Eden sucked in a breath in hopes she could stop what was rapidly becoming a losing battle. She pressed a hand against her roiling stomach, then lowered her head and blurted out, "Gotta go, Hale. We'll talk later."

She ran for the bathroom.

Two

"I think her first week went well," Eden confirmed as she sat with Hale in the living room after Ivory and Kenyon had left the dinner table. "Didn't she talk about what she's been learning when you were at the park, before dinner?"

Hale smiled. "No. But we're now kicked off the parent pedestal. Every other sentence was 'Nuh-uh, Daddy. That's not right. Teacher Cliff said this. Or Teacher Cliff does that.'" He chuckled. "Remember when Kenny said the same thing after he started kindergarten?"

"Now that you mention it. Kenny's so quiet. Is he still reading?" She pointed over her shoulder in the direction of her son's bedroom.

Hale rose from his seat and looked into Kenny's room.

"He's fine." Hale walked up behind Eden and rubbed her shoulders. "You look tired, hon. I know you haven't been sleeping well. You tossed a lot more last night than your usual. All week, actually. A sure sign something's on your mind." He kissed her nape. "If it isn't about the kids starting school this week, what is it? I know. It has to be about your job search. But I thought you said it was proceeding nicely."

Eden had been so confident she could get through another day before talking to Hale. But then came the feel of his lips on her neck, in that special spot that always sent tingles down her spine. His warm breath brushed her cheek, when he slipped his fingers under the neckline of her blouse to massage her neck and shoulders, and undid her resolve. She burst into tears.

"Whoa! What's the matter?" Hale sat down and pulled Eden into his arms.

Hale was her rock. Had been ever since they met in college. Through all manner of issues. But how could she tell him she already wanted this baby when she knew they couldn't afford one? How could she tell him that half of her was at war with the other half, one wanting the baby, the other wanting *not* to be pregnant? How could she not say what her obstetrician had confirmed after he'd inquired why Hale hadn't accompanied her after she saw him that afternoon, thanks to a convenient cancellation?

"Oh, Hale," she finally said in between quiet sobs, convinced she couldn't keep the news a secret any longer. "I saw the Dr. today."

Eden felt his sharp intake of breath right before he eased her out of his arms to gaze into her eyes.

"You're sick? Tell me. No matter what it is, we'll deal with it. Together. Like always." He wrapped one arm around her shoulders and clasped her hand in his.

She knew from his expression that he was thinking of his mother and her battle with lung cancer, a battle she'd lost less than two years earlier.

She shook her head and pointed to the box of tissues, inconveniently out of reach.

Hale leaned forward and placed it in her lap.

She wiped her eyes once, twice, then blew her nose and when that didn't halt her tears, she wiped her face again, moaning slightly into her hands. "I—I—" She gazed at her husband of a dozen years, aware that his light brown hair had begun to gray at the temples. She thought it made him look distinguished. But he'd complained that he was showing his age, would soon look like his father, if he lost more hair on top.

This new baby would be going to college about the time they celebrated Hale's fifty-sixth birthday. Which meant they'd both be over sixty before their last child graduated from college and was on his or her own. Would they never be able to retire? Thoughts that had twisted her in mental knots since she'd taken the pregnancy tests kept pushing her toward abortion as the only logical answer. But she couldn't see herself going through with it, and she was certain Hale would object.

"What did Dr. Shelby say?" Hale demanded. "If you won't tell me, I'll call him." He reached for his cell.

"Not Dr. Shelby. Dr. Ortiz. I'm pregnant," she finally blurted out an anguished whisper. She squinted at Hale, suddenly fearful that he might blame her for what had been a joint endeavor. An accident of their lovemaking, in which they'd both reveled, she recalled. Because he forgot the condoms and she told him it was her safe time. All because she'd said it was her safe time.

Hale brushed an errant strand of hair off Eden's temple, the tenderness with which he touched her generating another flood of tears. "Doc Ortiz confirmed it?"

Eden nodded. "He even did an ultrasound to date how far along I am. He says between four and six weeks. Plenty early to have an abortion."

As if in response to her words, Hale stared at her. "*That's* what you want?" his tone inferring he found it hard to believe.

She grimaced. "No, but we can't afford another child. And I know the statistics, Hale. The majority of abortions these days are sought by women just like me. Married or in a relationship, with at least one child, after contraception failure. Or in our case, failure to use. Not just teens who were careless or didn't know any better, were raped, or whatever."

"But—"

"I looked at the calendar and—"

His eyes widened. "Our last camping trip?"

She nodded. "I said it was my safe time." She sighed and blew her nose again. "Which means it's my fault. If I hadn't said that, would you, would we—"

Hale looked away for the first time since she'd mentioned the A word. "How can I answer that, babe? I love you, adore you. Enjoy making love to you, *with* you."

He reached for her hand again, his slender fingers stroking from knuckle to wrist. "Did you tell Doc Ortiz you don't want this baby? Our baby?" He let out a long breath. "But how you could *not,* Edie? We made this baby together." He stopped talking and glanced in the direction of their children's bedrooms. Ivory was singing along with one of her favorite Disney DVDs and Kenny was making train whistle noises. He must have finished reading.

Hale's voice dropped. "If we're going to assign blame, put it on me. I was the one who forgot the rubbers." He ran his fingers through his hair, causing a temporary spiking of several strands. "Aren't you still looking for a job? What's a baby going to mean for that plan? Another baby puts a lot of responsibility on you. Not just the pregnancy, if you go ahead with getting a job." He watched as his thumbs moved toward her fingers then back toward her wrists. "I never thought we'd ever go the abortion route. Never in a million years." He kissed her cheek. "But if that's what you want ..." He gazed steadily at her, the green of his eyes intense. "Are you sure you don't want this baby? I just never imagined..., " he murmured, as if her decision would be a personal rejection of him. Not just of the baby they had created.

"What I want is a *job*! Not a third baby, Hale. You know I've been counting the days—for months now—about going back to work, talking to adults again. Being more than a soccer mom, even though Kenny isn't that into soccer." Tears slid down her cheeks and she swiped them away, frustrated that she couldn't seem to control what now seemed to reflect her weakness at the very time when she needed to be strong.

He nodded. "Well, being pregnant doesn't mean you can't work. You worked when you were pregnant with Kenny."

She pulled away from him. "But I was a basket case, always having to run to the bathroom those first months, even into my second trimester. Not exactly what Andy appreciated and somehow I doubt he'd appreciate it now, either. Don't you remember? I kept wanting my nausea to stop, like it did for other women, after twelve weeks. Only, with me, it didn't.

That it probably meant I was carrying a boy. Even with Ivy, my morning sickness lasted a lot longer than for other women."

"Andy can be a real ass sometimes." He brushed her hair off her cheek again. "But I thought you ruled out wanting to go back to the finance office. You know, the nepotism thing."

He kissed her cheek. "Listen, we'll manage, hon. Don't worry about the money stuff. I'll go on line and advertise my services doing taxes for people. Like I did after my folks' accident, so we could help them pay those hospital bills. And after my mom got sick."

"And lose what few hours you have now with the kids? They love their time with you," she objected, knowing Hale was a loving and caring father, one who enjoyed being with his children.

"I'll work at night, after they're asleep." He sounded so hopeful, so willing to take on more responsibility, to work around their family life, a life they had both relished.

"You're such a wonderful husband and father, Hale," her tears causing her words to waffle uncertainly. "I don't want you to have to carry the entire financial load. If I can find a decent job, won't that make things easier? Please tell me you agree." Eden leaned her head against her husband's chest. His steady heartbeat, usually so soothing, seemed to mock her, that she would even consider not carrying this new baby to term. As if he sensed that she hadn't fully committed to mothering a third child.

"You know I do, hon. What's important is that you're happy. 'Cause when you're happy, we're all happy." He smiled down at her, lifting her chin and planting a kiss on her lips.

Hale ran a hand up and down her back. His slow strokes always made her feel better, Eden knew. Didn't he often do that when they lay in bed together, after they made love? As if he couldn't stop touching her, stroking her. She felt so cherished that Hale seemed to love touching her.

His voice rumbled in his chest and she felt as well as heard his quiet utterance. "How soon before you have to tell Doc Ortiz what you want?"

She leaned away from her husband and gazed at him. "He said it should be a joint decision. That both of us should be in agreement. He wants to see you, too, at that appointment. But he said a couple of weeks wouldn't up the risk very much."

Hale nodded. "Then we have time. You're still planning to look for a job, even one part-time?" He paused. "I think you should. No matter what."

Eden nodded. "I was planning to."

When Ivory walked into the living room, a book in her hand, Hale smiled at his daughter. "What is it, babycakes?"

"Time for my bath. And a story. Will you read this one, Daddy? I want *Kangaroo Kangaroo. Where are You?*"

"You bet!" He rose from his seat. "Honey, will you check on Kenny while I take care of Ivy here?"

"Of course." Eden allowed Hale to pull her to her feet.

The rest of the evening resembled the usual after-dinner happenings in the Brinker household with baths for the children, reading time after they were tucked into bed, all pink and warm and sleepy within minutes of the start of their respective story times.

After the children were taken care of, Hale opened his laptop and created an offer to do tax preparation. Once posted, he looked over at Eden.

"You want to take over and check for job postings?"

She took the laptop from him and scanned the sites she'd bookmarked earlier. A new ad had popped up, this one from the bank. Probably the one Hale had mentioned. And there was that ad from the new real estate office, recently opened in town, looking for a bookkeeper. She could do that kind of work in her sleep. But would it be possible to do it from home? She wondered if their failure to respond to her letter meant they weren't interested. Maybe her resumé had implied she was overqualified, would want a salary higher than they were offering.

"I sent in a letter and my resumé for this one. Even though it was totally blank for the last seven years. Which was probably the kiss of death."

"Did you tell them you've been a full-time mom, which means you have multitasking down to a science? I'm sure they'd understand. And if they don't, they aren't the kind of people you'd be happy working with."

"It would be nice if you're right." She sighed.

She stared back at the screen. But if she contacted them again, wouldn't that mean she was overly anxious? She looked again at the ads for the diner and that trucking company, though neither gave her positive vibes. Maybe she shouldn't be so picky. Minutes later, she attached her letter of inquiry and a copy of her resumé in response to both ads, hit send and closed Hale's laptop.

"I doubt those last two will bother getting back to me." She went into the kitchen and reached in the pantry for the cereal the children would eat for breakfast. After setting the table for what she knew would be another rushed morning, she headed for the bedroom.

"You're going to bed, hon? So soon?" Hale asked.

"It's been a big day." One harder to deal with than she preferred.

"I'll join you in a bit."

"Take your time."

As she lay on her side of the bed, she thought about that job at the new bank branch. *I know Paige. Maybe I should talk to her.* But did she want to work at a bank? She'd interned there her junior year and found the work less than exciting. Repetitive. But she'd only been a student intern. What they'd allowed her to do back in the day, under supervision, probably had nothing much to do with a branch manager's duties. The ad had mentioned managerial responsibility.

She climbed out of bed and went back to Hale's laptop, pulled up the classified ads section of the paper and reread the job description. *What the heck?* She typed up a letter indicating her interest in being considered for the assistant manager position and sent it. For good measure, she attached a copy of her letter to Paige Landvik with a personal note.

Hey, Paige. How are things with you? I noted that the bank is opening a branch south of town just in time for me to get back into making a salary now that my two rug rats are in school. How are your children doing? Wasn't your daughter the star of the middle school end-of-year play last year? Perhaps we'll be able to call ourselves colleagues again. Eden

"You decided to touch base with Paige?" Hale leaned against her just before Eden hit send.

"Figured it couldn't hurt to let her know that I applied. Even if nothing comes of it."

"Good for you." He kissed her nape before she stood up and turned to face him.

"I love you so much, Hale. Even when I'm an old grouch, that's never going to change."

"Then I guess that means I'll be loving a grouch when I'm a doddering old fogy," he murmured. "Want me to show you how I plan to love you, even if you're not an old grouch?"

"Would you?"

~ ~ ~

Two days later, Eden had just returned from taking Kenyon and Ivory to school when her phone rang. Caller ID showed Lexi's picture.

"Hi, Lexi. Let me guess. You're elbow-deep in flour or cake icing and needing a break. Or did you want to bring Chance over so he can play with Kenny this afternoon?"

Her sister-in-law laughed. "Good guesses, but I have another reason for calling. I just finished a wedding cake. Gave me ideas for when Chris and Teddy give us the word."

Why did Lexi sound so breathless? "Is something wrong, Lex? You sound out of breath."

"Nothing's wrong. In fact, everything's totally right." Lexi laughed into the phone. "Remember when we were at your place and I sort of hinted that Fletch and I might be pregnant again, but you had to keep my secret?"

Eden's heart slowly descended to her toes, though not before bumping into her stomach, which threatened to turn over and rid itself of the banana she had just eaten. Although eggs were not for her anymore, fruit seemed to settle her stomach. Before she could ask, Lexi blurted out her news.

"Since you've been my secret-keeper the last few weeks, I wanted to tell you first. Anyway, it's true! We're pregnant. It's for sure. As of today! And we can't wait to tell everyone on Sunday." Tears seemed to coat her next words. "You're the first to know." She giggled. "After Fletch, of course. Because you're my oldest sister! I'm going to call the others next." She chortled.

Eden felt for the nearest kitchen chair and leaned against it for a long minute. Knowing she should be happy with Lexi's news, even as her stomach knotted, she forced out the words. "Oh. That's … that's wonderful … news." She counted backward on her fingers. "So you're four months already?"

"Actually, just past the three-month mark, but the Doctor seemed to think it was unlikely we'd lose this one, so we decided to share the news now. Especially since I wasn't sure I could keep quiet much longer. And Chance knows as of this morning. He overheard us talking, so he's probably telling everyone at school that he's going to be a big brother. Including Kenny. Maybe even Ivory if he happens to see her on the playground."

Six weeks ahead of me. Eden sucked in a deep breath, determined not to say anything that even hinted at the announcement she and Hale would be making soon. "I'm happy for you, Lexi," she repeated, wishing she felt the same enthusiasm for herself, "and Fletcher. He must be ecstatic."

"He is. Thank you for keeping our secret. Listen, I need to go. Want to catch Deb before she turns her phone off. Do you know if Elaine will take my call while she's at work?"

"I'm sure she will. But if she doesn't, you can always text her. Better hurry if you want to catch Deb. She turns her phone off at eight."

Eden set her phone down and slid into the nearest chair. *She's happy, and Fletch has to be over the moon. Along with everyone else when they hear the news on Sunday at Mom's.* And she was, too. Really. She imagined sharing her pregnancy with her sister-in-law, knowing it would make their experience even more special. Not only could they commiserate regarding morning sickness, and those last weeks when being pregnant seemed never-ending, but the cousins would be close in age. Chance and Kenny considered each other to be special friends because they were cousins, practically the same age and in the same school grade. Eden felt certain Lexi would be thrilled to know her baby might also have a close-in-age cousin.

Hale continued to mention how much he wanted this baby, that he loved their other two and already loved this one. He'd taken to rubbing her belly every night, telling her he was saying hello to their little tadpole. But in the next breath, he insisted on assuring her that whatever *she* decided he would accept. Trouble was, she'd seen the sadness that coated his gaze at the thought that this baby might never be. And he'd agreed they wouldn't tell the rest of the family until she was sure about what they were going to do.

Why *haven't I told him I've already decided?* She didn't want to think she was trying to be deliberately hurtful. But unlike with her other pregnancies, Eden's mind remained blank regarding names. With both Kenny and Ivory, she and Hale had settled on names within days of the doctor confirming each pregnancy. As if her brain couldn't help but want to personalize the creature hidden deep inside her. That neither Hale nor she had mentioned names probably reflected her conflict and his assurances that he wasn't going to push her into agreeing to keep the pregnancy. Maybe that was why she hesitated to reassure him, the father of this baby, *her* baby. No, *their* baby.

But, funny how—after her admission to Hale that she was pregnant—she had experienced no more nausea. She'd perversely concluded that the baby was trying to tell her something. That this pregnancy might actually be easier than the others. That its presence would *not* prevent her from working, assuming she actually landed a job.

She looked down at her phone when it buzzed. Should she answer that unrecognized number? Usually, she let unknown callers go to voice mail. But curiosity impelled her to reply.

"Hello?"

"Is this Ms. Brinker?" A pleasant female voice inquired.

"Yes."

"This is Opal Springer, from the McCue Real Estate office. You sent him a letter indicating you might be interested in our bookkeeper position. Are you still available?"

Eden's pulse soared. *Oh, my gosh!* They called—after all this time? She swallowed then licked her lips. As if that would moisten her suddenly arid throat. "Um, yes."

"That's just wonderful! Could you come in for an interview today? Just between us, I'm desperate!"

Eden glanced down at her take-the-kids-to-school cut-offs and her blouse with the old mustard stain over her left breast. "What time?"

"Two-thirty would be perfect."

Eden's heart sank. "Oh. I'm afraid that's too late in the day for me. My children will be coming home from school about then and I have to be here."

"Oh." Disappointment dripped off the unseen woman's reply.

Eden held her breath, trying to recall if she'd mentioned her children when she'd keyboarded her letter of inquiry.

"Well then, how about one-thirty? Would that work better? Mr. McCue should be back in the office by then."

"Yes. That will work."

"Ducky! Excellent!" The woman's enthusiasm rebounded. "Could you please bring your resumé?"

"Didn't I include it?" Eden winced, hoping the woman on the line wouldn't take offense.

"If you did, it must have disappeared into cyberspace." The woman chortled.

"Of course I'll bring another resumé. I'm sure it was my mistake, not including it. My apologies." Eden stopped fidgeting in her seat and tried to conjure the address of that office. She came up blank. "I'll see you at one-thirty." She rose from her seat, quickly strode into her bedroom and rummaged in the drawer where she and Hale kept important papers. Had she retained a copy of her letter? But she couldn't seem to find it.

"Excellent!" Ms. Springer repeated.

"Um, could you please remind me of your office address? At the moment, I can't seem to recall ..." Eden crossed her fingers that the woman wouldn't conclude she was a loser for not even remembering where she'd sent her letter.

"We're in that new strip mall over on Cavanaugh Street. See you soon!"

"Oh, right. Thanks." Eden set her phone down, sat for a moment and then clapped her hands together. "Oh, my gosh!" she exclaimed to no one but the birds singing outside the window. She turned and went into her closet.

What to wear. Something nice. Something office-appropriate. But what did she have these days that fit that particular bill? She hadn't worked in an office since right before Kenny's birth, and the last clothes she'd had then were all designed to show off her pregnancy. Totally *in*appropriate. At least right now.

She considered and rejected one dress after another before stopping when she pulled out her navy blue jacket with the gold buttons. Did she still have the matching pencil skirt? Could she even get into it? Hadn't her hips widened after two babies?

Eden tossed the jacket onto the bed and reached for the hanger holding three skirts. *There it is!* She slid out of her jeans and pulled on the skirt. She was surprised that her hips seemed not to have spread, but the skirt was tight at her waist. Lucky for her, the jacket was hip length and would cover the top four inches of the skirt. She pulled it off and examined the waist. If she repositioned the button and left the zipper three-quarters closed, she should be able to wear it. Unless she took deep breaths, which would likely pop off a button.

Minutes later, she again tried on the skirt. *That works.* At least for now. If she got the job, she'd go shopping for more work clothes.

Over a quick lunch designed to prevent her stomach from growling, but not so heavy that she'd risk pregnancy-related nausea, Eden looked over the resumé she'd thrown together and then forgotten to include with her inquiry. She'd followed Hale's suggestion about playing up what she'd done during her last year in the finance office at Lambert-Knoll College. He'd told her not to include his name in the references section. Instead, she'd listed two former colleagues, one of whom still worked there, but in a different office. The other woman had gone on to a higher-paying job with a company located in a Seattle skyscraper.

Had her references already been asked for comments? Had she mentioned them in her letter or the missing resumé? She couldn't recall. Or was the real estate office holding fire about checking references until after an interview? She debated texting Hale and decided against it. In an effort to help, he might talk to his colleagues. That smacked too close to nepotism, and he knew her feelings about family assistance, especially from him, her dearly beloved.

After lunch, she showered and worked hard to make her hair presentable. It needed a cut, or at least a trim. During her working years, she'd worn it in a cute pixie style, easy to maintain. But, during her pregnancy with Kenny, she'd delayed her appointments with the hairdresser. Now her locks were shoulder-length with a slight wave. She'd never worn it in one of those classic chignons so many working women favored. She'd have to ask Deb how to do it. Rather than attempt it on her own now, Eden opted to simply brush her hair dry, turning the ends under and hoping they remained that way.

She opted for a pale blue blouse with the navy jacket and skirt, her best low-heeled flats, and a pair of understated gold studs in her ears that went with the pin she attached to her jacket lapel. As she drove to the real estate office, she fidgeted at every red light, alternating between fearing that she'd be late and appearing too eager if she showed up early. Although her phone GPS told her it was a mere ten-minute drive from her house, she'd opted to leave twenty minutes early. *Just in case.* At the last light, which seemed inordinately long, she was glad she'd given herself extra time when she pulled into the parking lot adjoining the building that boasted signs of recent renovation. A sign announcing "Another Lambert and Partners Construction Project" leaned against the wall.

Wow! Chris did work here? Did she dare mention that? Would it help if she did? *No! Nepotism, be gone!*

She took a deep breath and glanced at her watch. Six minutes early. She climbed out of the car that practically shouted Children's buggy! with its pair of worn car seats in the back and the distinct odor of French fries from a recent outing to a fast food drive-through. Eden sniffed her wrists, relieved that she'd selected her favorite understated scent, the one Hale said was hers and hers alone, at the same time hoping that her clothes hadn't picked up the aroma of days'-old fries. Why hadn't she noticed that odor when she climbed into the car? She'd clean out the backseat first thing after returning home.

She opened the door, which caused a two-toned bell to sound.

The woman at the reception desk looked up and smiled before shoving her glasses higher on her nose. She wore a paisley-patterned dress of mostly reds and blues, in louder shades than Eden would have chosen.

"Ah. You must be Ms. Brinker. You look wonderful! I'm so glad you could make it!"

"Thank you." Eden handed her the resumé. "My apologies for not including this with my letter."

"Not a problem. Have a seat. Mr. McCue isn't back yet, but I expect him any minute. He knows you were coming in. *Love* that outfit of yours."

"Thank you." Eden took a seat in the reception area and looked around. The place smelled of newness, and looked it, too. New paint, what looked like new trim around the windows and new display shelves along one wall, on which sat framed pictures of what she concluded might be new listings, as well as the photos of three agents.

"This is a new office?"

"Oh my, yes! We moved in two weekends ago and we've been going like gangbusters ever since!" The receptionist's gushing placed exclamation points after every reply. "Even Mr. McCue has been busier than a one-armed paperhanger!" The woman laughed. "Our other agents, too. You'll like them! See those pictures on our display shelf? That Jonnie Grayson is one terrific sales woman. Tons of experience! She mostly handles residential neighborhoods like those high-end houses backing up toward the foothills. She's real nice once you get to know her, though she about scared the pants off me when we first met! Not a smile to be had until I helped put her office in tiptop shape. That's when she gave me a big hug and said how much she appreciated all my help!

"Oh, and Dan O'Mara, the red-headed hottie in that picture over there? I call him Danny Boy, which he doesn't like, but me, oh my! He is one attractive man—I figure he'll bring in *lots* of women buyers! He's been spending his time holding open houses up the street and over the hill at that new group of condos going up. If you wander over there, just look for the sign that says Lambert and Partners. They're the builders. Same people who made this office livable. Do you happen to know them?"

Eden couldn't prevent a smile from curving the corners of her lips upward. "I believe I do," she murmured, before realizing she needn't have bothered as the talkative receptionist continued with her rapid-fire exclamations.

"I just *love* looking at those partners, like that one guy, Val, I think his name is. Too bad he's married and probably about twenty years too young for me. But then there's Christopher, the other owner? Whooee! God hit the nail on the "hot man" head when he made that young man! Lots of other good-looking men over there, too, if I do say so myself! 'Specially on those too-warm days we had in August when they were workin' here with no shirts on. I made a point of checking out the progress after the first time I saw them stripped down to their jeans and those tool belts. Oh me, oh my! I've been angling for the boss to let me go over to that neighborhood if things ever get slow here, just so I can ogle them some more! A girl's gotta get her daily fill of man candy, don't you agree?"

Before she could come up with a reply, the door opened, and a man Eden estimated to be in his midthirties walked in. He was followed by the woman Eden recognized from her picture. Ms. Grayson, her blond hair slightly askew, wore four-inch heels that sported mud nearly to where the leather stopped and her ankle began.

The man looked over his shoulder at the agent and said, "We'll go over your problem later this afternoon, Jonnie."

Unsmiling, the woman nodded and clomped down the hall.

Eden stood up. "Mr. McCue? I'm Eden Brinker, here to interview for the bookkeeper position."

The man's soft gray eyes flicked in her direction and a dimple in his left cheek peeked out. "Oh, yes. Right. Come on in."

Three

Two days later, Eden stood up after giving the children permission to leave the dinner table.

"So, how did your interview go at the bank?" Hale asked. He drained his coffee cup.

"It didn't." Eden reached for his cup and added it to the stack of dirty dishes she placed in the sink. She scanned Hale's face for his reaction. Would he be upset? Angry? She knew he thought her better suited to the job at the bank than anywhere else.

Hale stood up and carried the serving dishes and heavy soup tureen to the sink, proving once again to be the kind of helpful husband her friends so admired. His voice studiedly neutral, he asked, "Want to tell me what happened? Did you talk to Paige?"

"She wasn't in. And it was a phone interview only. I guess they thought I needed more recent experience. When I mentioned my last day at the college, they seemed to lose interest. If I had to guess, I'd say that woman at the bank is going to call me and say something like, 'Good luck. Try again somewhere else.' But the face-to-face interview went well, the one at the realty office. I'm keeping my fingers crossed that I hear from both of them," Eden concluded. "Or at least the realty office."

"Only it's just for bookkeeping, right? Won't you be bored to death if that's all it is? At the college, you were doing way more than data entry, making sure the numbers were in the right columns, squaring up income and outgo."

"I know, but it's been seven years, Hale. If I have to start over again, it might as well be as a bookkeeper."

"Which office did you say it was?"

"A new one. Chris's crew redid their offices. It still smells like new-cut wood."

Hale nodded. "Your brother has signs all over town these days." Then, cutting to the chase, he asked, "What kind of salary are they offering?"

She huffed out a quick breath. *The bottom line, the real reason I need to work. Not just that it's something I want to do.* As if her desire to be with adults at least part of the time was unimportant.

"It was just a first interview, Hale. You know how they go. Getting to know you, looking at my resumé, which I forgot to send in when I applied. They're probably checking my references now. Assuming they decide to consider me. A girl who looked like she just graduated high school walked in as I was leaving. I think she was applying, too."

She recalled the gum-snapping young woman, wearing a dress that ended well above her knees with a neckline best described as cleavage-challenged. It barely seemed to contain the breasts straining against the material. Well, that girl would fit right in with the receptionist and her wild color scheme and gushing manner, Eden thought. *I'm probably too conservative for them.* She sighed under her breath.

Hale's question broke into her thoughts. "Did you tell them you're pregnant?"

She shook her head. "No. And it's against the law for them to ask. Which they didn't. Not at the bank, or the realty office."

When Hale's gaze shifted to her face, Eden felt the burn on her cheeks. "What was the point, Hale? Unless I get the job, my being pregnant doesn't really matter." She felt like she'd morphed back into her pouting teenage self when her parents, especially her mother, had caught her doing something she shouldn't be engaging in. Eden had been the "good girl" of the family, even more of a rule follower than shy Debra. And way more a "good girl" than Elaine, who'd seemed to enjoy flouting their mother's restrictions even as she charmed her way around their father. Because she was the youngest girl, Daddy's girl, Nathan Lambert had declared so often. Eden sighed.

"I thought you—" Hale stared at Eden before looking toward the children's rooms when a half-hearted quarrel erupted between Kenny and Ivory.

His voice rose. "Kids, settle down. Kenny, if you're done with your spelling, bring it in here for me to check. Or your mother. Ivy? You ready for your bath?"

The sounds from Kenny's room subsided. "Not yet, Daddy," Ivory said.

Eden kept her voice low, imagining what Hale might have been planning to say. "You said we'd talk about it after we see the doctor," she said between clenched jaws. Too bad the tears she'd held back earlier were proving stronger than she was.

Hale rose from his seat and came around the table to stand behind her, rubbing her shoulders when she dipped her head and sniffed.

"Sweetheart." His hands felt so good, like they always did, but Eden didn't want his comforting, wished she could fight against what he was offering, his sympathy, his understanding.

"Why are you making this so hard? Your pregnancy matters to us. You and me. And it will to the kids, after we tell them. If you don't think it's important to tell your future boss, don't. But I think they should know. If you ask me, any one of those jobs you sent letters to would be perfect for you. Even if the bank makes a big mistake and chooses not to hire you. So you can talk to adults again, so you can complain over the dinner table just like I do." He gave her a lukewarm grin. "Wherever you work, I'm totally okay with it."

Now he was reminding her of the reasons she'd expressed so many times in the last two weeks?

She reached for a tissue and wiped her eyes.

"But don't you think you should at least ask? If that realty office offers you a job, will they let you bring the baby with you? Give you extra time off after the baby is born? You know how tired you were after Ivy. Don't you think you should know their views on that? So you can decide—fully informed—if you really want the job?"

Why did Hale have to be so logical? Of course, she needed to know that, but the thought of mentioning it gave her pause as she'd remembered how her former boss had treated her. Being thought of as a lesser worker because she also happened to be pregnant haunted her dreams, keeping her awake, rousing her long before she needed to be up, preventing her from concentrating when she was deep into meal-planning.

Eden scooted her chair back and stood up, bumping into Hale in the process. "You're right, but it's a question I can't answer. At least, not yet." She stared back at him, wanting him to acknowledge that she would ask when it was appropriate. "If they offer, I'll ask."

Hale backed out of her way. He glanced over his shoulder at his son, who stood in his bedroom doorway, the room that had served as a home office when both spouses were working and after Kenny's birth. Pre-Ivory. After her birth, they'd moved Hale's small desk into a corner of their master bedroom and sold Eden's desk at the church rummage sale.

"What is it, son?" Hale asked.

"Is Mom crying?"

"No, Kenny. Just got something in my eye." *And now I'm reduced to lying to my child?* Eden wiped her eyes and forced a smile in her son's direction. "It's gone now," she assured him.

"But you don't look happy. Not like when Ivy and I came home from school. You were happy then." Kenny stared solemnly at her before glancing at his father.

"Your mother and I were talking about important things. Sometimes such talks can be difficult, troubling," Hale explained.

Eden stared at her husband. Was he going to say what she didn't want anyone to know yet, not even their children?

But Kenny seemed satisfied. "Can I play a DVD? Ivy is done watching *Frozen*. I want to see *Cars* and it's on the shelf I can't reach. The one in the closet."

"Of course." Hale followed his son into his bedroom.

Eden gazed after her husband and Kenny. From the sound of their voices, she knew Hale had gone straight to the closet to retrieve the DVD she'd placed on the high shelf in hopes Kenny would forget about it. If she heard that theme song about life being a highway one more time, her head was going to explode.

She glanced at her phone, wishing it would ping a pair of messages. One from the bank, one from the real estate office. She hated being on tenterhooks. *Tell me you want me, or that you don't. Just don't leave me hanging.* Until she secured a job, she felt as if her life had taken a turn down a deserted pothole-ridden road, one that would never be smooth.

She had no real hope that the bank would come through, even if Paige did put in a good word for her. But she'd chosen not to leave her friend another message, didn't want to put her high school buddy —it seemed like such a long time ago— on the spot.

That job at the real estate office with the oh-so-enthusiastic receptionist was unlikely to be as demanding as what she'd accomplished in the college finance office, but at least it was a start. A restart, really. If they hired her and she proved herself, maybe she'd go after something more challenging. And Mr. McCue seemed like he'd be a nice boss, certainly nicer than Anderson Randolph.

First things first, she reminded herself.

First she had to land the job. Then she'd have to ask the questions Hale wanted answers to, answers that she admitted she also needed. She fully intended to ask the owner if she could work at home part of the time. That would guarantee she wouldn't have to spend money on a babysitter. *Working from home in the afternoon would be perfect,* she thought. Especially with three children. Maybe she would even be able to take the baby with her in the mornings. At least for a little while. Until the little one was crawling, anyway. Which meant she'd have to hire a babysitter. But she'd been hoping to devote her money to the childrens' college fund. For three children now, not just two. Elaine sighed.

But, first things first. In her pencil skirt, after she'd altered the waistline, she didn't look pregnant. She walked into the master bedroom, slid out of the skirt and unbuttoned her blouse, having worn that ensemble to another job interview, one she knew had been a mistake. As she hung her clothes in the closet, she heard the bedroom door close and felt the warmth of her husband's body as he pulled her close, her back resting against his chest, his arms coming around to hug her before his hands cupped her breasts.

Eden turned in Hale's arms and rested her head against his chest, the steady beat of his heart noticeable against her cheek. "I'm sorry I've been such a pill, Hale. It's just—"

"I know. You have a lot on your mind."

"It's just that I *need* a job. To pad our budget, even if only a little bit. To feel whole again. It's not something I expect you to understand, but I really *have* to do this. It's not that I don't want to be the kind of mother you and I agreed was best for our children. But you're with adults every day. I need the same kind of stimulation you seem to take for granted."

His chuckle seemed to rumble from deep in his chest before transferring into her body to circle her ribs. "As if that's what takes up all my time. Most of my day I wrestle with data on the computer. And the time I spend with students during financial aid interviews doesn't always seem like conversations with adults. Most of the time, I feel like Kenny could handle those sessions."

"I know, but I remember how it felt to meet with the students, helping them to solve those too-little-money, too-many-expenses puzzles that put their college careers in jeopardy. I loved helping them figure out how to make things easier. Besides, I want to be able to shoulder more of the fiscal responsibility for our family. It's not that I don't appreciate that you've always supported me being home with our babies. So many women don't have that luxury. But if I work, too, we could save more. Maybe enough to take a vacation longer than a weekend camping trip. Or fix up the house like we talked about after we moved in."

She slid her hands up and encircled his shoulders. When he lowered his face, she kissed him. "If I get this job, maybe we could ask Chris to come over and see what it might cost to at least bring the kitchen into the twenty-first century. I'm tired of those old colors and that awful green in the bathroom tub and sink. I sometimes wonder if we shouldn't have held off buying this place when it seemed like the best deal we could make because it needed so much updating. Maybe we should have gone with a brand-new house, one where the electrical repairs that first year wouldn't have almost bankrupted us."

"Water under the bridge, honey. Besides, we were both eager to prove we were adults to your folks and mine. Buying the house seemed like the best way. How were we to know that if we'd waited, we could have bought it for a lot less? No one knew about the recession or that we were buying at the top of the market, when so little was available in our price range. Even with us using your trust funds to get it."

Hale stepped out of her arms to pull off his dress shirt as he sat down on the edge of their bed. "I'm well aware of those extra bills we paid off so my folks wouldn't have to take out a second mortgage before my mom's surgery, which wasn't something they planned for."

She nodded. "I know. It's what families do. We take care of each other." She wiped a hand across her face. "I didn't question it then and I don't now. It's just that ..."

Hale shut the door and pulled her close. "Then let me be clear. I'm thrilled that we're pregnant again. Can't wait to share the news. Even though I know it worries you. But, sweetheart, with my new salary, we'll be making more than last year. As soon as the adjustment kicks in."

"But, why hasn't it? You got that promotion in April. It's already late September, six months later. That you haven't already received it makes no sense to me. What did Andy say?"

"Haven't asked. He's been on a tear for months, not the easiest man to approach these days."

Eden watched Hale slide out of his dress slacks and pull on a pair of worn and faded sweats. "Ivy just yelled again. Could you go see what those two are fighting about?"

Hale nodded, gave her a quick kiss on her forehead and headed for Kenny's bedroom.

~ ~ ~

Eden gripped Hale's hand as they entered the obstetrical office. Her stomach churned and she leaned close to whisper in his ear. "I need to visit the bathroom."

"You feel sick? I thought you said that wasn't happening anymore."

"Guess I was wrong." But to take care of the request the nurse was sure to make, Eden asked for and was given the small container for her urine sample.

She locked the door and leaned over the toilet, certain she was going to lose what little lunch she'd been able to eat after nearly two weeks blessedly free of that particular sign of early pregnancy. But nothing happened. Her stomach had quieted.

After collecting her urine specimen, Eden washed her hands and stared at her image in the mirror. *Good Lord. I look awful!* She cupped cold water in her hands and doused her face, hoping the dark circles under her eyes would fade, hoping she could hold herself together through the discussion with the doctor.

She knew what he was going to ask—of Hale and her. Their last conversation about how to make everything work, especially the household budget, had been interrupted by a pair of calls, one after the other— as if her phone was conspiring to give her hope that she would soon have a job. The two company reps, one from a marketing company whose PR person had mentioned they were expanding their finance department, and one from the local school district, had asked her to come in for an interview. She wanted to ask Deb if she had anything to do with the school district inquiry because she couldn't recall having approached them. She'd put off the human resources rep, saying she would be out of town over the next week, a lie that enabled her to focus on this all-important appointment.

She'd get back to both places as soon as this appointment … she gulped … was over. Both opportunities seemed worthy of serious consideration. Along with that real estate job. She thought of it as work she might enjoy, if only as a stepping stone to something more in keeping with her skills. Except they hadn't come through with an offer. Not yet anyway, even though her interview went well. Perhaps they were inclined toward someone younger, like that gum-chewing teenager.

After another receptionist called and asked her to come in for an interview, Eden concluded that she didn't want to work for a diner, imagining herself occupying the owner's office while a variety of stomach-churning scents wafted into the back office, guaranteed to send her fleeing to the nearest women's room.

That job at the trucking company was even less appealing as she imagined those men waiting for their weekly checks making lewd comments about her, particularly if she went ahead with her pregnancy and it became more obvious. Or would they come up with some crazy excuse not to hire her *because* she was pregnant? Even if that was against the law. *I should call them back and tell them I'm not interested.* Hale's protective nature had shown itself when she'd shared her concerns about working at the trucking company. He'd said he wasn't sure he wanted her working at such a place, although he repeated that the decision was totally hers.

Hale knocked on the bathroom door, his concerned words interrupting her thoughts. "You okay in there, Edie? They just called your name."

"Be right out." She patted her face dry, concluding nothing she did would erase those circles that confirmed she wasn't sleeping well. Uninterrupted sleep might do the trick, but it had eluded her ever since she'd taken the pregnancy tests.

Eden walked with Hale into the doctor's office, he smiling and relaxed, she serious and tense.

"Glad you both could make it," Dr. Ortiz began. "Before we go into an examination room, tell me what you've decided. Hale? You first."

"Shouldn't you be asking Eden? I mean she's the one who … you know." He placed a hand on her nearly flat belly.

"Actually, I was hoping what you had to say was a joint decision. Isn't that the case, Eden?" The doctor's hazel eyes peered in her direction under shaggy dark brows.

"We've decided to stay pregnant. Assuming I don't lose the baby. Like what happened to my sister-in-law," she blurted.

"Are you experiencing symptoms that suggest you might be at risk of losing the fetus? Anything out of the ordinary? Since you've been pregnant before, I'm sure you would have noticed. You know, abdominal pain, spotting or cramping? Any frank bleeding?"

"No. And not much in the way of morning sickness, either. At least not like with Kenny. Maybe it's a girl. My mother said she knew I was carrying a girl the second time. Because I didn't have as much nausea with Ivory. "

"Hmm." The doctor pulled open her chart then looked at her again. "Based on our first visit and what you told me then, I'm going to stick with my estimate that you're about eight weeks along now. Which places your due date somewhere in the vicinity of mid to late May or very early in June." He smiled. "A nice time to have a baby, don't you think?"

Hale beamed. "In my book, any time's a great time. Right, honey?"

"Spoken like a happy father," the doctor intoned. He rose from his chair. "Let's get you into an exam room, Eden."

A nurse escorted her into the room, and she changed into a gown before lying down on the table.

At the knock and her reply, the doctor entered, followed by Hale, who took a seat near the head of the examining table and grasped Eden's hand. She smiled up at him, her eyes filling as she squeezed his fingers. He answered with another squeeze and a smile.

The doctor washed his hands and donned gloves. He conducted a brief exam, pulled off his gloves.

"Everything's as it should be?" Hale asked.

The doctor nodded.

"So, are you going to do another ultrasound? So we can see the little squirt?" Hale asked.

"I'd rather we wait. At sixteen weeks, I'll have you go to the ultrasound lab at the hospital."

"Oh. Guess I forgot when that happened." Hale looked abashed. "What about the heartbeat?"

"We'll listen to that if you'd like. How old is your little girl, Hale?"

"Five. Just started kindergarten," he replied.

"And, I'm looking for a job. Any reason I shouldn't take one?" Eden inserted herself into the conversation, glanced at Hale as if reminding him that she had planned to ask the question.

Dr. Ortiz nodded. "There's nothing wrong with you keeping busy, Eden. Just don't plan on lifting heavy objects. Most sit-down jobs should pose no danger whatever, but I recommend that you get up and move around at least once an hour. That will reduce the likelihood of blood pooling in the legs, swollen ankles, other problems, too, particularly as you approach your due date." He looked over the tops of his half glasses and smiled. "What sort of job are you looking for?"

"Something clerical, I suspect," she said, wishing she sounded more definite.

"She's already received several requests for interviews," Hale crowed.

The doctor glanced over at Eden as he placed the transducer over her lower abdomen. "Good for you. Make them compete for your skills, Eden. Didn't you used to work at the college? Ah. There it is." He smiled when rapid-fire heartbeats sounded. "The littlest Brinker."

"Should it be that fast?" Hale asked.

"At this stage, yes. A good sign. A slow heart rate could be a sign of possible fetal loss. But this little guy is doing just fine." His gaze centered on Eden's face.

"Good to know." She gave Hale a quick smile.

Dr. Ortiz helped her sit up. "I'll let you get dressed, and see you in four weeks." He held out his hand to Hale. "Nice to see you again. Will you be attending all of Eden's appointments?"

"As many as I can," he replied, and gave Eden a quick grin.

"Nice. I like it when husbands are involved. See you two in a month."

Four

The next morning, Hale urged Eden to stay in bed, to rest. "I'll take the children to school today." He kissed her good-bye. "Check with you later."

"Hmm," was her muffled reply as she burrowed into the covers.

Hours later and shortly before heading for the college cafeteria to grab lunch, Hale pulled out his cell phone. But before he could ask how Eden was feeling about her job search, and the Dr.'s reassurances, she chortled in his ear.

"Guess what?" She sounded excited for the first time in weeks.

Hale felt a grin building, hoping his smile was transmitted in his reply. "Tell me, hon."

"That real estate office, the one I told you about? They asked me if I was still interested and could I come over if I was! I want this job, Hale. No matter what else happens. Please tell me you're okay with me taking it."

"Of course, I agree. But it's not my decision to make. If you want the job, take it. Feel my good-luck kiss," he said and smacked a kiss near the phone. "You're absolutely sure you don't want to reconsider those other places?"

"I'm sure. It might be nice to work downtown in a big fancy office, but I'm tired of waiting to hear from them. Want me to call you after my appointment? I'm supposed to be there at one. Today. In plenty of time to be home for the children." She laughed. "I guess that crazy receptionist remembered what I said about being home for the children."

"Why don't I call you?" he offered. "I'm not sure how long I'll be at lunch with Andy, to talk about my raise that never landed."

"Good luck. And, if you forget to call or get bogged down in that meeting, don't worry. I'll fill you in over dinner. Love you." She hung up.

Hale relaxed in his chair. *Finally, some news Edie's happy about.* After his meeting with Andy, he looked forward to reviewing the list of new scholarship contributions that had been received in the last month. *The Alumni Office has been particularly successful this term,* he thought. He picked up the office landline. Time to congratulate the woman in charge. Hadn't she graduated two years earlier? Maybe that was one reason for the largesse she'd managed to corral, in addition to her unbridled enthusiasm. He recalled how eager she had been to make contact with former graduates.

Hale left her a message and grabbed his coat. *Time for lunch.* Something he usually looked forward to. Not so much when he had to combine it with conferring with his irascible boss.

~ ~ ~

"Oh, Hale. What do I do now?" Happy Eden from three hours earlier had morphed into Worried But Excited Eden.

"What is it, hon? Could you make it quick? I'm about to go into another meeting." Hale ran his fingers through his hair as he watched the second hand on the wall clock slide from one number to the next. A meeting not previously on his calendar, after a call that sent his blood pressure soaring.

"I just got another call. From that company downtown, the one expanding their finance department? They asked me to come in for an interview tomorrow. And right after I hung up with them, the school district called. They kept referring back to my experience when I was at the college. The lady said she thought I'd be perfect for what they are looking for. *Now* what do I do?"

"Looks like those calls that you were worried about have paid off. I thought you were going to take that job at the real estate office."

"They called and delayed my meeting until tomorrow. Something came up and the owner can't meet with me today. I was going to tell them I'd take the job, but maybe I should hold off if there's a chance I'll receive other offers. Or am I jumping the gun? These calls today might just be to eliminate me from the list of candidates. You know, creating a second cut after seeing me, talking to me. Even if I go in for an interview, maybe I'll never hear from them again, like those other places that never got back to me."

"Which ones were those?"

Eden huffed out a quiet laugh. "Doesn't matter. I wasn't going to take them anyway, but these two look promising, more in keeping with what I used to do." She breathed into the phone. "I need to prepare for those other interviews, especially the one for the school district. I'm sure they'll understand that I need to leave early to be home when the kids come slamming in the door. Gosh! I never *dreamed* I'd get so many requests to interview!" she exclaimed.

Hale chuckled. "Hang in there, hon. Don't cancel your appointment for tomorrow. If that realty office makes you an offer, tell them you've had other offers, too, that you can't give them an answer immediately. It never hurts to play hard to get. Might even make them up whatever it is they plan to pay you."

"Good idea. I never thought of that. Okay. Bye." Eden hung up without her usual "Love you."

The excitement generated by Eden's job-hunting reminded Hale of how he'd felt before he landed his current position, a position that wasn't moving him into a higher salary level as he'd been hoping, or as rapidly as he wanted.

Hale had planned to stay long enough at Lambert-Knoll College to head up the Finance Department, to make overdue changes when it came to assisting needy students. But his immediate supervisor seemed determined to be hang on until he reached mandatory retirement age. Assuming he didn't die first. Andy's too frequent gasps for breath when climbing stairs gave Hale pause. One of these days, would Anderson Randolph pass out from overexertion even though he wasn't yet sixty? Retirement was possible at sixty-five, Hale knew, and mandatory at seventy.

But do I want to wait that long? Especially with raises coming so infrequently? The thought sent his stomach into freefall as he contemplated the possibility of losing financial ground with another set of unexpected expenses. Gearing up to take on private clients who needed help with their taxes seemed the only way to bring in more money, even if Eden did land a job. And if her job ended up becoming full-time, that would mean having to pay someone to watch the children. What would that do to the Brinker bottom line?

I should think about sending out my resumé. If only to test the waters. Even though he enjoyed his work at the college, especially now that he was second-in-command. The only major downside was the pay and having to follow Randolph's uninspired lead.

At least Andy had finally added another employee, who would be tasked exclusively with interviewing all students seeking financial aid when Hale wasn't available. Madison Hanover was shy, particularly with the more assertive students, but she seemed to be trying hard. And her questions were always on the mark, a sign Hale took to mean that she was intent on doing a good job. She was personable, enthusiastic and eager to please, the kind of employee he was happy to supervise, to encourage.

He stood up and shrugged into his suit coat for his meeting with the chancellor and president. Hale hoped this was about his still pending raise. For weeks, Eden had said he should push Andy to authorize it, but Hale had chosen to hold off. Too many other responsibilities keeping his mind on other issues. Besides, at lunch, hadn't Andy said it was "coming soon?" Too bad he hadn't defined what that meant.

Hale entered the conference room and took a seat across from his boss, who was bouncing a pencil against the edge of the desk in the president's conference room. Both the chancellor and the president seemed annoyed by the random click-clicking of the pencil on the desk.

The last time Hale had met with both leaders of the college, it had been to announce his promotion to second-in-command in the finance office. But Hale had anticipated that promotion, after the previous occupant of his current position had been hired away by a big accounting firm in Portland.

What was on today's agenda? Because Anderson was present, Hale felt in his bones that the upcoming discussion might become unpleasant. If only he was mistaken and it was good news. Like his long-awaited raise.

"Mr. Brinker. Glad you made it." Such unexpected formality from Anderson Randolph sent a chill of foreboding skittering down Hale's spine.

"I gather we're here to solve a problem," he replied, looking first at the president then the chancellor.

"Actually, to inquire what you might know about one," the president said when Anderson frowned.

Hale faced his boss, then looked to his left at the president, a man he viewed as the best leader of the college since he'd joined the finance office. Level-headed, totally supportive of the faculty and the student body, goal-oriented. Hale considered President Roger Ingraham responsible for the growth of the institution—in endowments, the number of buildings on campus, the percentage of the faculty with PhDs, and the number of students enrolled. Even the sports teams, whose presence Hale had never counted as a plus, had chalked up more wins than losses since Ingraham had been hired.

But what Hale had appreciated most about President Ingraham was his oft-repeated mantra about offering the children of low-income families a chance to go to college via scholarships that specifically targeted such students. At the convocation following Ingraham's investiture as president, he'd mentioned the Gates Foundation and their FLI program. Later that same week, he'd met with Andy and Hale and encouraged the finance office to seek out additional funding sources for such students. As a result, Hale had brought ten more local businesses into the fold of annual scholarship supporters. Two of those businesses had also agreed to take on summer interns, to give their scholarship students an opportunity to learn the skills necessary to running a business or working in one.

"I'll get right to the point," the president stated. "You were promoted last spring, along with a raise. Correct, Hale?"

"Yes, to the promotion, but I never received the raise." He glanced at Andy, who began fidgeting in his chair.

The president shifted his attention to Andy. "What's the explanation for that?"

Before his boss could reply, Hale, his brow furrowed, spoke up. "I was told there were budgetary constraints. Since I don't handle the office budget, I was unaware my promotion-related raise might pose a problem."

The chancellor leaned forward. "That's what you told him, Anderson?"

Mr. Randolph cleared his throat. "I, uh, I was concerned because we've had more than the usual expenses. Hired another person to handle student inquiries, which have increased dramatically in the last two years. I was concerned that enrollments this fall might not justify additional expenditures."

The chancellor rubbed one finger along the edge of the folder he was holding and then opened. "But enrollments have nothing to do with promotion-specific raises, Anderson. Surely you know that administrative expenses are managed out of different funding sources. If you chose not to authorize that raise but approved Mr. Brinker's promotion, you were in error. An error that must be rectified immediately, along with an apology to Mr. Brinker." He glanced again at the contents of the file folder. "According to Mr. Brinker's job evaluations here, which you signed off on, he's doing an outstanding job. Always has."

Andy remained silent. "But—"

The president buzzed his intercom, and his secretary entered, holding another document. "I've taken the liberty of looking at the budget for the finance office. It says here that Hale *has* received that raise, ten percent above his previous pay level." He stared at Andy and Hale. "How is it that these documents say he's receiving it, but you claim it wasn't authorized? And Hale confirms that his paycheck doesn't reflect it?"

"Yes, sir," Hale said. "Er, I mean, no, my pay hasn't increased." He glanced at the chancellor, knowing him to be a stickler for good governance. The president, too. When he'd come on board, he'd made numerous efforts to hire additional faculty, and had impressed Nathan Lambert with his attention to the administrative offices, as well, claiming that a college needed to be well run to attract and keep an excellent faculty, to attract outstanding students.

"Is your father-in-law aware that you didn't receive a raise?"

"I didn't tell him." Hale recalled Eden's insistent demands that he share that information with her father, but he'd always preferred to stand or fall on his own laurels. And he'd reminded her of her own opposition to nepotism, something about which they agreed.

"As I suspected. When I spoke with him, he knew nothing about what seems to have occurred here. Nor would he likely to be happy about it," Ingraham stated.

Oh, boy. Nathan's sure to pull me aside at Iona's Sunday dinner and demand to know why *I didn't talk to him.*

"He knows I'm not into leaning on family connections," Hale stated.

"Admirable, something your father-in-law applauds, by the way," the president continued. "But this problem should never have occurred. What puzzles me is the record-keeping error. That the Comptroller, whose people cut the salary checks, claim to have paid you while you haven't received this money. Makes no sense. Where'd that money go, if not to Hale's paycheck?" He gazed steadily at Anderson Randolph. "Perhaps you know."

But Andy simply shook his head, one hand nervously plucking at the edge of his suit coat.

Hale mentally totted up the amount of that raise and multiplied by six. Not a huge number, but one he and Eden could certainly use, especially with a new baby coming. He ran a hand through his hair before squeezing his nape. "May I make a suggestion?"

"Certainly," the president urged.

"If you authorize cutting a special check to cover what has been missing from my paychecks thus far, we could call it good. Especially if the error is rectified, beginning with my check at the end of this month."

"Of course. You are being more than gracious about this," the chancellor said. "Anderson, I want you to meet with the comptroller. Track that money down. Make sure you find the missing funds, and that it goes where it should hereafter."

Anderson's cheeks, previously pale, reddened. "I'm sure it was a problem of the comptroller. Or whoever in that office cut Hale's check. Maybe someone there stole it."

The president straightened in his chair, his frown mirrored by the chancellor's. "You're making a serious allegation, Anderson. Are you prepared to back it up with proof that you sent over the forms including the raise Hale should have been receiving since his promotion went into effect?"

Without waiting for Andy to reply, Ingraham said, "It appears I also need to have a conversation with the comptroller." He rose and held a hand out to Hale, who shook it. "I'll be in touch. Before you go home this afternoon, I'll have a check cut for you. Let me know if it is not delivered to you. Personally."

"Thank you, sir. I appreciate it." Hale glanced at his boss. Andy was standing, shifting from one foot to the other, as if anxious to escape.

"Malcolm, if you could stay for a couple minutes?" the president requested.

"Certainly." The chancellor took his seat again.

Hale walked into the hall, aware that Andy was right behind him. But his boss chose to say nothing, nor did he return to the finance office. Instead, he trotted in the direction of the stairs. Hale listened to the man's heavy footsteps as they approached the lower floor until they could no longer be heard.

~ ~ ~

That afternoon, the person from the comptroller's office who delivered Hale's check thanked him for waiting and announced, "I was told to tell you that all your checks will be delivered to you personally through the end of the year until we can find out how it was that the electronically generated ones weren't deposited into your account, even though our records show that they were."

"Please tell the comptroller I appreciate that."

Hale locked his office door and left the building, the check in his chest pocket. Maybe the kid from the Comptroller's Office was right. An error had occurred in the electronic submission into his bank account. Hale patted his chest pocket. Eden would be happy. Maybe she would relax and enjoy her pregnancy now that the raise was part of his paycheck. Except for the morning sickness that had plagued her so much with Kenny, she'd enjoyed being pregnant. Actually, reveled in it as the two of them had played with different baby names. Even though their first inclination in both cases had not changed over those weeks and months while her belly got bigger and the baby's kicks declared his or her presence.

Would she still be excited about her job prospects when he waved the extra check in the air? He suspected she'd give him one of those smiles that always melted his heart. Hale would remind her that things were working out just fine, like he'd said they would.

He pulled into the driveway, parked the car and entered the kitchen. "Hmm. What smells so good?"

"Dinner." Eden kissed him. "One of your favorite stews. You look happy."

"Look at this." He handed her the check. "The missing money from my pay over the last six months."

As expected, she beamed, then gave him a hug. "Nice. How'd that happen?"

"The president asked me to come to his office. Chancellor Middleton was there, too, and Andy, who didn't look at all happy. Anyway, until the end of the year, my check will be personally delivered. Maybe longer, if they can't figure out how things got messed up."

"You mean delivery by hand?"

He nodded. "Chalk it up to some kind of error in the electronic system the comptroller put into place when she came on board."

Hale chuckled. "What was weird was President Ingraham said the amount recorded by the comptroller's office— and he showed me the paperwork —had the correct amount, but that isn't what I've been receiving. To my knowledge, this sort of thing has never happened before."

"You think someone was diverting your raise?" She stirred the stew then lowered the heat and covered the pot before stepping away from the steam curling above the stovetop.

"I didn't think to inquire about that, but I have a feeling that's what Roger is going to find out. Edie, what would I do without you? Such logical thinking. I have to say, the way Andy was looking at me, I wondered if he was going to fire me."

"But why? You did nothing wrong. Seems to me he was called on the carpet with whatever questions Malcolm and Roger asked. Do they suspect a hacker?"

"Don't know. But I'm going to talk with the comptroller and ask her."

"But the college has an IT department. Didn't Dad say something about that a couple years back? You know, when a student was caught changing grades for those football players?"

"I forgot all about that. You're right." He pulled his cell out of his pocket and scrolled through the college contacts list. "Here it is. Bedrossian. Head of IT. I'll talk to her, too. Tomorrow. First thing."

~ ~ ~

The next day, Hale waited for Vanya Bedrossian in a small office in the basement of the oldest building on campus. The room felt crowded with the plethora of computers that lined the walls of the small space. Three people sat, their eyes glued to the screens, their fingers dancing across the keyboards, creating random bursts of sound as numbers flashed across the screens. Sounds of a printer in the next room spewing out paper resonated when the person nearest to the door hit a button and raised her hands off the keyboard, reminding Hale of a professional pianist completing a particularly difficult arpeggio.

Another door opened, and a woman entered, her waist-long black hair swinging as she turned and closed the door.

Hale's gaze took in the spike heels she wore, her mile-long legs with muscled calves that suggested she might be a runner, and the short black skirt that ended well above her knees. She wore a pale green sweater over a dark green blouse he thought might be silk.

He stood up. "Are you Ms. Bedrossian?"

"Yah. Am Vanya." The woman's pale blue eyes seemed to pierce his chest before settling on his face. "You are?"

"Hale Brinker, finance office. I just came from the comptroller's office, about what they think might be a hacking incident. Could we speak privately?" He allowed his gaze to circle the room. The three people previously working at warp speed seemed to have halted their pounding of keyboards. Was it his mention of hacking that had silenced them?

The woman nodded and motioned for him to follow her.

Hale entered a room that he was certain had previously been a storage closet. A battered desk and equally ill-used chair took up most of the space. A bookcase leaned against the wall, crammed haphazardly from top shelf to the bottom with what appeared to be manuals of different computer languages.

"Bring chair in," Vanya ordered while she shed her sweater and draped it over the back of her chair.

Hale retreated to the other room, grabbed a folding chair leaning against a nearby wall, hauled it into the room and straddled it. In doing so, his knees made contact with Vanya's desk. "Tight quarters," he murmured, more to himself than to her.

She nodded, a slight smile curving her lips. "What you said. Hacking. Why you think so?"

Hale sucked in a quick breath and began to explain about his raise, when it should have been received, that it had not been, but now had been taken care of via a special replacement check.

"I'm wondering if someone might have hacked into the system. According to the comptroller's reports, my checks should have included it, but they didn't. Oona Davies says she suspects a hacker. What do you think?"

Vanya Bedrossian hummed what Hale recognized as a Russian folk song beloved by his late mother, who had made a practice of collecting Eastern European music most of her married life. Hale listened, part of his brain wandering into musing if he still had some of that music in the boxes taking up space in the attic. Those boxes were there because his father wanted nothing that would remind him of his late wife.

In the silence that now seemed slightly strained, Hale glanced up at Ms. Bedrossian when she cleared her throat. "Sorry. Recognized the song. Reminds me of my mother."

"Oh? She is Russian?"

"Uh, no. Czech. She loved all kinds of Eastern European music. Collected it for years."

"Ah. A woman with good taste." Vanya lifted her hair off her shoulders before allowing it to fall down her back, reminding Hale of a blue-black waterfall.

"Your suspicion. Could be right, what Oona suspects. I get with her."

Hale nodded and prepared to stand.

"Wait. Please. Need information."

He eased back down and resumed straddling the chair, his arms resting on the back rest. "Of course."

"Your check electronically generated?"

"Used to be. Not anymore."

"Ah. If I create false account for you—to track what might happen—you okay with that?"

"As long as the Ms. Davies approves. You'll get with her?"

She nodded. "Phone, please," and held out a hand.

He placed his cell phone in her palm.

She entered her contact information and then sent herself a message, capturing his email address.

"Say nothing to anyone. I be in touch."

Hale nodded. "That's it?"

"Yah." She stared at him. "You have questions?"

"Uh. No. Well, there is one. Not just that some of my money never got to me. But also where it went."

"Part of same problem. Will find it. Not to worry." She stared back at him, giving Hale the impression she viewed him as dispassionately as a recently captured bug pinned to a piece of paper.

Okay. I'm dismissed. He offered his hand to the statuesque woman, rose from his perch on the too-small chair and man-handled it out of the tiny office. As he propped it against the wall, he felt three pairs of eyes follow him to the outer door, even as the word-processing rattles previously filling the room halted, their imagined echoes hanging in the air like so many gossamer shrouds.

Hale returned to his office, his mind occupied with his conversations with the two women he'd met that morning, and with what he had agreed to. He'd turned responsibility for a bogus account with his name on it to that impressive IT person who seemed to know her business. He wondered idly if she'd been sponsored by Nathan, who'd offered such sponsorship to immigrants hired by the college, making them a part of what he called the Lambert-Knoll family. Not that Iona approved. But Nathan was far more broad-minded, more expansive and ac-cepting in his thinking than Iona Bartholomew Lambert. May-be he'd ask at Sunday dinner.

"Yoo-hoo, Hale. Anybody home?"

Hale glanced up at Helen, who was framed in his doorway. "You need something?"

"Andy left early. You asked me to keep you informed. Re-member?"

"Oh. Right. Thank you, Helen. Could you please ask any-one wanting to see me this afternoon if they could wait until tomorrow morning? I need some uninterrupted time."

"Of course. Leave it to me," she assured him. "But it's nearly time for me to leave. Do you need anything else before I go?"

"No." He closed his office door against the sounds from other offices, appreciating that it was sufficiently isolated from the conversations often occurring around the secretary's desk and the open area where students filled out forms.

As soon as he sat down, he checked his cell phone. *Eden times two.*

He fired off a quick text. *Can't talk now. And I could be late for dinner.*

He opened his computer and scanned the spreadsheets from the several scholarship accounts, the most important of his many responsibilities. He'd be sending out requests for meetings with several of the local businesses in town that had previously provided financial aid or internship opportunities for deserving students. His eyes stopped scanning the lines when he spotted what looked like an irregularity. He picked up the phone.

"Greg! How are you? I was planning to hit you up for another internship opportunity next year, but first let me ask: how is your current intern working out?"

"Good to hear from you, Hale. Rachel's working out great! In fact, I've been discussing with her about working for pay, not just as an intern, as of the spring quarter, when she can give me more than the ten hours of work that internship provides."

"Mind if I make a note of that?"

"Not at all. Since you called, why don't you sign me up for another intern for next fall, too? I like that it gives me free help and the opportunity to identify a good worker. We're expanding again. Business has been great all year!"

"Good to know. Which brings me to why I called. According to my records for this academic year, your business never made a financial aid contribution in addition to the internship program. Not a lot of money, but enough that recipients had their registrations covered for whichever quarter they received aid."

"That can't be right. Let me check with my bookkeeper and get back to you. Maybe with everything else I've been handling these days, I simply forgot to have a check cut. If so, my apologies. I'll get that money over to you right away."

"Thanks, Greg. I'll wait to hear back so I can make sure our records match yours."

Hale sat back in his chair. Another person, like himself, so busy he'd neglected something that shouldn't have been missed?

He continued his scan of the internship list and the businesses that had stepped up. Five more than last year. Nothing else seemed to be out of order, so he went on to perusing the merit scholarship organizations. Nothing looked to be amiss there. All that remained was the list of new students receiving full rides from the Lambert Foundation. Nathan insisted that Hale handle all such requests personally. Which he'd been honored to do, even though he only set up the appointments with the Board for the students to address, if not directly, then by Skype. Twenty such students were currently enrolled.

Everything seemed in order here, too, until he reached the last student name in the alphabetic list of freshman Lambert Foundation Scholars. *Anthony/*prefers Tony *Walburn.* He'd learned that particular preference when he'd conducted a preliminary interview with the young man, who'd impressed Nathan and the rest of the board with his sincerity about going on to medical school. The kid wanted to become a doctor, because—as he'd said more than once—every person deserved top-notch medical care, something Tony's little sister hadn't received in time to save her life. Why then, was there no dollar amount confirming that the student's bills for the Fall term had been paid? Hale glanced at the student's name again. Had he transferred to another school? But that wouldn't have prevented his continued support from the Lambert Foundation. Maybe the student had dropped out.

He flipped back to that portion of the file listing the student's contact information, campus address and home address. He was an out-of-state student living off campus.

Hale dialed the student's cell phone.

"This is Tony. Leave a message."

"Mr. Walburn. This is Mr. Brinker in the finance office. I have a question regarding your Lambert scholarship. Please get back to me at your earlier convenience."

Hale hoped that brief missive would bring the student into his office, preferably tomorrow. He sat back in his chair, its squeak signaling a need for oil in the underparts. Hadn't he done that last month? Maybe the old chair should be replaced. The left armrest was loose, too, something he'd been unable to rectify, even with the assistance of someone from the maintenance department.

He closed his eyes and allowed his mind to ponder what he'd seen in the files. A possible error in financial aid funds, and now this student who was supposed to be receiving a Lambert Foundation scholarship?

Nothing like either issue had occurred previously, at least not since he'd been placed in charge of all student financial aid. He recalled when he had been hired. The accounting system previously utilized had been woefully inadequate in providing an easy way to go deep into student files. At that time, there'd been no direct link between student applications and financial aid sources. When Eden was hired, six months after Hale came on board, the two of them had worked out a system for creating such links, thus eliminating the cumbersome and time-consuming practice of checking different files. By hand. And since then, he'd steadily improved the system, bringing in new computer programs, speeding up the entire financial aid process, both when having to deny a student aid and when providing it.

Hale rubbed his neck, aware of the tension he felt after having discovered those two unexpected problems. As if his own raise, now resolved, hadn't been enough. Glancing at his watch and swearing under his breath at how much time had elapsed since he'd sat down in front of his computer screens, he shut down his laptop and reached for his suit coat. *Time to go home.*

Five

Eden smiled as Hale entered through the kitchen. "You're home, finally. I was beginning to wonder if you were going to sleep in your office tonight." She kissed his cheek before he pulled her closer, shifted her position and captured her lips against his in a way that felt almost desperate.

When Hale finally released his grip on her waist, she asked, "What was that about?"

"For being so late. And forgetting to call when I should have followed up my first text. Tell me about your day. How many interviews did you do? Did that real estate office ever get back to you?" He grabbed an apple from the bowl on the counter.

Eden laughed. "So many questions. Where do you want me to start? Never mind. I guess you're hungry. Didn't stop to grab something at the cafeteria."

She opened the refrigerator and took out a plate. "Let me warm this up for you." When the microwave dinged, she placed the plate in front of Hale and handed him a knife and fork.

She arched a brow. "I'm more curious about what kept you so long. It's been months since you've had to stay late. Please don't tell me Andy was haranguing you about something he should have handled."

"Andy was part of it. I wish he would retire. Every other week, he asks me to handle something that should be on his plate. I'm tired of doing his job *and* mine."

"Uh-oh. So it did have something to do with your responsibilities."

He nodded. "And I had a chat with the head of the IT office." He huffed. "If you could call where she hangs out an office. The woman works out of what I'm sure used to be a closet, and the room where she's crammed three people and twice that many computer screens isn't much bigger."

Eden's eyes widened. "Really? And a woman heads that office? What a nice change. What did she tell you?"

"She's going to see if she can figure out how my raise got screwed up. I have a feeling I'll need to see her again. Also found some other stuff that didn't look right."

Eden handed Hale a glass of iced tea and began to rub his neck and shoulders. "No wonder you were delayed."

"At the moment, I need more information. If I hadn't started scanning lists I usually don't get into until later in the year, I never would have spotted the problems. Which may not be a problem at all. What I'm hoping to find after one of our intern supporters and a scholarship recipient get back to me." He moved his head from one side to the other. "Babe, that feels so good. Keep rubbing. Oh. Right there." He closed his eyes as if to focus on where Eden's fingers were probing as she kneaded a sore spot at the base of his neck.

"You've got all kinds of knots back here," she murmured and concentrated her hands along his shoulders. "Lean forward, honey. Try not to tense up. I know it hurts, but if I could just get your muscles to loosen up."

Hale moaned softly in response. "Don't stop. That hurts so good. Now, tell me about your day," he murmured, his words barely audible as he lowered his head and leaned toward the counter.

"My news isn't nearly as interesting as yours."

"If it's good, I want to hear it. Dealt with enough bad news this week. Tell me something good. Something positive. Besides the kids doing well in school. I saw Kenny's paper with that big red 100 on the fridge. And Ivy's paper with the smiley face. So, did you get the job?"

Eden chuckled softly. "Let's see. Where to start." She slid her hands along Hale's shoulders. "I went to that downtown office first. My interview went well enough, but they are looking for someone who will work a full eight hours every day. I'd have to be there by eight o'clock, which means you'd have to drop the kids off at school. And we'd have to get a sitter for the hours before I'd be home." She sighed. "I'm not sure the HR person was all that pleased when I asked her if I could work from home in the afternoons. Anyway, if they pick someone else, I won't be unhappy."

"What about that school district gig?"

Eden nodded. "A much better fit. And the superintendent said they're flexible about my working from home. One of their other employees does that now."

"Good to know." Hale pushed his empty plate toward the center of the table.

"But they are just starting their job search. The person I spoke with hinted that they are interviewing *lots* of candidates. Probably several who haven't been home for more than five years like me. So, I'm not holding out a lot of hope that they'll get back to me."

"And you don't want to wait much longer?" Hale asked.

Eden smiled. "You know me so well."

"Which leaves the real estate office. What happened there?"

"Yes, that. They called me back just as I was getting home and asked if I'd come in today instead of tomorrow. The owner was already there when I showed up. Not like the last time." She paused, recalling how nervous she'd been when she'd pushed open the door to the real estate office.

"Anyway, the owner—his name is Quincy McCue—was really nice. He didn't say much about my resumé, but he did ask if I enjoyed working at the college. And then he said he was sure that being a mother meant I could probably keep everyone in his office in line." She giggled. "At first, I wasn't sure what he meant, but then he told me what I'd be doing. Recording money coming in via the purchase and sale agreements, keeping track of earnest money, disbursing checks after closing, that sort of thing. Actually, I'll only be handing out the checks that the escrow offices send over in addition to those I write to cover things like supplies and the like, which probably won't happen all that often. Most of the stuff they need, they order on line. It's possible I might be asked to do that, too, since the receptionist doesn't like doing it. When I was getting ready to leave, she said that whatever 'money stuff' she was handling she'd be happy to send my way.

"Anyway, Mr. McCue said that sometimes the agents collect their checks themselves, but when they do, they have to show me what they got and hand over the paperwork so that I can record the right amount. Stuff like that. It's really a simple bookkeeping job. None of the research stuff that I did with you at the college. Oh, and handling the phone when the receptionist is busy or on an errand for one of the agents."

Hale smiled. "Sounds like you're looking forward to being there."

Eden nodded. "Mr. McCue said he didn't think I would be challenged. Even asked me if I thought I might be bored. I told him there was only one way to find out and that was for me to do the work and let him know."

"Did he say you could work from home? You know, when it's closer to when you have the baby? And after, when you're recovering?" Hale wiggled his shoulders as if to show her the knots were gone.

Eden took a seat. "I didn't tell him." She glanced back at Hale.

"Don't you think he deserves to know you're pregnant?" Hale raised his head and turned in his chair to face her.

"The closest we got to that was when he said he thought I could get everything done in plenty of time to get home for the kids. He asked if I'd be okay agreeing to work from nine until about one-thirty or two. With only two other agents in the office, it doesn't look like things are all that busy. But, if he brings in more agents? My hours might change and I'll ask him if I can finish up at home. I told him it might be best if I agree to work for a month, after which he will decide if I'm the person they want. What I want, too." She shrugged. "If he still wants me, then I'll tell him." She glanced down at her abdomen, its slight rounding easily hidden in a loose blouse.

"So you have it all figured out?" Hale stood up, rounded the table and pulled Eden into his arms, holding her close, his warmth reminding her of the many times he'd comforted her during difficult times. How could she expect that he wouldn't be supportive now? To think she'd worried about how he might react after his extra-long day trying to solve vexing problems, especially the one called Andy.

"So … did he offer you the job? Sounds like he figured you'd say yes." He kissed her on the forehead.

"He agreed to a month-long trial. After I told him what you said. And that I'd had other offers. I asked if I could have until the end of the week to get back to him. I was afraid he might say he couldn't wait that long, but he agreed that would be fine." She giggled. "His receptionist told him he was a damn fool if he didn't hire me. I heard that as I was getting into my car. The window next to her desk was open and she has a loud voice." Eden chortled. "That Opal Springer. She's a real character."

"What'd he offer by way of a salary?"

"Oh, my gosh, Hale! I forgot to ask. I guess I should nail that down when I go in on Monday. Was that a mistake?"

"Maybe. Maybe not." He brushed a strand of her baby-fine hair off one cheek. "Your enthusiasm tells me it's where you want to work."

"I guess. Ever since I got home, I've been up and down about calling Mr. McCue back and saying I'll take it. And then thinking I shouldn't. Maybe my waffling means I'm not ready to return to the land of adults just yet."

"Nonsense. It's just been a while since you interviewed for a position. What about those other places where you sent off emails? Did you get any more calls?"

"Only one, and it would mean more than an hour commute each way. Too far for me to get home quickly if something happened with the kids. I told them I already had a job."

Hale smiled. "Then I guess you've decided. Real estate office, here comes Eden!"

She laughed. "Assuming Mr. McCue doesn't change his mind when I call him on Friday."

"What are you going to do between now and then?"

"Concentrate on my wardrobe. I'll start in my closet and see if I have enough clothes to wear at the office. It's been such a long time. Maybe I'll have to hit the thrift stores."

"Forget the thrift stores. Why don't you talk to Elaine? Ask if those stores at the mall are having sales. I'm proud of you, hon." Hale hugged her again then slid his hands down to her butt cheeks and gave each a gentle squeeze. "Want to join me in bed? I'm about ready to fall over and tomorrow's another big day, slogging through the data on my desk, getting back with that IT woman."

"Somehow, I don't think sleeping's all you have in mind," Eden replied with a grin. She took his hand and they walked into their bedroom.

~ ~ ~

On Friday, the home phone was ringing when Eden returned from dropping off the children and then Hale.

"Hello?"

"Ms. Brinker, it's Quincy McCue. Any chance you're still willing to take on our bookkeeping chores?"

Eden's pulse picked up. "It's Friday, isn't it? I was just getting ready to call you. And my answer is yes."

"Terrific! Can you come to the office today, so we can nail down the details? In maybe half an hour?" He lowered his voice to a near-whisper. "Opal's been on my case since I opened the door and I'm close to breaking."

Eden stifled a laugh. "I think I could make it by then," she replied.

"Great. I'll let her know you're on your way."

Eden ran a quick comb through her hair, glad she'd dressed for the office just in case. After donning a light sweater, she drove to McCue Real Estate and parked in the nearby lot.

The sign for Chris's business no longer leaned against the building. *I guess he got my text.*

Minutes after Eden was ushered into Mr. McCue's office, he smiled, wrote a number on a piece of paper and passed it across his desk. "Your suggestion that we try this for a month is something I'm comfortable with. I hope you're willing to start at this salary."

Eden looked at the amount he offered, pleased that it was higher than she'd expected. She cleared her throat.

"And you want me here every day?"

"Only Monday through Friday. My agents and I often come in on the weekends. Any completed contracts and related paperwork that comes in over the weekend, we'll just drop on your desk for you to take care of on Monday. And if you get behind or need help, Opal will scan them into the electronics record." He stopped tapping his pen on the desk and gave her a bemused glance. "Any questions?"

"Only one. You mentioned that your contracts are all entered into the computer, either by me or Opal. I just wanted to make sure you're still okay with me working from home some of the time. Mostly in the afternoons. You know, when the office gets busier and there's more work for me than I can cover during my regular hours." As he opened his mouth to reply, she added, "So that I can be there when my children arrive from school." She imagined how they might feel if she wasn't home to welcome them. She and Hale had long ago decided that their offspring would not become latch-key kids.

"Let's try out that arrangement during this first month and see how things go. When you're not here, Opal will scan in the contracts, like she does now. And you can access them from home. She'll give you the security code." He stood up and extended his hand. "Let's shake on this one-month probationary period. I hope that at the end of that time, if you're happy, and we're happy, we'll make this arrangement permanent."

Eden shook his hand, relieved that her request hadn't killed this first opportunity to work outside the home. "Thank you. And I start on Monday?"

"That would be perfect. Opal will be thrilled. She really hates bookkeeping. Hasn't been her usual smiley-face since she had to start keeping the books after my divorce." Quincy grinned.

"Your ex-wife did the books?"

Mr. McCue's face assumed the look of someone who'd just tasted a lemon. "She did. Rather badly, too."

Not going to touch that topic again. "Well, then I'll see you on Monday. At nine sharp."

Eden grinned as she left Mr. McCue's office.

"Did he do what I told him?" Opal asked sotto voce, when Eden passed her desk.

"We're trying things out for a month."

"Yes!" Opal raised a fist ceiling-ward. "Wonderful!"

~ ~ ~

When Hale arrived home, Eden beamed as she announced, "I got the job. With the realty office. At least for a month."

"Your salary?"

"Less than I was getting at the college, but more than I expected he'd offer, *and* I can work at home in the afternoons if I can't get everything done before I leave. Starting Monday. It's really only part-time, about five hours a day if I don't do any work at home. But I'll be keeping track of my hours. And no benefits this first month. Mr. McCue said we will revisit that at the end of the month, assuming he wants me to stay and I agree." She gave Hale a halfhearted grin. "Which gives me tomorrow to shop for more business-appropriate clothes."

"You mean maternity clothes? But don't you still have those?" He stepped away from her and crossed his arms over his chest.

"Don't you remember? I took them to the secondhand store after Ivy. After we decided two was our limit." She squinted at him, recalling how she'd felt that day, half happy that her maternity clothes and other items no longer in fashion wouldn't be cluttering up their precious closet space, but half sad that she'd never be pregnant again.

After Kenny's birth, she'd *wanted* to stay home, and couldn't imagine going back to work after Ivory was born, either. How was she to know that, four years later, she'd change her mind, feel as if life was passing her by?

"What's the matter, Hale? Why do you look so growly?"

"Let me get out of these business duds." He left her in the kitchen.

In the midst of making dinner, Eden looked down when Ivory pulled on her hand. "What is it, sweets?"

"Can I go shopping with you? Like you told Daddy?"

"No, dear. You're going with your father to watch Kenny play soccer tomorrow."

"I don't want to. It's booooorrrrriinnnng," she pouted through the elongation of the word.

"You can help me pick out what earrings I should wear when I get home. How about that?" Eden asked, hoping that little chore would mollify her daughter.

"Are you going to be like Auntie Debra and Auntie Elaine?" Ivory asked.

"What do you mean, dear?"

"They get dressed up every day. 'Cause they have jobs."

"Auntie Lexi has a job, too."

"But she doesn't have to get dressed up. She just has to put on a big apron and that funny hat."

Eden nodded. "It's still a job. And I have a job already. Taking care of you and Kenny," Eden countered.

"But that's a mommy job. I mean a different job, a *real* job. Not at home."

Eden nodded. "Then I guess you're right, I'll be like them. Because my new job is at an office, too. And I'll be like Auntie Lexi, too. She has a mommy job along with her other job, the one at the bakery."

"Is that why she yawns so much?" Ivory asked.

Eden chuckled. "Probably, but I think she yawns because she's going to have a baby and some days she gets really tired. Don't you remember when she said Chance is going to be a big brother in a few months?"

"Are you going to yawn, too, Mommy?" Ivory's blue eyes widened.

Eden's pulse raced for a moment. Had Ivory overheard her conversation with Hale the other night about when to tell the children about the new baby?

"You know, because you'll have two jobs?"

"Just like them, except that I will also work here when you and Kenny come home from school. Which means you'll have to be quiet if I'm on the phone or working on the computer. No yelling at your brother. Think you can do that when I'm doing my new job at home?"

Ivory stared, big-eyed, at her mother. "I guess. Can I go out and play before we eat?"

"You may, but please stay in the yard, Ivy."

"I will." The kitchen door slammed.

Hale wandered into the kitchen after having changed out of his business suit. "This new job of yours isn't going to become a problem, is it, hon?"

"Don't think so, since I'm really only working part-time and sometimes at home." She stared at her husband, unwilling to change her mind about what she would be doing, starting Monday. She placed her hands on her hips as he met her gaze.

"Do you *not* want me to work, Hale? Is that it? Or is it the money? I wish it was more, but maybe it will be after I show *my* boss I can do the work. I'll bet you've already figured out what we need to keep this family together with three children to feed, and clothe, and send to college. And that what I'll be making isn't going to be enough. Or is it that you really prefer that I stay home?"

Those furrows in his forehead returned. "I didn't say that. You know I support you and this new job." Hale reached for her hand. "My real concern is that it's way below your skill level, what I know you can handle. I already agreed that whatever money you earn, we'll put in the children's college fund. And since my raise is finally in place, I was thinking we should apply that check to the kitchen remodel. I know you've been wanting an upgrade. Maybe even before the new baby comes. Want me to call Chris for an estimate?" He kissed her cheeks and lips before sliding down to nibble on her neck.

Before she could answer him, Hale continued. "Besides, your salary's not what has me tied in knots right now. It's what's going on at my office. Didn't want to say anything, but I wanted to let you know. So you'll understand if I seem distracted. More than usual, anyway." He gazed at her. "I have a sick feeling that someone may be stealing scholarship monies."

Eden gasped. "*That's* what you're dealing with? How long has this been going on?"

"I don't know, and I couldn't get back to the head of the IT department today like I wanted. She was at some big conference. To make matters worse, when I tried to talk to Andy, he put me off, too. Said that scholarships are my responsibility since I'm in charge of all things having to do with student financial aid. That he didn't want to be a part of whatever was bugging me." He shook his head. "I never imagined I'd ever have to deal with such a problem."

While Eden prepared dinner, Hale reviewed with her what he did know, what he wanted to find out, and the information he was still waiting for. After he finished talking, she covered the dishes still simmering on the stove and walked around the kitchen island to stand in front of him.

Eden pulled Hale into a hug, wanting comfort herself as much as to show him that she cared about what he cared about, that she loved that he wanted to share what was bothering him. Just like when they'd worked together.

"You've got some big issues to deal with at work. What can I do to help? Maybe if we went through those files together, we could figure out how this might have happened. And stop it from happening again. Like we used to, before Kenny was born."

"Our systems are different now, Edie." He sucked in a big breath. "This is serious. Financial aid funds, scholarships. I hate to think that we might be dealing with a hacker. Someone from the outside who somehow got into our system. Or worse, someone on the inside."

"Oh, sweetheart." Eden's heart ached for Hale. He, like her father, thought of the students, faculty and administrative people connected to the college as one big family.

"I love that you want to help, but this is something I need to try to figure out. Now that we have an IT team, I'll talk to them. I'm sure that's why President Ingraham made them an early addition to the administrative staff. To protect us." Hale stroked her back. "But we should be celebrating tonight. Your new job. Right?" He kissed her again.

Eden nodded then gave him a quirky grin. "And you deserve to think about something pleasant, to relax, at least for tonight, maybe even through the weekend."

"Oh? You have something in mind?" He chuckled as he slid one hand down her torso and patted one butt cheek while the other hand teased her breast.

Eden closed her eyes, her focus turning to what her husband was doing. "I think I do," she murmured breathily.

"What, exactly are you thinking, Eden Brinker?" he asked between nuzzles.

"In case you hadn't already figured it out, I can't get pregnant tonight, so why don't we live dangerously—you know, after dinner and the kids are in bed."

Hale smiled. "Sounds like something that might improve my mood. To something pleasant, like you said," he repeated, his voice roughening right before he answered her latest kiss with one of his own, only deeper, longer, more passionate.

After dinner, he helped Eden get the children ready for bed. Earlier than their usual hour, Hale and Eden showered and tumbled into bed together. After several minutes of the kind of foreplay that Eden loved and Hale did so well, he entered her, sending Eden's pulse racing as she climbed to a peak and soared over the edge, taking him with her.

Six

Hale munched on his lunch as he studied the list of student appointments Helen had printed out for him. Helen had dropped another five names onto his desk, all sophomores inquiring about financial aid for the winter session.

He pressed the intercom. "Helen, see if Madison can talk to these students. I have to dig into other problems."

"Yes, Mr. Brinker."

He set the list to the side, scanned through the series of questions he'd planned to ask each of them, and emailed those questions to Madison. She was good at interviewing, and at assuring the students their requests would be handled expeditiously.

After that troublesome finding regarding Tony Walburn's scholarship, Hale worried what he considered a bigger bone. Missing financial aid money. Had he happened on an embezzlement scheme? Had any other student scholarships been taken?

He was still waiting for Vanya what's-her-name to get back to him. Tony, too, had failed to respond to Hale's request for a return call. Impatiently waiting. Not something he found easy. *If only Walburn's the only one.* If that young man didn't get back to him by the end of the week, Hale would talk to Nathan Lambert. As president of the Board for the Lambert Foundation, maybe he could explain what had happened to the student's scholarship.

On a hunch, Hale pulled up the entire list of Lambert Scholars. In doing so, he was surprised to see how many students had received aid from the family source. Hoping that Tony Walburn was the only one affected, Hale checked each name against the funds granted, beginning with the masters candidates and gradually reviewing all the other class groups, ending with the freshmen, those on campus for the first time this fall term. Some of the students had received small grants, likely to cover books only. Still others had received aid covering room and board, while others were recipients of merit scholarships of varied amounts. Only twenty had what Hale knew to be those coveted full rides, for four years of study.

Shit! Walburn's not the only one! Hale's gut clenched. The amount for other Lambert Scholars didn't gibe with what was supposed to be in their college-managed accounts. Were the students aware of the missing money? And what about their parents? Would he be hearing from them?

As he looked over the screen to his far right, Hale lifted his fingers off the mouse.

Hale called Helen. "Is Madison free?"

"She's talking to one of the students you asked her to speak to."

"When she's at a convenient break time, could you send her in to see me, please?"

"Certainly."

Minutes later, Madison Hanover knocked on Hale's door. "You wanted to see me, Mr. Brinker?"

"Have a seat, Madison. You're probably familiar with the students who've made application for financial aid since you came on board."

"Yes, sir."

"Remind me when I asked you to begin doing that. Was it in March, right after spring break, when you were first hired?"

"Yes, sir. It's what I've been doing ever since, except when Ms. Arsenault needs me for things, like entering data when she's busy with other things."

Hale nodded. "Of course." He glanced back at the right-most screen. "How are you at remembering the names of the people you interviewed?"

Madison beamed. "Pretty good. Ms. Arsenault said I have an eidetic memory. Whatever that means."

"Good to know. Would you happen to recall a student by the name of Brenda Cochran?"

The young woman's forehead bunched and she nibbled her lower lip. "I'm not sure. When would I have seen her?"

"Probably last spring, maybe early summer. It appears she was awarded a substantial scholarship for the current academic year. My guess is she probably made application in writing before you were hired, although it's possible her paperwork arrived shortly after you started with us. Big awards usually receive numerous applications, often during the student's senior year in high school unless they were early admits." He clicked several keys and stared at the screen. "And you enter their personal data, on-campus address, home address, that sort of thing?"

She nodded. "After I see the students who come in for aid, if they are new, I create their personal file. If they already have one, I update it to show when they applied and what they applied for. And if they receive money, I add that information to their file, too. What was that name again?"

"Brenda Cochran. She's a sophomore."

Madison shook her head. "Sorry."

"What about Matiás Corrillo?"

Madison nodded. "I remember him. A transfer student from an Oregon junior college."

Hale hit several keys and nodded. "Ms. Arsenault is right about that eidetic memory of yours." He smiled at Madison. "What else do you recall about him?"

"He told me he wants to go into politics. Why he's doing a double major in American History and Political Science. We laughed about whether his accent —I think he said his parents are from Guatemala— would be a help or a hindrance."

"Right again." Hale closed the student's subfile. "That's all for now, Madison. If Helen has that file, please bring it to me."

"Of course, Mr. Brinker." Madison left his office, pulling the door closed behind her.

A good worker, personable, and attractive enough that others had probably noticed. Would she be here five years from now, or would she, like Eden, fall in love with a faculty member or one of the administrative staff and leave to start a family? He'd check with Helen about when Madison was coming up for a personnel review so that he could add his comments.

Minutes later, Madison buzzed Hale. "Mr. Brinker, Ms. Arsenault doesn't have that file you were asking about, for Matiás. But she does have the files for Nick Cochran and his sister. Nick asked to see you."

Hale glanced at the Lambert Scholars list he'd set to the side. Nick's name, and his sister's, were both on the list. "Right, if you could bring me those files."

Minutes later, Hale studied the older sibling's file, which seemed to be in order. Nick Cochran, a master's candidate, had a teaching assistantship in the Math Department. But the merit scholarship awarded to his younger sister, Brenda, represented one of those problems that had arisen. She had graduated in June from a parochial high school in Seattle near the top of her class. The copy of the letter notifying her of a full year scholarship was dated early May. But the reporting of monies used to cover her expenses represented only about half of the correct amount. Everything else in her personnel file seemed to be in order.

He fired off an email to his contact at the bank handling Lambert Foundation funds. Rather than alarm the man, he asked only for confirmation of the dates when the monies were wired to Lambert-Knoll College to cover Ms. Cochran's first year. The email he received verified what he suspected. The monies had been received in June, to be applied to the student's expenses her first year, and a confirming receipt had been sent back. So, the loss had occurred sometime between June 20 and the start of the fall term. Information he didn't have before. Was that when the other thefts had also occurred?

Hale scratched his head. Three of the long-term employees in the finance department were on holiday during different weeks in the summer months. A decision of Anderson's making, to take advantage of the limited academic activity between June and September. Because he insisted on scheduling staff vacations when their absence from the office was least likely to be missed. Even Hale had taken advantage this year, in August. The family's second camping trip of the summer, during which Eden had conceived.

He studied the names of all the employees in the office. Were any of them likely to make mistakes entering the data relating to student financial aid packages? Hale doubted it. The employment of two of the people predated his own hiring. He trusted them implicitly, had never had reason to mistrust them. Only Anderson had been here longer than they had. And Hale eliminated Madison from consideration as the guilty party. Her only access to the student files was to enter contact information. She couldn't access the subfiles involving the transfer of funds in and out of accounts.

That left him and a part-time student who spelled Helen at the front desk. But that student didn't have access to the subfiles, either, only the phone and intercom system. And Helen always locked down her computer when not at her desk.

Hale's phone buzzed in his pocket. When he saw that it was the IT head, he breathed out a sigh. *Finally! Please tell me that the security issues in your last report to the president and administrative offices are all in place. And if not all offices, at least for* this *office.*

"Mr. Brinker."

"Yes?"

"You left message?"

"We have a problem. Could—"

"Not we. You," the woman claimed.

Hale rolled his eyes, not caring that no one saw it. "All right. *My* office has a problem, one that seems to have expanded. Could you meet me here so that I can show you what I've discovered?"

"When?"

"As soon as possible. How about now?"

After a pause, she replied, "I see you in one hour."

Hale glanced at his phone. The woman had hung up on him. Okay, he'd wait one hour and if she wasn't here, he'd go to her closet, er, office, even if he had to straddle that godawful folding chair again.

~ ~ ~

Hale stared over the shoulder of Vanya Bedrossian as she scanned the student accounts he'd flagged.

"Hmm, hmm," the woman murmured as her fingers flew around the keyboard, opening and closing windows faster than Hale could follow. He felt dizzy trying to keep up with her.

Her fingers rose. "I see problem here. You see it? This student replied to fake antivirus message. Bad." She shook her head and began pounding the keyboard.

"And this one? Replied to a friend request. Looks fishy to me. Not salmon or trout. P-h-i-s-h-y." She chuckled low in in her throat.

Hale grimaced. *Very not funny.*

"That's how the thief got in?"

"Not all of them." She leaned back in his chair, pushing him painfully against the wall. "You have problem."

Duh. "Looks like more than one to me. What do you suggest we do?"

"Need outside help. Cyber professional."

"But you have people. Can't they take care of this? I mean, isn't your office supposed to be making sure everything is secure?"

"More than my people can do. Too busy creating security in campus offices. Not student accounts. They've been hacked."

Hale backed away from his desk so that Vanya could sidle past. "How soon can the professionals get here?" He'd thought *she* was the professional who could solve the problems he'd encountered. "Tomorrow, maybe?"

"I call them. Tell them it's emergency. Since it involves money." She stared at the back of the trio of computer screens on Hale's desk, as if she was able to able see the screens. "You have big problem. Call students. Tell them to come to me. My people will fix their email accounts, unfriend bad people, that kind of thing." Under her breath, she muttered what Hale interpreted as "Stupid students," as she shook her head.

"I can do that." He preceded her to his closed office door. "What else do you want me to do?"

She shook her head. "Wait. Professionals will fix this."

"You're sure about that?"

The raised left eyebrow above her implacable stare told Hale the woman was unlikely to reply to any more of his questions. "All right. I'll wait." He reached for the business card holder on his desk, and handed her two cards. "For the professionals. When you call them. After you see them. Assure them I'm at their service." He mentally crossed his fingers that they would be on the phone to him within the hour.

Vanya opened the door and stalked out, the click of her heels on the hardwood floor reminding him of a drum cadence accompanying a criminal to a firing squad.

Hale followed her and halted at Helen's desk.

After an interminable thirty-second delay during which the woman's footsteps could be heard moving down the hall, Helen said, "That woman is just plain scary."

Hale laughed. "You said it. She's contacting cyber professionals, whatever that means."

"FBI, CIA, NSA?" Helen snorted. "Those guys?"

"Whatever kind of people know how to catch hackers. Some of our student accounts have been hacked."

"When do you suppose those people she mentioned will show up?"

"Sooner rather than later, I hope. Put them right through when they call, or if they just show up. I want no more delays. The sooner I get this cleared up, the better."

~ ~ ~

Hale didn't have long to wait. The next day, Helen escorted two men into his office. Each looked serious enough to chew nails. They set their briefcases down next to the chairs they took before leaning toward Hale. He'd never forget their demeanor. No smiles. One with a light brown crew cut, the other with blond dreadlocks pulled back into an unruly ponytail, his face pockmarked with acne scars. Both wore black shirts and pants. Mr. Dreadlock's motorcycle boots were decorated with silver chains that jangled with each step. Sir Crewcut pulled what Hale concluded was an i-Pad from his briefcase and propped it on the edge of Hale's desk.

After introductions, he answered their questions, identifying the six students whose accounts had been hacked. He handed over a piece of paper containing each student's contact information, address, the class they were in and major, if that had been declared.

"What are you going to do, if you don't mind my asking?"

Mr. Dreadlocks, who had what looked like a razor nick on his chin, spoke up. "We'll talk to the students. The ones who answered fake messages warning them of a virus probably already had their computers scrubbed by Bedrossian's crew. We'll double-check. Make sure they have new passwords and antivirus protection installed. But that only takes care of two of your victims."

Sir Crewcut, whose black eyes reminded Hale of shiny marbles, spoke up. "We'll check first for obfuscation technology."

"What's that?"

"A way to disguise the IP address of whoever's breaking into those accounts. We'll look for constants in the hacker's behavior, not just how they got in, but what they did there."

"We already know what they did. They rerouted money out of those student scholarships."

"They may be after more than the scholarship funds. Leave it to us. We'll find 'em. Usually these guys make a mistake, sometimes the first time they get in where they don't belong, sometimes later, after they feel confident they won't be caught. As for those two students sent messages about a virus, we'll look for aliases. Along with that student who received the odd-looking Facebook friend request."

Hale nodded. That much he understood. The other information was as clear as mud.

"We'll install intercept software, too. For that, we need to know how many students received scholarships this year."

Hale's eyes widened. "Lots."

"How many sources?"

"You mean where the money derived?" He held up a hand. "Just a minute." He checked the screen with that information. "Over a hundred sources, but some only provided one scholarship or some other form of financial aid, like free books or covered room and board. Only twenty provided more than one scholarship, and eight provided more than fifteen."

"Get us a list of all the funders and all the students they supported, no matter the amount."

Hale nodded. "On paper or in an email?"

"We'll take it on paper for now. I'll send you an email address to an encrypted account, the only one you should use to communicate with us from now on."

"What about other people in this office? Should they have that account, too?"

Mr. Crewcut frowned. "You're our contact person. No one else."

Hale gulped and nodded, feeling guilty. As if it might have been his fault that the thefts had occurred.

"I understand. Will you be on campus very long today? I'm guessing you'll meet with Ms. Bedrossian in our IT department?"

Nearly identical cryptic grins slowly emerged on the faces of the two cyber experts. Both nodded.

"I guess you already know her?" Hale asked.

Both men's grins broadened.

"While you're talking to her, I'll work on getting those lists together for you."

Sir Crewcut stated, "When it's ready, call Bedrossian's office. One of us will come back for the paperwork."

"Of course." Hale watched as the two men rose as one, picked up their briefcases and moved toward the door. "May I ask another question?"

They turned and faced him.

"How do you suggest I deal with any parents or students who've been hacked? Assuming there are others before you're able to track down whoever's doing this? Should I refer them to you?"

"No. They're your responsibility at this time. But get us their names if you spot more thefts," Dreadlocks ordered. "Feel free to send out letters of apology and assurance that you're on it."

"Right." Hale was certain they were thinking, *but we're the ones who are really on it.*

Each man shook Hale's hand and left. Unlike Vanya, they nodded respectfully in Helen's direction before leaving.

Hale stopped at the secretary's desk. "They didn't ask to speak with Andy?"

She huffed out a soft snort. "No. But I'm thinking that the Russian spy—"

"Helen!" Hale grinned even as he protested her characterization of Vanya Bedrossian.

"That's what she reminds me of." Helen patted her neat coif. "Anyway, she probably told them you're the one who asked for their help."

"Andy's door has been closed all day. Where is he?"

"Out sick. Or maybe it's his son that's sick. I overheard enough of one conversation last week that tells me that kid may be back into drugs again."

News I didn't want to hear.

"And if you're thinking of alerting him, don't bother. You know what Andy'll say. That this is your responsibility."

"He's still the boss, Helen. He deserves to know what's going on."

"That may be, but what's the point of saying anything until he's back in the office? If you ask me, you're the one who does most of the work around here. I wish you occupied his office."

Hale stared at Helen. She'd never been so forthright before. "Has Andy done something that you disapprove of?"

She pursed her lips. "I've said too much already. Please don't hold it against me."

"Of course not. Where would I be if I couldn't depend on you to keep this office running like the proverbially well-oiled machine?" He smiled at her. "Which reminds me. I'd best get to the lists those guys want." He turned on his heel to head back to his office then reversed course and faced Helen again. "Just so you know. Those cyber guys don't want anyone other than me communicating with them. So, if Andy or anyone else should ask who they are, pretend you never saw them, don't know who they are, or why they wanted to see me."

She saluted smartly. "Got it."

Then with a sly grin, she asked, "Are you sure they're not ex-FBI or CIA? And if you asked, think they could find out if that IT lady is really a Russian spy?"

Hale chuckled. "I'm not going to ask either question. Nor should you." He returned to his office, but found himself wondering how long he'd have to wait before hearing from the cyber techs again. *Please make it be good news, that you caught whoever hacked our system. And that it won't happen again.*

Seven

Eden kissed Hale, relieved that he was finally home. "How was your day? Have you talked to my dad? He got a call from the manager of the foundation with some news he said was disturbing. Know anything about that?"

"It's part of the problem I mentioned earlier. But until I have something positive to report, I'd rather not talk about it. The IT office has brought in a pair of hacking experts, which means it's out of my hands, at least for now."

"That sounds serious, hon."

"I'm hoping it doesn't get worse. So far, it involves six student accounts. Your father would probably prefer to keep things quiet until we can happily announce we caught the crooks and got the money back." Hale popped a cherry tomato into his mouth and grabbed a carrot stick from the plate Eden was filling with raw vegetables. "I could use a good laugh. Tell me something funny that happened at your work."

She grinned. "Nothing really out of the ordinary. Opal wears the most outrageous outfits. I could never get away with that, but the clash of colors seems to fit her." She handed Hale another carrot stick.

"I hope you're looking forward to Kenny's soccer game on Saturday. He's finally showing interest in playing and not just kicking around stones in the backfield." Eden grinned. "And sitting through Ivory's tap class."

Hale groaned. "Aren't you coming, too?"

"I'm behind on all things domestic, like picking up the dry cleaning so you'll have a clean suit for next week, and restocking the pantry. If you take over Kenny's game and tap class duty for Ivy this weekend, it'll help me catch up."

"I'll probably be the only dad at Ivy's class." Hale's hangdog look played briefly on Eden's sympathy.

"Wrong. One of the girls has a single dad. He's there every week." Eden brushed her hand along Hale's cheek. "You can commiserate with him."

"Want me to bring down those boxes of baby clothes in the attic so you can go through them while I'm with the kids tomorrow?"

Eden placed her hands on her hips and straightened her back. "Is asking about the clothes your way of saying you want to find out the baby's sex ahead of time? Even though we never did that with the other kids?"

Hale shook his head. "I like how we did it before. Being surprised. You know I don't care about the sex. Another healthy baby is what I want, and to live with and love my beautiful wife, who's a wonderful mother." He grabbed Eden's hand and pulled her down to sit next to him. "You do know that, don't you, Edie?"

Her lids burned with unshed tears as she slewed her gaze away from her husband's face, the love that shone in his eyes, in his expression. She wanted to tell him how much he meant to her. Why was she hesitating?

Afraid her voice would emerge as a croak, she nodded and gulped. "I'm not ready to go through the baby clothes. Could you call the kids inside and supervise washing hands?"

He nodded and headed for the back door as the phone rang.

Eden grabbed the landline. "Hey, Deb. What's up?"

"I have some important news. What each of us Lambert brothers and sisters need to know."

"And you can't wait to share it at Mom's on Sunday?" Eden glanced at the calendar, noting that she'd planned to bring a fruit salad.

"No, we need to strategize about this before laying it on the folks. Especially since Lexi's pregnant again. She did call you, didn't she?"

"Yes." Eden's heart thumped in her chest then began to race. "She's not going to lose this one, too, is she? I thought she said everything was fine."

"No. Ask Hale to stay with the kids and come on over. Tonight. I've already asked Fletch and Elaine to come, too. Even managed to reach Chris, although he says he may be late. Something about a last-minute issue at his big jobsite."

"Hale just got home and we're about to sit down to dinner. I can make it around seven-thirty. Is that too late?"

"Make it closer to eight. Todd just walked in the door."

"Eight it is. See you then." Eden slid a finger into the waistband of her favorite skinny jeans. *Already?* What she'd been comfortable in last week now felt too tight. No changes above the waist that she couldn't manage for now, although she knew she'd need a larger bra soon.

The kitchen door banged open and Ivory's and Kenyon's querulous voices snagged Eden's attention.

"Knock it off, you two," Hale ordered. "Time to wash your hands and come to the table. Any more arguing means no story time tonight."

"That's not fair, Daddy. Kenny started it," Ivory whined.

"But Dad …"

Kenny's put-upon sigh was loud enough to be heard in the hall as Eden walked toward the kitchen.

She watched as the children headed for the hall bathroom, looking morose before they exchanged death stares. She glanced at Hale.

"Deb has some big news. She insists us Lambert sibs have to talk. Tonight."

"Hmm. And you're going?"

Eden nodded. "After we eat. Which means you'll be super-vising both baths tonight, depending on how long I'm at Deb's."

"Not an issue. It'll give me more Dad time with Little-Miss-Lower-Lip-Sticking-Out and Young-Mister-Scowler."

Eden snorted. "They've been testy since they got home from school. Maybe you could find out why."

"I'll do my best."

Ivory returned to the kitchen holding a book. "This is what I want you to read, Daddy."

When Kenny followed her into the kitchen, he reached for the book. "Not that one! We read it last week! I want one of my Harry Potters."

"What did I say about arguing and no story tonight?" Hale replied.

"But Daddy," Ivy whined.

Eden stared at her son. "Kenny, you heard your father. Best not to say a word." She paused. "Don't you have home-work to do?"

"Just some spelling," Kenyon replied.

"Your father will quiz you on the words," Eden said.

"But, Mom. You usually do that."

"I have to see Aunt Debra."

"Can I come, too, Mommy?" Ivory asked.

"Not tonight, sweets. Weren't you going to practice your alphabet? Daddy will help you. He's good with letters and words," Eden said. "Right, Hale?"

"I'm an alphabet champ," Hale replied with a grin and a wink at his daughter, who giggled.

~ ~ ~

Eden knocked once and walked into Debra's home. Todd stood near the window overlooking the side yard, conversing with Fletcher.

Debra grinned at Eden. "I'm glad you're here, sis. Some-one who won't freak out."

Eden's pulse jumped. "It's that bad? Where's Elaine?"

"She's picking up Chris. They ought to be here soon." Debra glanced at her watch and took a seat on the couch next to Eden. "Your kids were so cute when I stopped by their school on Monday just as it was letting out. Full of information about what they did that day. How's your new job? Kenny said you're working for a Realtor?"

Eden's heart clutched, knowing now that word of her job was out. She'd planned to share that tidbit on Sunday. "It's going well. I like it."

"Ivy said you're just like me now, a working woman." Debra chuckled. "Hey, wipe away that frown. I haven't said anything to Mom. No way would I steal your Sunday thunder. I'll bet Hale's happy. When you're happy, he's happy. Because he loves you." She grinned.

Eden relaxed. "He does and he is." *But he's been so busy at work, not so happy about that.* Another bone she was also worrying.

She glanced at her younger sister and patted her hand. "Are you sure it's wise to keep whatever you're going to share with us away from Mom and Dad?"

"I just want us to discuss *how* to tell them, *when* to tell them. It's not something they can do a thing about, which is what bothers me the most."

"Sounds ominous."

The door opened with a whoosh and Elaine entered, followed by Chris. He slid out of his muddy boots and tossed them onto the porch.

"Okay. We're all here. Let's get this show on the road," he announced after scanning the room and appearing to count noses. "I need to get home, get cleaned up. You got any food, Deb? I'm starving!"

All three sisters laughed.

Deb looked over her shoulder. "I guess that means you haven't been home for dinner. Todd, will you dish him up something? Don't we still have some of that turkey chili you made the other night?"

Her husband grinned. "Coming right up. Have a seat, Chris."

Elaine joined the other Lambert siblings in the living room. Chris adjusted his chair at the dining room table so that he could eat while he listened to Debra.

"Okay, spill it. Tell us why you asked us here," Elaine ordered. She took a seat next to Fletcher.

"Do you want dinner, too, Ellie?" Todd asked.

Elaine shook her head. "Already ate. Alone," she added, anticipating the question she knew hung in the air. "You know I've sworn off men. Come on, Deb. Speak."

"Okay. Todd and I want to start a family." She blushed and glanced in his direction as he took a seat in the dining room near Chris. "But we decided to check to see if there was any reason why we shouldn't. You know. Bad genes, that sort of thing. Especially given that his mother had Type 1 diabetes, which contributed to her heart problems."

"I thought she died of cancer," Fletcher said.

Deb nodded. "And it wasn't the kind that has a genetic link, either."

Eden's pulse started to climb. *Oh, God. They found something bad. I know it.*

"Anyway, we ordered some genetics tests, the kind where you spit in a tube and send it in and a report comes back, something you can check on the internet, too."

Elaine leaned forward. "And you found out that Todd has bad genes?"

"Not him, me. At least one, anyway." Debra paused to let that news sink in.

"You? Like what?" Chris asked. "So you're not going to try to get pregnant? That's what you're trying to tell us?"

"Not exactly."

Chris finished off his chili, slid the empty bowl toward the center of the table and took a seat in the living room on the other side of his twin.

Deb glanced in Todd's direction. "I found out that I'm a CF carrier. Which means I don't have the disease. Fortunately, Todd's negative for that gene mutation, so there's no danger to any children we might have."

"CF carrier? What's that?" Elaine asked.

"Cystic fibrosis," Deb replied. She looked around the room at her siblings' serious faces. "Todd and I have been all over the internet since we found out. It's an inherited disease that affects the lungs. Both parents have to be carriers if any of their children are to have the disease. Even then, there's only a twenty-five percent chance that a given baby will have it. There's a fifty percent chance he or she will be a carrier like me, and a twenty-five percent chance he or she will be negative, like Todd. Because he isn't a carrier, but I am, any of our children will either be carriers or totally in the clear. No risk of the disease in our children."

"That has to be a relief," Elaine said.

"But since you're a carrier and a Lambert kid, you think we might be, too," Chris declared.

She nodded. "Bingo. I think that every one of us Lamberts should be tested. And our partners—to make sure. To know if there's a risk."

She looked at Eden. "Your two kids are healthy, so it's likely you aren't a carrier, or if you are, that Hale isn't. But if he is, you lucked out with both Kenny and Ivy. Missed that twenty-five percent chance of having a baby with CF."

"Scary," Eden breathed out, sliding one hand close to her belly, hoping no one noticed.

Debra continued. "I talked to Dad the other day. Just in general terms, to learn more about our grandfather Lambert and his sister. They were the only ones in that generation of the family to live to adulthood. There's no way for us to know, of course, but maybe our great-grandparents on the Lambert side were carriers. It's possible some of their children might have been affected and that's why they died so young, some within months, and others, according to Dad, before their second birthday. That's what he remembered. He didn't have much detail, since most of his siblings died before he was born. Only two were born after Dad and before Annoria, and neither lived very long. But CF wasn't even identified until the late 1940s, long after they died."

Fletcher nodded. "Sounds like a possibility. Okay. Lexi and I will get tested. If she's a carrier, we'll test Chance, too.

Just to make sure. What about you, Chris? Want to spit in a tube? Even though you and Teddy aren't pregnant yet?"

"Or married." Chris frowned at his brother before turning his gaze on Eden. "You're awfully quiet."

"I wish I'd known this before … Maybe our kids should be tested, too, even if they are healthy now. There's no chance they could show signs of it later?"

"It doesn't work that way," Debra said. "CF usually shows up at birth or shortly thereafter. I read nothing that said it would show up after five years."

"But we should know if they are carriers." Eden's heart thumped against her lungs then plunged against her stomach. What if Hale was a carrier? And if she was, too, this new baby … What would they do now, if their child had CF?

"There's lots of information on the web for you to check out," Deb added. "Most people born with it have a much longer life expectancy now than used to be the case, but still, it's kind of scary to think about. CF affects the lungs. Requires special meds, special treatments, too, from what I read."

"Does insurance cover the treatments?" Chris asked, ever the practical one.

"Probably depends on the policy," Todd replied. "Ours does. I already checked. I think it falls in the preexisting conditions category."

Chris stood up. "Now that I know, I'll head home. And fill in Teddy. Send me what I need to know about getting that test kit."

"No need," Todd said. "We already did. Hang on a sec."

He detoured into the guest bedroom and came out carrying three pairs of testing kits. He handed two to Chris, two to Fletcher and two to Eden. "I didn't think about your kids when we ordered these, but there's a form inside. You can easily get two more to have Kenny and Ivory tested. Fletch, there's a form in your kits, too, so you can get one for Chance."

"Even if I'm not a carrier, we'll do that," Fletcher said. He opened one box and handed the order form to Elaine. "I know you've sworn off men, but maybe you'll want to order a test for yourself. Just to make sure. Even if you never need it." He grinned.

Chris laughed. "Yeah, sis. Who knows when you'll get serious about someone? I'm betting that happens next month. Maybe even next week." He winked at his twin. "We know how you are."

"How I *used* to be," Elaine retorted with a frown. "Didn't I say I'm done with men?"

Debra and Fletcher laughed. "Riiigghhht."

"Okay, okay, I'll order a kit. Even if I never need to share the results with anyone," Elaine grumbled. She headed for the door. "See you at Sunday dinner. Come on, Chris."

"Wait! We haven't discussed how to tell Mom and Dad," Debra countered. "Don't you all agree that they should be told? I mean, Logan's our youngest brother. He probably should be tested, too. Trouble is, I didn't think we should dump this on him without first talking to Mom and Dad."

"Mom is going to freak out, insist she couldn't *possibly* be a carrier," Chris declared. "But Dad should definitely be told, since he's a Lambert, and he's probably how we got the gene, assuming any of the rest of us are carriers, like Deb."

The discussion continued for another ten minutes before Elaine and Chris headed for her car.

Eden departed shortly thereafter. On her way home, she held back tears. More medical bills weren't something her family needed. Even with her new job and Hale's raise. And more worries weren't something she wanted to deal with. Not now, not for the foreseeable future.

She had a feeling she knew what Hale would say about this news. Unlike her more cautious approach, he was a glass-half-full kind of guy, always looking optimistically at whatever challenge they faced. He'd probably spend hours on the internet and then quote her those statistics Deb had spouted, numbers and percentages that gave her little comfort.

Eden thought of Kenny and Ivy. Neither had exhibited any signs that they might be ill. At least not with a genetically related disease. Which meant they were probably in the clear, or maybe only carriers. She glanced down at the test kits perched on the passenger seat. She wanted them tested them right away. To assure herself that her two babies were safe. After that, she and Hale would get tested. Even though the answer regarding her special secret, her pregnancy, remained unanswered.

Eden pulled into the garage and clumped into the kitchen. She heard no television. Nor was the house resounding with children's noises, signaling that Hale had managed to get both children into bed on time. She hoped they were asleep so that they could talk without fear of interruption.

As she shut the door behind her, Hale turned in her direction from his perch on the couch and smiled. "All's quiet on the Western front," he murmured. "They went down without a single argument. Kenny knows his spelling words and Ivy aced her alphabet, big and little letters."

"Good," she managed to croak before her face crumpled.

His smile disappeared into a concerned mien. Hale rose from his seat, strode toward her and opened his arms to her. "Honey, what's wrong?"

"We shouldn't have agreed to keep this pregnancy." She dropped the test kits onto the dining room table.

"Why? What in the world did Deb say?"

"Cystic Fibrosis. We may be carriers. Debbie was tested. And she has it. I mean, she's a carrier. But Todd isn't, so their kids will be spared, but if I'm a carrier like her and you are, too, this baby could have it." The other words she wanted to say disappeared in sobs she could no longer contain as she clung to her husband.

The steady beat of Hale's heart, the warmth of his chest against her breasts, the gentle stroking of his hands up and down her back represented safety, but what about the baby she carried? Was it not safe from the Lambert genes she carried? Genes her mother was always crowing about, that the Lambert family— early settlers in Pacific Knoll and descendants of the college founder —and her, by marriage, were entitled to be looked up to. But according to Deb, at least one of those genes might be defective. What would her mother say about *that*?

Hale walked Eden over to the couch. "Let me talk to Deb. Did you share *our* news when you were there with your sisters?"

"No. Didn't we agree to tell everyone at Sunday dinner? Fletcher took two kits so that he and Lexi could get tested. I doubt Lexi will be happy. After all, she's pregnant, maybe as much as two months further along than me. Maybe she's in the clear, since Chance is healthy. But if Fletcher's a carrier, Lexi could be, too."

Hale dialed Debra's number and spoke briefly with his sister-in-law before returning to the living room.

Eden sat on the couch, hugging both decorative pillows to her chest, as if their presence would make her feel better.

"I want us to test the children first," she said.

"But they can't be more than carriers, according to Deb. If you're worried about this baby, don't you think we should get ourselves tested first? If we're both carriers, we'll have a decision to make. About the new baby. I'll talk to the Dr.. Find out if there's a way to test him ahead of time. Did Deb say anything about that?"

Eden shook her head. "She said there's a form in each box for ordering more tests."

"Good. We'll spit in the tubes, and fill the out the forms for more tests. And I'll mail both kits. I'll fill out the order form first thing tomorrow. When those new kits come, we'll test the kids."

"You're probably right." She sat up and hugged him. "I was hoping you and I could think about names. We haven't done that yet. Now, though, I think we should wait."

Hale kissed her cheek then angled her face to center on her mouth. "Something we should have done right after we listened to the heartbeat."

"But with names already picked out, we …" A sob muffled her words, muddied her thoughts. She sniffed more tears away. "I'm so lucky to have you for a husband, Hale. I don't know what I'd do if I had to face this by myself." She swiped her fingers across her moist cheeks.

Hale waited until Eden was no longer wiping her eyes. He retrieved the kits and opened them. "Let's do this. Right now." He and Eden spit into the tubes, following the directions. He filled out the form for additional kits, sealed up the boxes and laid them on top of his briefcase.

He gave Eden a reassuring smile. Hale, ever the optimistic one.

"We'll face this together, Edie. Just like everything else." He kissed her. "You never ate dessert before you scooted off to Deb's. Want some now? The kids thought your chocolate cake was terrific!"

"You'll have some, too?"

"Already ate two pieces, one before homework and one after our little monsters were in bed." He grinned. "Didn't want to set a bad example for them after they brushed their teeth."

Eden gave him a wan smile. "I could probably eat a small piece."

"Let me get you one."

"Actually, I think I'd like to soak in the tub first."

"You're making this a bubble bath night?" Hale asked.

"How'd you guess? It always makes me feel better."

"Then I'll have your cake ready for when you're out of the tub."

Eight

After eating the cake and placing her plate in the sink, Eden climbed into bed. Several minutes later she set aside the information about CF and burst into tears. She and Hale talked about Deb's news again, but the information he'd printed off from several internet sites—the ones he considered legitimate, trustworthy, up-to-date—only ramped up her fears. Eden was thankful she had such an understanding husband, one who didn't pooh-pooh her anxiety. But she imagined the tiny bundle she carried being attacked by that recessive gene, rendering her child a victim of cystic fibrosis. She imagined her new baby daughter unable to breathe, her lungs unable to provide needed oxygen, dying a slow and painful death. Hale said that what he'd printed off for her to read was assuring. Scientists knew so much more now than decades earlier. But Eden felt anything but reassured, even though she knew no one who'd borne a child with the disease. She was convinced that Fletcher was right. CF had killed her paternal grandfather's siblings before they even had a chance to live.

"But didn't you read how much better things are now? Besides, we don't even know that our kid is in danger." Hale slid next to her and reached for Eden.

She knew he hated it when she wept. Almost as much as she did. She despised feeling so helpless. *Damn these preg-*

nancy hormones! Was that why she was so easily rattled these days by good as well as bad news?

The call from Mr. Wyecliff minutes after Eden arrived home the other day had also provoked tears. Her usually compliant daughter had been placed in the time-out chair for two minutes on Wednesday morning after she snatched a book from a classmate and refused to say she was sorry when asked to give it back. Eden's crying jag that afternoon was barely over before the children tromped up the porch stairs. When asked, Ivory remained stubbornly mum until Eden confronted her with the teacher's report. Then both had wept. At least Kenny hadn't reported anything untoward. Instead, he'd handed over his spelling test with a bright blue "100%!" accompanied by three stars parading across the top of the paper.

Hale patted Eden's hand. "Maybe I should call Dr. Ortiz and ask for a referral to a genetics counselor. One of those articles mentioned that. Would that make you feel better, even though we don't know anything yet?"

"What can they say without the results of my spit test?"

"It takes two carriers, Edie. You heard Deb, read what I printed off. If you're feeling guilty that you might be a carrier and our kid has CF, I'm guilty, too. But, even then, there's only a twenty-five percent chance that this baby has it. You're making a mountain out of a molehill that may not even be true."

"But Hale, we can't *afford* a child who's sick. Yes, we're lucky we have two healthy children. But what if this baby inherited our bad genes? What if he or she has CF? It's not just a financial burden for us, but one for Kenny and Ivory, too. They might not be able to go to college if we have to spend all our funds on medicines to keep this baby alive."

Hale stared at her. "We don't know that our insurance won't cover those meds. Or if we'll even need them. You're jumping to conclusions without confirming evidence."

"Yet. But every day that goes by, this baby gets bigger. I'm already growing out of my clothes. The pants I wore today were so tight I had to undo the zipper after I got to work. I know we were going to say something on Sunday, and I have a feeling Deb and Elaine already suspect. I so wish there was a way for us to know the baby's status ahead of time."

Hale held up a sheet of paper that described chorionic villus sampling. "There's this."

"But, the risks, hon. What if we ask Dr. Ortiz to do it, and we lose the baby and then we find out he wasn't affected? We'd have killed our child for no good reason."

"Then we'll just have to wait and do that other test. Amniowhatever. The one we decided not to do when you were pregnant with Ivory."

"But I have to be four, maybe even five months along before we can do that one. By that time, everyone will know. And if she has CF and we choose to abort, how can we help the children to understand?" She sighed and ran a hand through her hair, pushing it behind her ear.

"Then maybe not knowing is the better option." Hale kissed her forehead. "I mean, we didn't know before, with Kenny or Ivy. And you loved being pregnant with them."

"But I never imagined anything would be wrong. That was before this particular genie was out of the bottle." She punched her pillow and reached for the covers when she shivered. "I wish Deb and Todd had never done that stupid spit test," she huffed.

"But if they hadn't, we wouldn't know the risks. Besides, it's only a twenty-five chance at the very worst. No, babe, Deb and Todd were right to tell us. Even if they don't know we're pregnant. And I'll bet Fletch is glad, too, even though Lexi's further along. Think they'll do that amnio thingy?"

Eden shook her head. "I have no idea. Maybe they'll wait for their results. Want me to ask her?"

Hale leaned back, pulling Eden closer. "Only if you want to. When did you say Doc Ortiz wants to see us again?"

"At our regular appointment, in three weeks. I doubt we'll have our results by then, but at least we can talk about the amnio. I made the appointment for the afternoon, so I won't have to tell my boss. He'll just assume I'm going home, like usual."

Hale leaned over and kissed her cheek. "If you'll lie on your side, I'll massage your back and shoulders. That always helps you relax." His gaze seemed to consist of equal parts tenderness and sexual heat.

Eden slid onto her side. When she felt his warm hands on her shoulders, she teared up again. "My mom was right about you, Hale. You're the best, a perfect husband, a wonderful father. How could I have been so lucky? " she murmured jerkily in between sniffs.

"Living right, I guess." He kissed her nape and leaned over her shoulder, grinning crookedly at her. "I was the lucky one. When I found you. Let me check on the kids. I'll be right back." He scrambled off the bed, exchanged his boxers for a pair of pajama bottoms and walked down the hall toward the children's rooms.

Eden listened for sounds that confirmed the children were awake. But she heard nothing except the closing of their doors and the soft pad of Hale's feet in the hallway. Eden climbed out of bed and wandered into the dated master bathroom. It seemed to show its age more each year.

She counted rooms, wondering how the house could be expanded to provide another bedroom. Right now, one room would have to hold two boys, or two girls. They would need bunkbeds after the little one graduated out of the cradle and then a crib. Three children would mean more toys in the living room, effectively pushing the adults out of a space she'd wanted to reserve for quiet conversation and occasional TV-watching.

Kenny's larger bedroom sometimes served as a playroom for both children. Ivory didn't mind sleeping in the smallest bedroom in the house, only slightly larger than an oversize closet. Would Kenny be as accommodating if they had a second daughter and he was moved into Ivy's room so that the bunkbeds for the girls could be housed in his current space?

The baby will be in our room for at least a few months, she reminded herself. Would that provide time enough to convince the children that change was good? That it might even be fun? If only they could sell this place and buy something more spacious. But that was out of the question, and she refused to raise the issue with Hale. She sensed he'd feel badly that she craved a larger home, knowing they couldn't afford it. *If only I hadn't insisted on using my trust fund to buy this place when prices were so high.* But they had wanted to be in a real home, a house, after they were married. And she'd insisted that she didn't want to raise their children in an apartment.

Eden climbed into bed, but pushed the covers off, feeling too warm for comfort right before Hale followed her into the master bedroom.

"What about it, sweetheart? Ready for a massage?"

She nodded, aware that with just his voice, Hale could send her hormones soaring. Or was this another example of her pregnancy alerting to his male presence? "External only, or internal, too?" she asked, wanting to lose herself in his loving.

Hale reached for Eden, his body telling her what he must have been thinking, what he wanted.

She helped him pull her nightgown over her head. "I love you, Hale. Never doubt that. The kids, too. It's just that—"

"I know, hon. But we're a team. Remember? Whatever we have to do, we'll do together. Right?" He kissed her then chuckled.

"Are you laughing at me?"

"Not at all. Just thinking that you being pregnant means we can save some dough for a few months." He smirked. "No need to stock up on condoms." He slid his hands down her body, heating her. "Good thing, too. You're always so hot to make love when you're pregnant. Not that you aren't when you're not. Which is why we're growing a baby again, right?"

"Hmm." Minutes later, Eden closed her eyes, no longer needing a massage to relax.

~ ~ ~

The next day, Eden drove the children to school determined to think positively about Ivory playing nicely with her schoolmates. She penned a note to Mr. Wyecliff that she had spoken with Ivory about her behavior and hoped that her teacher would see an improvement in her willingness to share. When she kissed her daughter good-bye, she gave her a do-as-I-say look. Ivory had looked appropriately mollified.

"You have a good day, too, Kenny. See you at home this afternoon."

"Okay. Come on, Ivy." He grabbed his sister's hand and headed for the building. "Hey! There's your teacher. Maybe he's looking for you."

Eden heard Ivy's pouted, "Is not," when she pulled her hand away as she followed her brother up the steps. But Mr. Wyecliff's words were for Ivory alone as her daughter handed him Eden's note before scampering up the stairs and walking into the building.

At the real estate office, Eden sat at her desk and took several deep cleansing breaths, determined to look on the bright side, as Hale had suggested. She glanced at the calendar. Three weeks until her Dr.'s appointment. She mentally crossed her fingers that the DNA test results would be back by then, although Hale had said it might take longer. Which meant she'd have to decide about the amniocentesis without knowing if it was necessary. She squeezed her eyes shut at the thought of that big needle penetrating her womb.

"Hey? Are you okay?" Opal asked.

Eden straightened in her seat. "Yes. Just doing a little meditating." She forced herself to smile at the receptionist, who was garbed in a bright purple tunic with ballooning sleeves and a black-and-white striped pair of Capri pants.

Opal pointed. "Check out all the stuff I stacked on your desk before I left yesterday. Lots of deals this week. Our people must have struck gold or something."

Eden glanced at the pile of paperwork that threatened to teeter into her lap. "I'll get on this right away."

"And I'll leave you to it. I know how you like to get home on time to your kiddies." Opal left, her overly sweet perfume seeming to cling to the air near the door.

Eden opened the window, craving freshness, determined to counter Opal's favorite scent so that it wouldn't send her rushing to the bathroom at the end of the hall. After gulping air, she turned back to the work awaiting her and began to enter the information from each purchase and sale agreement.

Two hours later and halfway through the stack of papers ready to be filed, she stood up and walked around the office, easing the strain on her lower back. She'd neglected to set the alarm on her cell phone. She sat back down and smoothed her big shirt over her belly, glad that she'd chosen to wear her newest pair of slacks, the ones with the expandable waist.

She continued working until her growling stomach told her it was time for lunch. She pulled out the bag she'd packed that morning and sipped her tea, still hot in the small thermos she'd popped into her lunch bag. As she leaned back in her chair, she checked her cell phone and was surprised she hadn't heard it announce that she'd received a text.

Wedding's on! Call me quick!

From Elaine. Eden thumbed a quick reply. *Chris and Teddy? Can you talk now?*

Her phone rang almost immediately.

"Are you on a lunch break like me?" Elaine inquired.

"Yes. What do you know?"

Elaine laughed. "Not a whole lot. Teddy texted and asked if we could meet her tonight. All she said was she and Chris have set a date, but to keep it a secret from Mom. You know how she is, would probably want to have a great big to-do. And neither Chris nor Teddy want a flashy wedding. Maybe she wants what Fletcher and Lexi did. You know, a justice of the peace at the courthouse."

"Did she say that?"

"No. Just that she needs help from the Lambert sisters. Anyway, can you come over to their place tonight? I told her I'd call you and Deb. Already touched base with Lexi. This is her day off at the bakery, so no problem there. I'm free any time after six."

"I'll make sure the kids have eaten. But I may be late if Hale is delayed. His work has been total madness lately. Or maybe I could drop the kids off with Fletcher, since he'll probably be taking care of Chance."

"Whatever. I'll tell Teddy you'll come as soon as you can."

"Okay. See you tonight." So Teddy and Chris were finally getting married. She wondered how Chris had convinced Teddy.

Eden shoved the remains of her lunch into its bag and glanced at the clock. Less than two hours before she had to leave. *Back to work.*

She focused on the rest of the paperwork and was relieved when, with five minutes to spare, she added the last sale agreement numbers to the spreadsheet she'd created.

"You got them all done?" Opal asked as Eden walked past her desk. "I was betting it would take you *days* to finish that pile!"

"I concentrated. See you tomorrow, Opal." Eden trotted to her car and climbed inside, mentally planning a quick dinner that Hale could supervise if he was home on time. And, if he wasn't, she'd call Fletch, just in case.

~ ~ ~

Eden dropped Ivory and Kenny off at Fletcher's house and drove with Lexi to Chris's place. Elaine and Deb were already there, wreathed in smiles and laughing at something Teddy had said.

"Come on in, Eden. Chris, you can leave now," Teddy declared. "This is a girls-only gathering. Right, ladies?"

"Women, Teddy," Elaine remonstrated. "The Lambert women, of which you are now one. Bye, Chris." She waved her twin toward the studio across the driveway from the home he shared with Teddy.

"I'm going, I'm going," he growled, though with a hint of a smile. "If Lexi brought something good to eat, save me a piece."

"I did and we will," Lexi assured him.

Each Lambert sister found a place to sit around the kitchen table. Eden spoke up first. "So, Teddy. Who decided you were getting married? I know how Chris is. He's never been all that interested in doing things by the book, especially if it involves Mom's rules."

"Actually, it was me who kept saying I wasn't ready," Teddy admitted. "So, I guess you could say your brother wore me down."

"You're not pregnant, are you?" Lexi asked, rubbing her small baby bump under the cover of the table. "Not that that's any reason to get married."

"Nope," Teddy declared. "Not that I'm against it exactly," her cheeks reddening. "But we decided to wait before adding to the Lambert population explosion." She grinned at Lexi, who laughed.

Eden breathed a quiet sigh of relief. Lexi being pregnant was enough pressure in that regard. She could only imagine what her mother would say when she heard Eden's news, assuming it was positive. But would it be? Her heart gave a little kick against her lungs, a reminder of the decision she and Hale might have to face when they saw the Dr..

"So why now? And when's the big day?" Deb inquired.

"December 31. That way, we'll have fireworks every anniversary." She joined the hoots of laughter that ringed the table. "And so he won't forget the date," she added.

Debra beamed. "That's wonderful. Todd and I loved having a December wedding. I'll bet you picked it because the construction work slows down around the holidays."

"That, too, although we're both doing more in the studio this year than last. Hardly a seasonal dip."

Eden scanned the women's nods of agreement. Chris's furniture orders and Teddy's glass-making and carving commissions now represented a sizeable percentage of the work of Lambert and Partners Construction.

"So, tell us what kind of wedding you want. I gather the reason you asked us over is because you'd prefer that our mother isn't involved in the planning," Debra said.

"Right," Teddy replied. "Chris said he'll run interference if he has to. But I don't want your mom to be mad at him. Or me. It's just that she wouldn't be on the same page with what Chris and I want. I'm still hoping she'll accept me. Chris says that our being married might help with that."

"If that's the only reason you're getting married, don't do it," Deb replied. "Even if Chris wants it."

"That's not the only reason," Teddy grinned, her cheeks looking burnished by the sun. "You know we love each other. And we're living together *and* he keeps asking. So I finally agreed."

"Are you going to keep your surname?" Deb asked, "Like I did? Mom was offended at first, but I think she's used to it now."

"Probably because you're still a Lambert," Elaine broke in. "Besides, she loves Todd, and would never say anything that would get her on his bad side."

Teddy shook her head. "Haven't decided. Wanted to talk to Yancy first, since it's his name, too. He's the other reason we picked December 31. He'll be home then. Chris knows I'd never get married if my brother wasn't here, too."

Eden nodded. "So, tell us what you want, where you want it, what you want to wear, that sort of thing. In other words, how can we help?"

Teddy smiled. "You're going to think we're crazy."

"No, we won't," Elaine said. "Just tell us. I, for one, love unusual ceremonies."

"Okay." Teddy beamed. "Well, to begin with, Chris wants all of you to be his attendants."

"What? You mean us sisters? Not just his brothers?" Elaine asked.

Teddy nodded. "Fletcher and Logan *and* his Lambert sisters. That includes you, too, Lexi. Oh, and we'd like Kenny and Chance to be our ring bearers and Ivory to be my flower girl. That kind of tradition, I'm totally okay with, and your mom would like that, too." Teddy giggled. "Come to think of it, those three little kids have way more experience than me. I've never even been in one wedding!"

The sisters laughed.

"Ivy'll be thrilled," Eden affirmed.

Teddy glanced at her hands as her fingers nervously tapped the edge of the table. "We want our wedding to be small. Just family and friends."

"But who will be your attendants if Chris has his brothers as ushers, and his sisters as his groomswomen?"

Teddy grinned. "You're probably going to think we're nuts, but I asked my crew to be my attendants. Chris wants them to wear tuxes with work belts on their hips. The two women in my crew will probably wear the same dresses as you." She giggled. "Don't know yet if they'll also don their work belts. And I haven't made up a list of our friends, but I'll get on that real soon."

"When you say your crew, you mean the guys at Lambert and Partners?" Elaine asked.

Teddy nodded. "Flint and Val and George, and Benny. Oh, and Zeb. He's kind of new, but he's been part of Flint's team and mine, too, for months now. And the two women, who aren't as new as Zeb. And the guest list will definitely include Val's wife, Paula, and the wives and girlfriends of the crew in the guest list. Yancy, of course, will walk me down the aisle." Teddy blushed again. "He insists. So do I."

"In his dress blue uniform?" Eden asked. "Mom would like that. She loves men in uniform."

Laughter ringed the table again. "He'd probably prefer that to a tux, but we haven't talked about it yet."

"An intimate friends-and-family-only wedding as another Lambert bites the dust," Elaine added drily. "Will Mom ever recover? What about the location?"

"We decided to have it at The Bluff, that restaurant where he asked Val and me to be his partners. It has a room upstairs that's just the right size and it won't interfere with the regular New Years' Eve crowd. We've already reserved that room for the wedding, which will be in the afternoon, the reception to follow right after. That way, if anyone wants to stay for dinner, all they have to do is make a reservation and walk downstairs." She giggled. "Oh, and Val's brother is a minister. He said he's happy to make everything official."

Lexi stood up. "Sounds like you two really didn't need us at all. This calls for a toast and a cutting of what I brought over."

"Something special, I hope?" Elaine asked. "Although everything you make is wonderful."

"Chris loves my lemon cake and Teddy is partial to the raspberry chocolate. So I made both and cut them in half. Only thing they share is the icing, a butter cream that works for both."

"Oh, yum," Eden murmured. "Which side is which? I love raspberry chocolate."

Lexi grinned. "Can't remember, but when I cut it, it'll be obvious."

"I should text Chris to come back if we're going to dig into the cake," Teddy said.

"Tell him to hurry. I may want a slice of each side," Elaine declared.

An hour later, after Chris and Teddy added a few names to the guest list, Debra and Elaine left, followed shortly by Lexi and Eden, who returned to Lexi's house to retrieve the children. On the way home, Eden told Ivory she was going to be a flower girl again.

The little girl cheered. Kenny accepted his role as a ring bearer with nonchalance.

"Is this the last time?" he asked.

"Probably. That is, until Aunt Elaine gets married. By the time it's Logan's turn, you'll probably be an usher, maybe even a groomsman."

Eden wondered what Hale was going to say when she told him about this Lambert wedding, so much smaller and more casual than when they had exchanged rings and vows. But, she'd been the first Lambert child to tie the knot. A very traditional gathering.

Eden sighed, recalling how her father had patted her cheek when she'd tearfully complained that Iona had taken over, with Hale's mother as her eager accomplice, that it no longer felt like the wedding she and Hale had talked about.

"Let her have her fun, sweetie. You're her eldest daughter and she's been counting the days since you started dating Hale. As soon as he rushes you down the aisle and you're off on your honeymoon, your life together will your own. Mothers of the bride— and groom, it seems —love spectacle. Think of it as your way of making both mothers happy."

She'd spotted what she thought might be a tear in her father's eye. "Even as she waves good-bye to her little girl." He'd cleared his throat once, twice. "You'll always be our precious first daughter."

It was no surprise that Chris and Teddy were doing things their way. Her younger brother had always marched to his own drummer. Maybe he also had learned from Fletcher, who wrested the reins of control from their mother when he married Lexi. So, too, had Debra when she wedded Todd, although their surprises had come at the end of what had been a mostly traditional ceremony.

With her grandchildren a part of the wedding, Iona would probably command the first row again to remind them to behave during Chris's nuptials. But Teddy hadn't mentioned her colors or what style of bridesmaids dresses she expected the Lambert sisters to wear. *I'll have to ask.* Lexi would be displaying an obvious baby bump by the end of December. Eden glanced down at her own belly. *Me, too!* That is, if the amnio showed her baby wasn't afflicted with cystic fibrosis, a cloud that threatened nearly every thought she had about this pregnancy.

She'd taken to wearing skirts with over blouses in the past week, opting for comfort rather than style. It wouldn't be long before she'd have to start donning maternity dresses and slacks.

Eden smiled. She didn't think Teddy would care about a baby bump or two. *But I'll have to ask her about colors.*

Nine

Hale called the Dr.'s office. He was pleased that he didn't have to wait long for Dr. Ortiz to return his call.

"What's on your mind, Hale?"

"Last week Eden got some news that means we might have to rethink keeping this pregnancy."

"What news is that?"

"Her younger sister had one of those ancestry tests done, the kind that reports DNA findings. Turns out she's a carrier for cystic fibrosis. She gave us two kits to see if we're carriers, too. I was wondering if you could convince her to find out before the baby's born. Edie's pretty clear she doesn't want to bring a baby into the world who's seriously ill."

"Hmm. Says here in her chart that we talked about CVS when she was pregnant with Ivory. Eden said no to that after we talked about the risks of spontaneous fetal loss, miscarriage. And, frankly, I'm not sure we'd get enough fetal cells with CVS to rule out CF. If she's already done that DNA test, why don't you wait for the results? Did you take the test, too? It requires two carriers to make a baby with CF."

"Yes. Eden wanted to test the children, but I told her we should do it first. When I sent them in, I ordered two more kits. For the kids."

"Your other children are healthy, so I'm inclined to think that only one of you is a carrier, if that. In which case, you needn't worry about the fetus. At the most, the new baby would only be a carrier."

"What if both of us are carriers?"

"The only other opportunity for a confirming prenatal diagnosis is through amniocentesis. It also poses a small risk of miscarriage, though less than with CVS. That's why I prefer to wait until at least sixteen weeks."

"So it's risky, too."

"Every prenatal test poses risks, Hale. Small, but there."

"And she'll be showing by then. The kids will know."

"Very likely, especially since this is her third pregnancy. I gather you don't want the children to look forward to a baby brother or sister and then have to tell them it isn't going to happen."

"Right. When our sister-in-law had a miscarriage, her little boy— he was six at the time —was pretty unhappy. We don't want our kids going through that." Hale paused. "Can you tell if the baby has CF some other way than by sticking a needle into Eden's belly?"

"Sorry, Hale. CVS and amnio are the only means of ascertaining a prenatal diagnosis. And, the symptoms don't always show up immediately after birth. CF severity can vary widely. But treatments today have lengthened the average life span of affected persons. Wait for the results of that spit test. If it's positive, I'll refer you to a genetics counselor for the latest information. Don't just scan the internet. Some of those sites aren't accurate."

"Good advice. Eden still wants the kids tested."

"Since both are healthy, they either don't have the recessive gene or are only carriers."

"Okay. Thanks, Dr.."

Knowing that Eden was at work and not wanting to distract her, Hale texted her a short note that the Dr. had encouraged them to wait for the spit test results, their own and the kids'. *He was encouraging, babe. We'll talk more tonight.*

He returned to reviewing the remaining recipients of financial aid, a task he'd taken on even though the cyber experts had told him to leave everything to them. If only they'd get back to him. The waiting game wasn't easy.

Helen knocked and opened his door. "The college attorney is here."

Hale set aside the pages with student names crossed off or highlighted in yellow, thankful that the highlighted lines numbered far fewer than those crossed off.

A fifty-something gentleman with flowing white hair and piercing blue eyes entered, the color of his eyes intensified by the blue of his tie against his white shirt and charcoal gray pinstriped suit.

"Don't get up," the attorney said. "I don't believe we've met except over the phone. James Abernathy." He extended his hand.

Hale shook it and nodded. "I think my father-in-law may have mentioned you."

"Nathan Lambert. He left me a message. He's why I'm here. At first, I didn't connect you with him. But now, it makes sense." He pointed to the window behind Hale's shoulder. "I gather you entered the building from the rear this morning. Missed the contretemps on the brick walks in front of the two newest lecture halls."

Hale swiveled his chair and looked out the window. "What's going on?"

The lawyer rose from his seat and joined Hale as he looked out the window. All along the sidewalk leading to the front of the building and extending into the lawn that bordered the trees and the memorial forest, students were marching, several with signs. Their chanting was muffled by the windows, but it was clear they weren't happy.

Hale sucked in a breath when he spotted a poster with his name on it. Nearby, two other signs reading "Finance Office = Thief!" festooned the posters in large black markers. "They're blaming me? This office? But we're doing our best to get to the bottom of this."

Mr. Abernathy returned to his seat. "I'm sure you are. I suspect you're so named because you've been reaching out to the students to find out what they knew. My office has been besieged with phone calls from parents and, as of this morning, from one local donor, and another from out-of-state, both funds set up by alumni. They want to know how their names can be prevented from being sullied by this mess." The attorney placed his hands on the edge of Hale's desk. "How close are you to identifying the culprit or culprits?"

"Wish I could give you an answer. You probably know that the IT office has turned everything over to outside experts. I've been waiting for them to get back to me. Damn hard to do, this waiting. So, I've been going through *all* the financial aid recipients, hoping no new names pop up. Some have. Which I passed on to the cyber guys." He turned the paper around so that the attorney could see what he was referring to. "I suspect some of these cases can be explained away via bad math, since the dollar discrepancies are small. But the greatest number of cases include larger amounts."

"What have you done thus far to try to stem the damage to the college?"

"I secured the president's permission to allow all the affected students to continue with their studies. We won't penalize them. After all, it's not their fault. They've been allowed to register, buy books, or do whatever was represented by the stolen monies. I assume our insurance policy will cover those scholarships until we find out who took the money and we can get it back."

"But you have no idea when the thefts began? Nothing new that the cyber company doesn't know about?"

"What I found out, I've passed on to the experts. But I don't know what they're doing about it."

"From your father-in-law's call, I gather most of the students affected are Lambert scholars."

"Most of the undergrads, and about sixty percent are freshmen. But two students are master's candidates. I've been looking for a pattern, haven't come up with anything yet. The undergraduates with declared majors, for example, are all over the board. See this?" Hale pointed to several names. "This one's an English major, this one in applied health— that young man wants to go to med school —and three others are biology majors, but none of those students know one another. I asked when I spoke to them. And of the three biology majors, one is a sophomore, the other two are in their third year. I met with the older brother whose finances weren't touched, but his younger sister's entire scholarship was taken. Several of the students are the first of their families to go to college. That's not a surprise, given how many freshmen are involved. The Lambert fund tries to support as many of those students as possible. And most of the financial aid given to needy students reflects that status. Those receiving merit scholarships tend to be sopho-mores or juniors, and they received money from sources other than the Lambert Foundation." Hale sucked in a deep breath. "I agree with the IT group and the experts that we have a hacker. But who it might be, I have no clue. Don't even know if it's a local person."

"You don't suspect anyone in your office?"

Hale shook his head. "All but two of our team have been with us for years. I can't imagine that they would be involved. Of the two new employees, one handles the new students mak-ing application, but she doesn't have access to the subfiles. The other one is a part-time worker. He actually alerted me to two of the early irregularities when the students asked to see me. I find it hard to believe he would be the thief if he did that."

Abernathy reached a hand over Hale's desk. "Mind if I take that paper with me? The one with the students names?"

"Let me make you a copy. I was going to get back to all of them. Doing my own investigating." Hale copied the page and handed it over to the lawyer. "I've also taken it upon myself to send the students to the IT office to learn about security sys-tems they should be using. Something mentioned to me."

"What is that office doing?"

"Last time I spoke with Ms. Bedrossian— have you met her? —she confirmed they are proceeding apace with creating security systems throughout the campus. Starting with every academic department. I've been doing my part by checking and rechecking the student lists. I'm looking for a link between the victims, some kind of pattern. But all I've got out of this thus far is a headache."

Abernathy's blue eyes twinkled in the light from the window. "I have assured the parents who contacted me that you were taking all appropriate steps to resolve the situation."

"Thanks. The sooner we can catch this crook and make sure it doesn't happen again, the happier I'll be." Hale stood up and shook the attorney's hand for the second time that morning.

"If any other parents call you, feel free to refer them to my office for follow-up, let them know we're on it." The lawyer glanced out the window. "Maybe that will reduce the likelihood of continued demonstrations like what's going out there."

"I'm for that." Hale breathed a small sigh. The thought of having to endure calls from irate parents had already kept him up several nights in a row. "I'll alert Helen, too. She's doing her best, acting as my protector."

Abernathy chuckled. "The sign of an excellent administrative assistant."

The rest of the day, Hale checked off two more names and highlighted others. When he had completed that chore and assured several students by text that they would not be asked to leave the college owing to nonpayment of the bills they had thought were covered, he copied the list and gave it to Helen to fax it to the attorney's office. He then used the encrypted email they'd set up for him and sent off the same to the cyber guys, men Helen had taken to calling Click and Clack.

When Hale was sure that Eden would be home, he called her. "How was your day, honey?"

She laughed. "I'm really liking these agents. And they like how I've streamlined the record-keeping. I just finished setting things up so they know where they stand at the end of each week. My biggest problem is not being interrupted by Opal. The lady receptionist. She talks a mile a minute and *loves* to talk."

"Don't you have your own office?"

"Yes, but she's always stopping by and opening my door to say something. I finally had to ask her to please not do that when I'm entering numbers—so I don't make a mistake. I told her that if I switched numbers and it was on her end-of-the-month check, she might end up being shorted what she was owed. That seemed to get through to her."

Hale chuckled. "Good for you, hon."

"What about you? Making progress with the problem that cannot be named?"

"I met with the college attorney. He says your dad called him. I hope he's not unduly worried about this."

"You know he trusts that you're doing everything possible to find the crook and bring him to justice." Eden said, her voice softer. "I was thinking we'd have salmon steaks tonight. If you call me when you leave the office, I'll put them on then so we can sit down as soon as you're here."

"You want me to pick up salad fixings or something special for dessert?"

"No need. I put the salad together before I went to work this morning. And I have all the makings for a strawberry compote for dessert."

"That sounds like something we'd have for a special event. What are you trying to tell me?"

"Nothing, Hale. I'm just trying to think positively about everything. We're overdue for a relaxing meal and nice dessert." Her smile surrounded her words.

"Absolutely. I'll call you right before I leave the office. See you then. Love you, Eden."

"Love you, too," she murmured.

Hale leaned back in his seat, ignoring the complaining squeak of his chair. A pregnancy with the possible complication of cystic fibrosis. *But Eden's thinking on the bright side. That's good.* He wondered if her putting that special dessert together meant that she was going to make an announcement to the kids. Even though she'd insisted they should wait until after the Dr.'s appointment or the arrival of the DNA results.

At least her job seemed to be working out, keeping her on the happy side of the life ledger. He'd always wondered why she tended to see the glass as half-empty and mused that it was her mother's influence.

Iona was more inclined to see the negatives before acknowledging the positives of people and events. At least she was an enthusiastic and loving grandmother, something Hale had never enjoyed in his youth. None of his grandparents had lived past his infancy.

But he considered it his husbandly duty to help Eden see life with rosier glasses than was her wont. Not that she didn't adore their children. He couldn't ask for a more devoted mother. And a loving wife, too, always passionate in her responses to him. He'd just have to work a bit harder to help her through the possibility that their third child might have cystic fibrosis.

Even as he tried to put a positive face on the difficulties he was facing at work. He glanced out the window. No longer were the sign-carriers on the front lawn of the campus. He wondered if news cameras had caught the action. And would he then have to explain to his children why his name was on one of those signs?

He glanced up at the knock on his door. His boss entered, frowning.

"What is it, Andy?"

"You talked to the college attorney?"

"I did."

"I suppose you saw and heard about that dreadful demonstration this morning."

Hale nodded. "As long as they don't storm the building, I'm not worried. First amendment stuff, you know." He smiled, hoping his lighthearted remark would soothe the man into a less fearsome mien. "And not all that unusual on a college campus. Don't you remember? Before and after the 2016 election, we had demonstrations almost every week."

"But those signs demeaning the department, *my* department!"

"Because we're a convenient target, Andy. And the only name on a sign, aside from the ones mentioning the office, was mine. I'll bet this all blows over as soon as we catch whoever took the money. Think of the students whose aid was compromised. They're the ones most hurt by this—even though the college is covering the missing money."

"Because President Ingraham doesn't *dare* have anything happen on *his* watch," Andy declared, his words more vehement than Hale expected.

"As he should. I for one am pleased the president cares enough about the students to provide such assurances. And the reputation of the college—"

"His reputation, you mean!"

"That, too, I guess," Hale replied, surprised that his boss was so uncharitable toward the college president.

Anderson paced from Hale's door to his desk. "I wish it was all over, that this hadn't occurred, wasn't happening now."

"We're of a single mind on that. But the cyber experts are on it. They'll find the crooks, how they gained access."

"If you mean the campus IT office, what can they do? Those techie dweebs! Totally useless, if you ask me."

Techie dweebs? Really, Andy? They know a helluva lot more about cyber security than you or me.

Hale stared for a moment at Anderson. "Perhaps that's why the IT office called for outside help, because this was beyond their expertise." He reached for his suit jacket, slung over the back of his chair. "If they know when to call for assistance, that tells me they know their business. And, although I hate having to play a waiting game, I have every confidence the culprits will be caught. In the meantime, I'm doing my best to keep our funding sources calm, so they don't pull back from supporting deserving students."

"Hang the students and their funding sources! It's *my* department I'm worried about!"

Unable to come up with the right words to calm down his boss, Hale shrugged. "Everyone who's an expert is doing their best, Andy. Which means we just have to stay out of their way, let them do it."

Anderson turned on his heel and departed, his frowning countenance telling Hale his attempt at affecting a positive approach was lost on his boss.

Hale locked his office and waved at Helen as he headed home.

~ ~ ~

As he drove home, Hale's conversation with Andy weighed on him. His boss's erratic moods were worrisome, and not just because of his over-the-top reaction to the current situation. The fact that Andy was concerned about the reputation of their department, but not about the students the thefts were affecting most directly, or the college's relationship with the funding sources, struck Hale as off.

Was Andy's angst related to his personal life, his marriage, or his no-good son, Piers, who'd been in and out of trouble for years? Or was this an indication that Anderson Randolph was no longer the best person to lead the finance office? Maybe he didn't want the responsibility any longer, but wasn't sure how to go about stepping down gracefully? He wasn't near retirement age, but that didn't mean the man might not want to retire. Hale toyed with the notion of asking Helen if she knew what was behind Andy's weirdness of late. Surely she'd noticed, but would she confide in Hale?

After dinner, his mental exhaustion translated into an overwhelming desire to nap on the couch after dinner instead of helping Eden get the children ready for bed. But he did his duty before leaning back on the cushions and closing his eyes.

Eden joined him on the couch. When she remained silent, he opened his eyes and squinted in her direction. She sat nearby, her arms crossed, looking unhappy.

He sat up and reached for her hand, intending to angle her close enough for a kiss.

But Eden's last-minute shift meant his lips met her cheek instead.

"Are you mad at me, hon?"

"You barely said a word at dinner. Even Ivory noticed it."

"I've been distracted. First by the attorney's visit. And Andy. He's acting really strange."

Eden's tone softened and she shifted close enough to brush a hand across his brow. "It's not like you to bring your troubles home so much that you ignore the children."

"Sorry about that. But Andy's behavior really bothers me. And I found two more students whose aid has been stolen. Not large amounts, but still."

"You turned over their names to those outside experts?"

"Yep."

"What about Andy?" Eden squeezed Hale's shoulders.

"He overreacts. That demonstration today? I thought I was going to have to haul him off the ceiling. He acts like the thefts are designed to give *him* a bad reputation. He used to care about the students we help. But now it's all about him and the office, but mostly him *because* he runs things." He huffed out a disgusted breath. "At least he used to. Most days, he just asks me to handle whatever the issue is at hand and walks off in a huff. I have no idea what he does all day. And he's been AWOL a lot of the time. Leaving me up to my ears in stuff we both should be handling."

"You think he's losing it?"

"Maybe. And I don't need that right now, in addition to everything else I'm dealing with." Hale ran a hand through his hair, already spiked from an afternoon of that nervous habit. "Today was not exactly a great day. Not like yours. I love it that you sound so happy. Even when you complain about Opal's interruptions. Please tell me I'm right, that your day was great. Fulfilling. Fun. I *need* to hear that kind of stuff."

"Consider it said." She leaned over and kissed his cheek. "But I think this particular cat's out of the bag, or will be." She pointed to her middle.

Hale's gaze widened. "How's that?"

"I went over to Lexi's to retrieve the kids. She picked them up for a playdate this afternoon. While I was helping her hang new curtains in the baby's room, my shirt flew up and both boys saw my baby bump. Chance pointed and said I looked just like his mom, and did that mean I was going to have a baby, too. Kenny turned around and asked, point blank, if Chance was right. I lied, Hale. You know we said we'd never lie to our children. And Lexi was right there, too, looking more pregnant than me, but still … She didn't say a word, but I knew what she was thinking."

"What did she say?"

"After we sent the kids outside, we talked. I had a good cry, and she promised not to say anything, that she would talk to Chance. She agreed news like a new baby was something the mother should be the one to announce. I told her we were going to do so at Mom's on Sunday. I asked her if her spit test results were back."

"And?"

Eden shook her head. "She said Fletcher marked the calendar for ten days from now, the day he thinks everyone will hear. Assuming we all sent off those little tubes on the same day."

"Maybe I should have sent ours express. Didn't occur to me. And we can't expect the children to keep news that big to themselves. We should tell them the truth, so you don't have to lie." He smirked at her.

"Then our two got into a fight on the way home. You can guess about what. Kenny started it by saying that if I have another baby, he wants a brother. Then Ivory said it had to be a sister, that there were too many boys in the family already." She faux-glowered at Hale. "And don't you *dare* say I can solve that problem by having twins!"

Hale unsuccessfully covered his scoffing chuckle with a cough. "Always a possibility, hon. After all, your mother had twins."

"Don't remind me," she huffed. "I just wish we already had those test results."

"Two more weeks and we see the Dr.. Maybe to do the amniocentesis."

Eden sighed. "But that means waiting another two weeks for *that* result." She leaned her head against his shoulder. "I really hate waiting. Don't you?"

"I do." His mind raced at the thought of how many things he was waiting on—the hackers to identify the thief and stop the hacking, the spit test results, maybe even the results of that prenatal procedure.

"Maybe the DNA tests will come in early, so we don't have to do the amnio—unless you want to know if it's a boy or a girl. That's something I'd be happy to tell the kids." He grabbed her fist when she playfully threatened to push against his chest.

Eden shook her head. "If the results are what we hope for, you'll only have to worry about the problems at the college, all that money that's been taken."

"I feel guilty that our system wasn't as secure as I thought, as it should have been. If only I'd insisted on upgrading sooner."

"You've been fighting Andy for the changes you've been making for at least two years now."

"I know. But if we'd done it sooner, maybe he wouldn't be acting so weird. I've never seen him so crazed about a problem that he basically turned over to me. Instead of focusing on what we've already done, he keeps harping on how we need to make sure that the administration knows he had nothing to do with it."

"Is that the only thing bothering Andy these days?"

"I don't think so. Maybe his bad mood is related to his son. Madison let slip that the kid was picked up by the cops last week. Don't know how she knew that, except that news travels fast around here. But if that rumor's correct, it could be he's back into the drug scene again." Hale shook his head. "And if he's living at home, Andy could be privy to whatever the kid's been doing. Has to be hard, having a kid drop out of school, get caught up in all kinds of bad behavior."

He stroked Eden's hand. "I've been wondering if one reason our system was vulnerable is because of the frequency with which the students are all teched up—you know, doing everything on their phones, being linked to their college accounts that way, too. Maybe that's why the IT crew is busy creating firewalls, so people can't get into the system that involves grades and stuff. And money transfers. Never occurred to me that we'd be in this kind of a mess."

He stood up, rubbing his neck. "I'm beat. Time for a shower and bed."

Eden followed Hale into the bedroom, where he stripped and headed for the shower, hoping the hot water would relax the muscles in his upper back and shoulders.

When he returned to the bedroom, Eden was already in her nightgown. He pressed a hand onto her abdomen, aware that her shape was changing.

"How's this little guy? Have you felt him move yet?"

"Not yet. And I've had almost no morning sickness. Maybe it means I'm having a girl. Ivy'll be happy, even if Kenny doesn't share her joy." Eden's mouth quirked up in a crooked grin. "I keep thinking about the amnio. It would tell us the sex. Maybe we *should* find out this time. And get the kids used to whatever we're having."

"And you won't abort, even if we find out the baby has CF?"

"Every time I think about it, I can't imagine not letting him be born. You were right. We made this baby together." Her eyes welled. "Maybe it was meant to be. No matter what."

Relieved, Hale nodded and began tapping her abdomen. "Hello in there," he murmured. "Think this little guy knows we're talking to him? About him?"

"Or her," she reminded him. "Remember when you asked if I shouldn't go through the baby clothes we stashed in the attic?"

"You said you weren't ready." Hale climbed into bed and gestured for Eden to join him. "You want me to bring those boxes down now?"

"I don't want to put it off any longer." Her eyes filled and she swiped a hand across her face. "Even if the news is bad." She rested her hand on her belly.

Hale stroked Eden's face. "I'm glad, hon. Whatever happens, we'll deal with it. Like we always have. The doctors know lots more now than they used to."

"I know."

"I love you, Edie," Hale murmured. "For always and ever." He reached across his wife and turned out the light.

"And I love you, Hale Brinker, financial analyst par excellence. Father of the Year. Best lover ever, my husband." She rolled over and slid her arm under his chin then onto his chest.

Hale's lids burned with unshed tears, imagining that the simple weight of Eden's arm told him she supported him in everything, even as he tried to solve the weirdness that was Anderson Randolph these days.

Eden kept assuring him he'd find the thief of that scholarship money. She would love their new baby, too. As much as she loved their other two children. Even if the little one came out needing special care. Which they would provide. Together.

He listened as Eden's breathing slowed and she slid into sleep. But even after he closed his eyes and willed himself to believe that somehow his upside-down world would soon be righted, Hale couldn't seem to relax. And when he woke the next morning, he felt as if he'd run a marathon all night long, leaving him more exhausted than when he'd arrived home.

Ten

The next day, Hale arrived at the office early, intent on reviewing his spreadsheets before calling Vanya Bedrossian for an update. He wanted her assurance that the entire finance office was secure, protected against any new cyber intrusion. Next he planned to approach Helen. What did she know about Anderson Randolph that Hale should be aware of? But the secretary wasn't at her desk.

When he opened his office door, several Post-its affixed to the back of his center computer screen started fluttering as if seeking his attention. He pulled off the notes and placed them, one by one, onto his desk, slid into his seat and scanned the messages. Three were quickly disposed of with email replies. One requested a call back from James Abernathy.

Hale hoped it was good news, that the hacker had been identified, and that the money would be returned forthwith.

"Mr. Abernathy. It's Hale Brinker. You wanted to see me?"

"I'm about to go into a meeting. How about we meet over lunch, say, 12:30?"

"You bet."

Hale powered up his computer and waited for the screens to reveal what he didn't want to see. Since his first awareness that someone had attacked the financial aid accounts, he'd created a program that alerted him to any change in the student subfiles. Each time he found another discrepancy, he passed the student's name on to the cyber guys, Click and Clack, and to Vanya's crew. Bedrossian's employees contacted the students and worked with them to create new passwords. Hale spent the rest of the morning scanning the new scholarship accounts.

Then, because he sensed he was missing something, he created a new spreadsheet, to which he added all scholarship funding sources. If he concentrated on where the money was coming from for deserving students, perhaps he'd find a clue. He'd given up trying to find a pattern via the recipients of the aid that had been tampered with. He was about to stand up and stretch his back when he received a text alert.

Oh, shit! Not another student account. The Lambert Family Foundation—to the tune of more than $50,000! How could that have happened? He'd intended to ask Nathan about the security measures used by the bank managing the foundation monies, but he couldn't recall having done so. He rubbed his hand across his forehead, sweating.

When had the Lambert account been attacked? His fingers pounded out commands as he searched the file and stared at the dates when activity had occurred. Last week, those monies were fully accounted for. Since the first theft had occurred, he made a point of checking every Friday before closing the office and going home. Last week all was well. But today that hunk of money had disappeared. Had he checked last Friday? And if he hadn't, why had it slipped his mind?

His office was the only one with direct access to the Lambert Foundation subfiles. Correction: his and that of the bank manager. Before calling the bank and ruining that man's day, he needed to check his own calendar.

Had anyone gained access to his office when he wasn't there? Where had he eaten lunch last week? With whom? After the week following the discovery of missing money from student accounts and those meetings with Vanya, and later Click and Clack, he'd followed their advice and tried to concentrate on his regular work. Which meant he'd resumed meeting with different department heads, sometimes over lunch, knowing that budgetary issues would be coming up, to be discussed with the various deans. Those gatherings usually included Hale's boss, or more recently, him.

With several key clicks, he scanned his daily calendar for the previous week. Monday: lunch with Dean Acheson. They'd talked about the retirement of one full professor and the anticipated hiring of two instructors, one to focus on philosophy classes, the other to collaborate on research with one of the historians on campus.

Tuesday: a meeting with the English professor who'd assumed chairmanship duties, filling in for the designated chair, out on maternity leave. Their conversation had revolved around how to maintain small classes during the winter quarter if she remained on leave. Hale recalled adding a line item to the English Department's budget request, along with a note to alert the chancellor to that addition.

Wednesday: lunch with Anderson. Hale frowned. They'd disagreed on what to say about the missing student monies with those parents who were calling. Andy was fearful that the press might get wind of things and bad publicity would result, particularly involving him as the Finance office chief. Hale was all for total honesty.

He recalled his conclusion of their conversation. "You turned it over to me, Andy. The parents aren't going to come after you. It's my signature on those letters assuring each of the students and their parents that the missing monies will be replaced."

But Anderson was not mollified. He'd slammed out of Hale's door and, according to Helen, left the office early.

Thursday? No meeting scheduled. *I guess I ate at my desk.*

Friday? Oh. Hale talked to Eden, debated meeting with her so that he could meet her boss. And he wanted to meet Opal, too, to add a face to the name Eden mentioned so often.

But Eden asked him to wait until after Mr. McCue asked her to stay on, *if* he asked. Hale had no doubt that the man would. Thinking of Eden brought to mind their earlier conversation, when she'd said she was less and less comfortable with the idea of doing the amnio.

It was time to talk to Anderson, time for Hale to talk to Nathan, too, about the latest theft. Hale rose from his chair and traversed the hall to his boss's office. He knocked on the door then grasped the knob. Locked. *Damn!*

He went back to the reception area, pleased to see that Helen was at her desk. "Did Andy not come in this morning?"

"No. He may be ill. Want me to call him?"

"Don't bother, but could you let me know if he has appointments that I need to take? Also, how is Madison doing with the students coming in with questions about aid for the winter term?"

"She's on top of things. Very efficient, that young woman. I hope she plans to stay."

"She didn't sign a contract?"

"Oh, she did, but now she's talking about grad school. Once she has the money, I suspect she'll leave us in the dust."

"I didn't know that. Too bad."

If Madison confirmed what Helen had said, he'd have to alert Andy about starting a new employee search.

But every recent encounter with his boss had been unpleasant. Was it a sign that the office money problems were really getting to him? Or a reflection of something else, like Andy's worries about that son of his? In jail, out of jail, a school dropout, the kind of kid Hale imagined would prefer to live in his parents' basement while turning it into a pigsty rather than assume responsibility for himself. Not something Hale intended to allow in *his* children.

He reached for his phone and dialed the bank, asked for the manager of the Lambert Foundation and learned that he'd stepped out. Hale sighed, chose not to leave a message, and said only that he would call the man back later.

As the hands on the wall clock approached the time he was to meet with the attorney, Hale printed off proof of the missing Lambert Foundation money, and folded the damning page.

Hale trotted down the stairs and strode toward the college attorney's office.

He approached the secretary's desk. "I'm here to see Mr. Abernathy."

"Go right in, Mr. Brinker. He's expecting you."

The lawyer must have heard his approach. He was standing near his office door, sporting a suit Hale estimated would have paid for at least five of his own work uniforms.

"How about we go to the Campus Club?" the man suggested. "We ought to be able to take over one of the smaller rooms while we eat."

"I'm for that."

After securing a food plate, Hale followed James into a small conference room. He shut the door after securing a "Do Not Disturb" sign on the doorknob.

The attorney sipped his coffee before speaking. "Now then. What new information do you have for me?"

Hale handed over the paper with the information about the Lambert Foundation. "This is new as of this morning. Big money this time. I tried to reach the manager of the fund, but he wasn't in. I'll try again this afternoon. And I need to alert my father-in-law so that he can take immediate steps. Only he or his eldest son is authorized to change access to the Foundation accounts. I've been meaning to ask him to do that."

The attorney's eyebrows rose and he nodded. "Of course. I'm going to guess that this means those IT wizards haven't yet managed to secure all the programs your office can access."

Hale nodded. "I'm afraid you're right, although it never occurred to me that they could get into the Foundation monies. I've been wanting to update all our systems processes for two years, but it took me some time to convince the head of the office. Obviously, my efforts didn't include the kind of security that would have stopped a hacker. His skills seem way above my pay grade."

"Don't beat yourself up, Hale. Your office wasn't the only one. President Ingraham saw what needed to be done right away. That's why he brought in Ms. Bedrossian and authorized her to hire the people she needed to get the job done." He looked up at the knock on the door of the small conference room. "Come in."

Hale stifled his surprise as one of Vanya's employees, looking more cleaned-up than Hale recalled. Instead of a scruffy beard, the young man was clean-shaven and wearing what appeared to be a clean shirt and pair of Dockers. Only the scuffed boots on his feet reminded Hale of the slovenly look the young man had presented when Hale had passed his work station in the IT office.

Hale watched as the young man set up his laptop. Then he leaned to one side so that the lawyer and Hale could see the screen.

"You remember Reggie, Hale? He's one of Ms. Bedrossian's best people."

Hale nodded at the young man, whose cheeks reddened at Abernathy's praise.

"Yo. Want me to get set up?" Reggie asked the attorney.

"Yes." James focused his gaze on Hale. "I asked him here to help us understand what they are trying to fix."

"Done," the young man muttered. "Now what?"

The attorney smiled. "Why don't you begin by showing us how easy it is to hack into a college email address. How about an email for one of the people working in the finance office?"

Hale glanced at James. "I don't like where this is going."

"Not to worry. Just a demo," Reggie said. He crossed his arms over his chest. "Okay, that new girl, Maddy."

The lawyer nodded.

Several keystroke flurries and Madison Hanover's email opened.

"Two minutes, fifteen seconds," the lawyer announced after clicking the stopwatch on his smart phone. "That was fast. How'd you do that?"

"I tried some obvious passwords. Hers was a little trickier than most, longer than four characters, but we're in." Reggie smirked at the lawyer.

The screen showed a recent email note from Madison to her mother, enumerating how many months she needed to work to cover initial grad school expenses.

Hale waved a hand. "That's a personal email. Can you get out of there?"

Reggie nodded. Several clicks and the screen no longer showed Madison's communication with her mother. "Done. And she won't know we saw it. I'll talk to her, get with her to create a better password. What else?" Reggie asked.

"How about the back end of Mr. Randolph's website, the one that features the finance office?" the lawyer asked.

"This isn't a good idea," Hale objected.

"Just another example," the attorney assured him.

A few more flurries and there was the version of Anderson Randolph's landing page, enabling the user to make changes.

"Forty-five seconds. Even faster than before," James said.

"Because he has a really stupid password. 1 2 3 4 5 6. Dumb," Reggie scoffed. "You have no idea how many people do that. Or they make it their address or their birthday and never change it. Stuff like that."

"Let me dictate an email to Mr. Randolph," Hale insisted.

"Go ahead," Reggie replied.

"Mr. Randolph. Your website was hacked. Please call the IT office for assistance changing your password. Use upper and lower cases letters and several numbers. Please do not make it obvious, such as your name, your address, your birthday, a pet's name, and the like. If you need help, please contact me as soon as possible. Sign it with your name, please."

Reggie grunted assent.

"I'll ask him if he's done that, or have Helen remind him," Hale stated.

"That should take care of him," the lawyer said. "Let's do one more."

"Do we have to?" Hale muttered. "I'm beginning to see that we need a major overhaul to make things secure in our office."

"Bear with me, Hale. Let's check *your* account. I doubt it will be as easily accessed, since you are aware of security issues," James said.

Reggie got to work, biting his lip with several flurries on the keyboard that netted him little dings Hale concluded were an indication of no access. Finally, Reggie was in. "There!" He sat back proudly.

"Why did it take you more than six minutes?" James asked.

"Well, Mr. Brinker uses a really long password and, like he said to Mr. Randolph, it included big and little letters, numbers and two different symbols. That slowed me down, but once I saw the pattern he uses, I got in." He closed down Hale's email.

Hale shook his head. "And I change my password every month."

"What you used was effective. Would probably stop most people," Reggie beamed. "I suggest you use a different password generator, one that employs a random scatter of symbols, for example. If you come to my digs, I'll show you what I mean."

"Definitely." Hale glanced at the attorney. "What, exactly, were you getting at with this little exercise?"

Before the attorney could answer, Reggie said, "Oh, shit! Look at that!"

All three men focused on the screen. As they watched, they found themselves looking at a screen Hale immediately recognized.

"Someone's into my system. It's not you?" Hale asked Reggie, who shook his head, his hands hovering well above the keyboard. "Your cursor is moving on its own. He's trying to get into a student subfile. And I closed myself out before he got in. Look! He's in!"

Reggie pulled his laptop in front of him and began pounding the keyboard, beads of sweat popping out on his forehead as he worked. "Damn, damn! He's fast!" He slammed a palm down on the table hard enough that the coffee cups rattled in their saucers.

Reggie looked over at the attorney and at Hale. "Another account messed with. And now we have confirmation how he's getting in. Via your office account."

"My email again?"

"Worse than that. Your access code to the subfiles. Makes it look like you're doing it." Reggie stared at him. "But you're not. 'Cause you're here."

The attorney frowned. "Mr. Shepherd, I suggest you get back with Ms. Bedrossian immediately. Tell her she needs to shut down all access to those student files from Mr. Brinker's office."

"Even the new accounts, students making application for future aid?" Hale asked.

"Yes."

"But that sends us back to the dark ages. Paper entries." Hale glanced up when he felt the attorney's gaze on him. "Go ahead. It can't be helped. I'll get with my people immediately about this change and why we're making it."

The attorney slid his chair back and stood up. He turned to Reggie. "Thank you for that demonstration. I consider it a lucky break that we actually observed the thief in action. Why don't you get cracking on shutting down Mr. Brinker's system?"

Reggie mumbled something, his fingers flying. "Done. Disabled. At least for now." He shook the attorney's hand and then Hale's.

Reggie grabbed his laptop and left.

Hale felt a headache coming on. He looked at the lawyer. "I feel sick that they used my office to access all those accounts."

"Wasn't your fault. You saw how long it took that whiz kid to break into your email. We should be thankful that you are one of the few people with access to the subfiles. Who else can do that? Used to be able to do that?"

"Helen, our admin person, for sure. And Anderson, but he hasn't bothered in months. When those first student files were accessed, I double-checked that no one else could open them, even though I never suspected it was an inside job. I felt we needed to have all the security elements in place before expanding the list of people with access. Never thought it might be me letting that thief in."

The attorney emptied his coffee cup. "Telling your father-in-law what we now know isn't going to be pleasant. And with the major theft of funds from the Lambert Foundation, I'm guessing that Mr. Randolph won't be happy to hear about it, either. He mentioned that the Lambert Foundation is one of the largest of the multiyear scholarship awarding sources."

Hale rubbed his nape. "Andy'll be furious. He's already deeply upset, concerned that he'll be blamed, worried about adverse publicity. Even though I took responsibility for replying to the parents, telling them what we're doing about it. Reassurances, mostly. I need to talk to Nathan and the fund manager."

The attorney nodded. "Did Anderson happen to mention that I met with him about a week ago?"

"No. Helen said he called in sick last Friday and he didn't show this morning, either."

"Why don't you ask Reggie to change Anderson's password today? Leave him a note with your admin person so that when he does arrive, he can at least open up his email."

"Not something he'll appreciate, but I'll take care of it."

Hale stood up to leave.

"We're not done yet." The attorney pointed to the document Hale had placed on the table relating to the Lambert Family Foundation. "I suggest we ask Mr. Lambert to meet with us now. Think you can convince him to join us?"

"Shouldn't be a problem." Hale picked up his phone and dialed his father-in-law, but all he got was voice mail. He left a message.

"I have a feeling he might be on the golf course. That being the case, he won't get my message until he's home. Leaves his phone there on days when he plays."

"Then I suggest you talk to him as soon as possible. I'm open to joining you if he wishes me to be present for that conversation."

"Of course. Being one of the top donors to students here is something Nathan is proud of. He claims it's the family's responsibility to support as many students as possible. Views it as a legacy honoring his grandfather's founding of the college."

The lawyer nodded. "Not surprised he feels that way." After emptying his coffee cup with a long sip, he said, "This particular theft is a major felony. Not that the total amount missing from all the students' accounts doesn't also qualify. How do you think your father-in-law is going to react to this news?"

"He'll be shocked. Nothing like this has ever happened before. But he's not one to panic. I suspect he'll want to talk with the manager at the bank immediately, the person who handles the fund. See what they can do to provide additional protections. And stop all transfers for the time being. Which is what I'm going to suggest."

"Good idea. Will he continue to offer scholarships?"

"I'm sure he will. Nathan is the kind of man who would first look into whether new scholarships were planned, how much, and when they were scheduled to be awarded. That sort of thing. You know, to determine if there might be a link to the removal of that huge chunk of money and any new grants scheduled for the winter and spring quarters. Somehow, I doubt that, but he's sure to check." Hale ran his fingers through his hair. "The missing money represents way more than what is usually provided in a given quarter. Nathan will know that, too. Nothing he'll be happy about."

The attorney pushed his empty plate to the center of the table. "I suggest we go back to my office and call Professor Lambert. Maybe alert his man at the bank. You know his name?"

Hale nodded.

"Good. I'll have my secretary do that. Can you clear your calendar for the rest of the day in the event we reach your father-in-law?"

"No problem." Hale pulled out his cell phone and texted Helen. *Please move my afternoon appointments to later in the week.*

The smiley emoji she sent back confirmed she'd received his message. If only he felt like smiling, too. The day was turning into a nightmare unlikely to end on anywhere close to a happy note.

Eleven

Hale and Eden entered the Dr.'s office and were sent into an examining room. When he reached for Eden's hand, she pulled it away, but not so quickly that he didn't feel her cold fingers. He glanced at her as she took a seat. She refused to meet his gaze.

"Honey, relax. Think of it as a regular visit. Just to find out that the baby is fine."

Eden's face crumpled and she covered her eyes with her hands. "I can't do this," she moaned.

"You can't do what?"

"Don't let them stick a needle in me. I can't. I won't." She turned her tear-stained face toward Hale, her eyes so wide he could see the whites of her eyes. "Help me up. I have to get out of here! Before the doctor comes in."

But the knock on the door and turning of the knob told Hale they were too late.

"Dr. Ortiz," he said. "I'm sorry. It seems Eden's changed her mind."

"Oh? You don't want the amnio? But I thought—"

"No. Can't do it," Eden declared. She reached for the tissue box Hale held toward her and blew her nose, once, twice. "I'll just wait for that spit test. Like you suggested. Come on, Hale."

She brushed past her husband and the doctor who backed away from the door.

Hale apologized to Dr. Ortiz and followed her to the car. When he slid behind the wheel, he turned to Eden. "I thought you said you *wanted* to know. Even though you hate needles. Last night you said we should go ahead, because then we'd know the sex, too. Why didn't you tell me you changed your mind? We could at least have avoided coming here and wasting the doctor's time."

"And our money. Isn't that what you were really thinking, Hale? Because this was a special appointment, not part of the regular OB package?" She sniffed, wiped her eyes and motioned him to put the car in gear. "Go! Drive! Take me home! I don't want to be here another minute!"

Hale turned the key in the ignition and stared at her. "Who's watching the kids?"

"I called a babysitter. I didn't want Mom to see me like this and no one else was available." She pressed a hand against her belly where her baby bump was visible, her gaze stubbornly focused on the road. She sucked in an audible breath.

"Fletcher called me," he stated quietly. "With their results."

"And?"

"Both of them are negative. Elaine has hers, too. She's a carrier, but since she's not—never mind. And Chris, too, a carrier, I mean. But Teddy isn't, so any children they have are safe."

"When were you going to tell me?" Eden's tone was accusatory.

He felt her eyes on him. "I was hoping our test results would be here, too."

"*Why* aren't they? We're the ones who *need* to know. I so hate waiting."

"Maybe it's in the mailbox." Hale gazed back at Eden. "But if it isn't, I'm sure it'll be here soon. With everyone else getting their results ... You're fifteen weeks along, hon. And it's pretty obvious that you're pregnant. Which the kids are happy about. Even if they can't agree about what you should have." He glanced back at the road ahead.

Eden sighed, her voice quieter. "Can we please just go home, Hale?" She covered his hand as it gripped the wheel. "Sorry, love. I shouldn't take out my nasty feelings on you. I'm just so tired of waiting."

"I get it." He faced forward. "On our way."

When they arrived in their driveway, he asked, "Want me to take the sitter home?"

"She lives just around the corner. It's Katya."

"Oh. Right. Haven't seen her in months. She's a senior this year?"

"Junior."

"Okay. I should go back to the office. Or do you want me stay until you're feeling better about ... everything?"

"I'm okay. Go." Eden slid out of the car and headed for the kitchen door.

No good-bye? No kiss, either. Hale grimaced. *Another downer day.* He backed out of the driveway and headed for the office, determined to check in with the IT people. Surely they were making progress now. Each day without news was draining.

~ ~ ~

That evening Hale glanced around the dinner table. The children had been unusually quiet. Were they as aware as he of the tension that seemed to coat the room? Eden hadn't said more than two words to him, directing brief remarks only to the children and mostly in curt orders, unlike her usual loving urgings to eat their vegetables, to wipe their mouths.

He cleared his throat. "It's time to tell you something, kids. Put your spoons down and listen up." Hale waited for Kenny to stop stirring his ice cream into mush.

"What is it, Daddy?" Ivory asked, loving innocence shining from her marble-like blue eyes.

"You know we're going to have a new baby," he said, unable to stop smiling at his daughter. "But we'll have to wait to find out if it's a boy or a girl."

"Why's that?" Kenny asked, the corners of his mouth drooping.

"It's a surprise. Only God knows what it will be."

"But we're still getting one, aren't we? I want a baby," Ivory cheered. "Chance is getting a baby. He wants a brother. But *I* want a sister! Mommy, if you ask real nice, will God tell you?"

"No, honey."

"Don't want the baby, Mom?" Kenny asked.

His question seemed to bring Eden up short. She stared at her son for a moment then stood up abruptly. Her voice shaking, she said to Hale, "Take care of things, will you?" and fled to her bedroom.

Hale wanted to follow her, but she needed alone time. "Come on, kids. Help me take care of the table. Finish your ice cream, Ivy. Kenny, if you're done, take your dish and your mother's over to the sink."

For the next several minutes, he supervised the children as they took turns clearing the table. While Hale rinsed the dishes, Kenny wiped the kitchen table and Ivory pushed in the chairs.

After the dishwasher was loaded and humming, Hale reached for the book Ivory asked him to read. He considered it the height of irony that she'd handed him *Where Did I Come From?,* a title Eden had bought for Kenny when he was four and asking questions. After they finished reading it, with Kenny taking turns reading some pages and Ivory giggling over the funny drawings, Hale said, "So, do you guys have any questions?"

Ivory wriggled closer. "Mommy wants the baby that's in her tummy, doesn't she?"

"She does. Just like when Kenny and you were in her tummy. Very much."

"Is it dark inside Mommy's tummy? Maybe the baby is afraid of the dark. If I talk to her, should I tell her it's okay, 'cause it's light outside and she'll see that when she comes out?"

"That would be nice, but I don't think the baby is afraid of the dark. She hears Mommy's heartbeat and that makes her feel safe."

"Do you know if it's a girl, Dad?" Kenny asked.

"Not yet we don't."

"But you said 'she,'" he insisted.

"Just because it was easier. Your mom and I want to be surprised, like we were when you and your sister were born."

"Do Uncle Fletcher and Aunt Lexi want to be surprised, too?"

"You'll have to ask them the next time you go over to play with Chance." He ruffled his son's hair and watched as Ivory slipped off the couch.

"Time to get ready for bed, kids. Who wants to climb into the tub first?"

"Me!" Ivory said and scampered toward her bedroom.

Hale glanced at Kenny who remained where he was.

"Are you sure Mom's not mad?"

"No, son. She's just got a lot on her mind."

"She didn't look happy at dinner."

My son, so sensitive to others. "But she's not mad."

"The last time we were at the bakery, someone made fun of Aunt Lexi and Uncle Fletcher looked all mad and everything. Even though he didn't say much. Chance said it was about his mom, because she looks kind of funny in that apron she wears. Her middle really sticks out now." Kenny giggled. "Chance said it makes him think she swallowed a balloon, even though he knows she's hiding a baby inside."

Hale chuckled. "You were smart not to make fun. Maybe you could tell Mom how we're all here to help her, especially on days when she needs to rest. Pregnant moms need to do that, you know, especially toward the end, before the baby is born."

Kenny nodded. "Did we do that before Ivy was born?"

"We did. And Mom liked that you napped with her when she needed to rest."

"But I don't nap anymore, Dad. I'm too big for that."

"I know, but maybe you could remind Ivy to play quietly when Mom needs to rest."

Kenny looked serious for a moment. "Okay."

Hale rose from his seat on the couch. "Water's running in the bathroom. Time to check on Ivy. It's your turn next. Why don't you grab your pj's?"

Hale helped Ivory with her bath. He emptied the tub and refilled it for Kenny. When both children were dried off and tucked into bed, Kenny asked if he could read. Hale agreed, but only for a half hour. He headed for the master bedroom to talk to Eden.

~ ~ ~

Hale climbed onto the bed and slid his body close to Eden, whose eyes were closed. But her breathing told him she wasn't asleep. "Hey, babe. The kids are bathed and in bed. Guess what book Ivy chose tonight?"

She shrugged.

"The one about where babies come from. Seemed appropriate, given our announcement, don't you think?"

She opened her eyes, scooted onto her side and faced him. "I'm sorry I've been such a grouch, Hale. Can I chalk it up to pregnancy hormones?"

"I think it's because you were extra tired from work *and* being pregnant *and* worrying about the amnio."

"The way you say it, no wonder I've been such a bitch all day." Eden's mouth finally curved up into a slow grin.

"Doesn't mean I don't still love you." He kissed her forehead then nibbled her nearest earlobe and planted his lips on hers for a tender kiss. "Kenny may have more questions."

"I'll answer every one." She sighed. "I just wish … I really want to know those results. Even if it's too late to do anything about it. This baby is so active. A few minutes ago, I felt what has to be a little leg kicking." She grabbed Hale's hand and placed it on the center of her rounded baby bump. "Right here. Feel that? Not a kick, exactly. More like he's rolling from one side to the other. I keep hoping he's telling me that he's fine or she's fine, that I've been worried for nothing."

"The baby's probably all right, even if the results aren't here yet. Maybe we should have gone with that cheaper test, the one where the results are posted online."

"But, remember what Deb and Todd said? They wanted to make sure the information was accurate, and that the more expensive test gave written results that seemed more reliable, more detailed. The kind of report their Dr. recommended."

"You're right." He shifted to a sitting position when the doorbell rang and he glanced at Eden. "You expecting anyone at this hour? Forget to pay Katya? It's past eight."

"No."

"Never mind. I'll get rid of whoever it is." Hale grabbed a robe and went to the door. A fifty-something gentleman stood on the porch, holding a package.

"Sorry I didn't get this to you sooner. We've been out of town. When we picked up our mail, this was in our stack. Letter carrier must be new, or maybe he just didn't read your address right. Your number's 689 and ours is 698. One street over, too. Anyway, I hope it's good news."

"Thank you." Hale took the package and shut the door. When he saw the return address, his heart skipped a beat. *The spit tests.* Finally.

He strode into the master bedroom. "Eden! They're here. The results. Got mixed up with some other people's mail. Let me help you up. We'll read it together."

Eden paled as she swung her legs over the side of the bed and stood up. "There's a pair of scissors in the junk drawer."

She walked with Hale into the kitchen and retrieved the scissors. She held her hands in the air. "I'm shaking like a leaf. What if it's bad news?"

"Have a seat, hon. It could very well be good news. Maybe neither of us have the bad gene or only one of us does. Only three of your sibs are carriers. Fletcher isn't. You might be like him, negative."

"Okay." She pointed to the package. "You open it. I'm too shaky."

Hale slit the edge of the large envelope and slid out several pages. "For some reason, I thought the results would be one-liners."

"Because we paid more, we got more," she replied, smiling for the first time since Hale had joined her in the bedroom.

They leaned their heads together and read the first document. Eden was a CF carrier. She blew out a slow breath. "Just like Elaine and Deb. And Chris." She pressed a hand along the side of her belly.

Hale set that page aside and read the document identifying his markers. After a moment, he said, "Me, too," and looked at Eden. A single tear slid down her cheek as she gulped.

"That means …"

"I know. This baby could have CF," he declared. "Or maybe not. It's only a twenty-five percent chance, honey. This baby could end up being negative. Twenty-five percent chance of that, too. Or more likely, just like us, a carrier." He wrapped his arms around Eden. "I wonder why we haven't got those tests we ordered for the kids. They should have come by now, too."

She pursed her lips together. "Maybe they're in a separate mailer."

"Will you talk to the doctor again? Or do you want me to call him? Didn't he say we should meet with a genetics counselor? I'll call in sick if I have to, Eden. Just tell me what you want to do."

"After I take the kids to school, I'll call Dr. Ortiz." She leaned into Hale's chest, seeming to take comfort from his closeness. But her heart was racing, and the fingers stroking his nape were ice cold. "I so didn't want this news."

"But weren't you the one who said we'd also find out about any other risks, like for diabetes or heart disease? We lucked out there. No genetic markers for either of those health problems."

Eden sighed. "No, but we may have doomed this baby."

Hale placed a hand on Eden's rounded belly and tapped a finger, as if saying hello to the tiny baby inside. "We have to think positively about this, Edie. The odds are on our side."

Her drawn-out sigh and her bereft expression told him she was terrified. He kissed her and considered it a positive omen that Eden didn't pull away when he hugged her close.

~ ~ ~

The next morning, Hale climbed out of bed, feeling as though he'd barely rested. Eden, too, looked tired. She'd tossed and turned most of the night. He hadn't been able to settle, either. His mind couldn't seem to stop whirling with imagined medical bills, perhaps not even covered by his insurance.

Just before dawn, after Eden's most recent trip to the bathroom, Hale fell asleep after concluding that he should start scanning for a better job, one that paid more than what he was making at the college.

He'd set those plans aside when the hacking issue had taken up so much of his time. And he didn't want to be thought of as abandoning a damaged ship before it was fully righted. What would Nathan Lambert think of him then?

Hale showered and dressed for work, aware of Eden in the kitchen, talking with the children as she prepared breakfast.

When he entered the kitchen, he asked, "Will you drop me off at work this morning? I'm not in the mood to walk."

"Of course."

"Mommy, can I tell about our new baby during sharing time?" Ivory asked.

Hale watched a series of expressions flash across Eden's face. Finally, she smiled and nodded. "Of course. Are any of your friends at school big sisters already?"

"Uma is. She has twin sisters," she proclaimed. "Now I'll be one, too. Just like Kenny."

"I'm a big *brother*," he corrected her, bumping his sister's shoulder.

"The principle's the same," Hale said. "Come on, kids. Grab your backpacks." He herded the children out to the car and took the passenger seat so that Eden wouldn't have to get out of the car after dropping off the children.

When she stopped behind his building, he leaned over and kissed Eden. "When you talk to the Dr. and get an appointment for the genetics counselor, let me know so I can get it into my calendar."

"I want one as soon as possible. And I'll ask for a waiting list slot, in case of a cancellation."

"Good idea. Are you going to talk to your sisters? Or Fletch and Chris?"

"I'll call Deb first. She's less likely to freak than Elaine. Debbie said something about presenting a united front with Mom and Dad, even if we have to convince Mom to get Logan tested. He and Dad are the only Lamberts left who have an unknown status."

"We'll work on a strategy for convincing them." Hale waved at Andy, who was walking toward him.

"Okay."

"Try not to worry, hon." He patted her shoulder and shut the door, remaining where he was until Eden pulled away from the building.

"Hale, any word yet?" Anderson asked, not having to remind Hale of the news he asked about almost daily.

"No, but I'm going to the IT office after I check in with Helen."

Andy grimaced. "Every day that goes by makes this more of a big deal. One I don't want to have to deal with."

Which you aren't, because you dumped it all on me. Hale nodded and watched as his boss strode into the building, then peeled off as if headed to the president's office on the main floor.

Hale continued upstairs, quickly reviewed the emails in the queue and confirmed with Helen that he wasn't scheduled to see any students before lunch. He pulled out the sheets of paper on which he'd written the names of all the students whose scholarship monies had been tampered with.

As he studied them, his pulse suddenly picked up. He stood up so suddenly that his chair banged into the window behind his desk. To confirm what he thought he'd found, he opened the top drawer of the file cabinet and pulled out the folder containing the list of all scholarship funding sources.

I'm right! Why *didn't I see this before? Was it because two of the students had different funding sources?* He grabbed his suit jacket and pulled it on, not bothering to shoot his sleeves. As he passed Helen's desk, he said, "If anyone asks for an appointment with me before lunch, send them to Madison."

Without waiting for her reply, he jogged out of the office and up the stairs to the college attorney's office. But the man was ensconced with someone the receptionist said could not be disturbed. Hale impatiently cooled his heels in a chair, palming a magazine too dated to include anything interesting.

When James Abernathy appeared, escorting a man who had the look of a plainclothes detective past the receptionist's desk, Hale rose from his seat.

"Can I have a word with you?"

"Certainly." The two men repaired to Abernathy's office. Hale shut the door.

"I think I found something. In fact, I know I did. Can we bring in that IT guy who was here at our last meeting? He should be in on this."

"Let me call him." James pulled out his cell phone and texted a quick message. "Serendipity. He was already headed here. Should be right in."

He'd barely got the words out when a knock sounded and the young man entered.

"Have a seat, Reggie," the attorney said. "Mr. Brinker appears to have news he wants to share."

Hale reviewed the number of students whose accounts had been affected and what he'd just noticed. "I went back and double-checked and we're dealing only with two different scholarship sources. But I think the hacker's really after the Lambert Family Foundation. Only two, both kind of smallish thefts, affected another source, and it isn't local. Well, within state boundaries, but not a city-located giver. And they occurred a good week before most of the thefts. Probably why I didn't see what now feels so obvious to me." He glanced again at the hacking expert, who listened, his eyes scanning the list. "Think this might help you find whoever's been stealing from us, from the students?"

"Maybe. Good to know." Reggie's voice reminded Hale of a rusty buzz saw. Rough.

"So. What do we do now?" Hale turned again to the lawyer.

"I say we share this with the outside experts, too. And any other students who received aid from the Lambert Foundation. Can you get me a list of those names?"

"Of course! I'll get right on that." For the first time in weeks, Hale felt more hopeful that real progress was being made.

James glanced in Reggie's direction. "Have you any other news?"

"Not me, but the experts texted me this morning." He leaned forward and outlined what they had discovered. Only the first two thefts had occurred in the week immediately preceding the first week of school, when new students were registering and when previous students were making changes in their courses for the fall term. The Lambert monies had been accessed on the day after upperclass registration began, thus interfering with the aid recipients in all classes, including those in master's candidacy.

"Think you can you get the money back?"

"Don't know that, either, but the outside guys are looking into what they think is a fake account."

"Where does that leave us?" Hale's frustration level showed in his tone. "My father-in-law is beside himself about all this."

The lawyer spoke first. "I'm sure he is. I've been in touch with the other scholarship source whose student recipients were affected. Steps have been taken to safeguard their scholarship accounts."

"How?"

"New passwords. Double verification that said accounts are secured and now require two different signatures before monies can be released. That sort of thing. I suggested the same elements to Professor Lambert. He said he'd be in touch after he speaks with the Lambert Family Board. I gather that includes you, Mr. Brinker."

"Not me, my wife. But she hasn't said if the Board has met yet. I'll ask her."

Hale glanced at Reggie. "I thought what I found by way of a clue might be helpful."

"Could be." Reggie left the lawyer's office.

Hale's left brow rose. "Hmm. That kid reminds me of his boss. Is he always that closed-mouthed?"

Abernathy smiled. "As long as he does his job, I don't care how silent he is. You may be onto something, that so many of the students are Lambert Fund recipients. Have you had complaints from parents or students about the foundation?"

"None. One of the perks of handling financial aid requests is how happy that makes the students. The ones turned down are disappointed, but I've never had occasion to worry that they might take any action against the foundation or our office. And I try, as often as possible, to steer those students toward other forms of aid."

Hale shook the attorney's hand. "I'll let you know what my father-in-law has to say. And what the Board agrees to do regarding those new safeguards we talked about."

The attorney nodded.

"I just wish Nathan would move a little faster on all this."

"Maybe he has and just hasn't said anything."

"From your lips to his ears." Hale departed for his office.

Twelve

Two weeks later, Hale returned home to find Eden putting the final touches on the holiday decorations on the porch.

"It's almost Christmas, Eden. We *have* to say something to your family about those tests we all took, especially since we now have the kids' results—Kenny being negative and Ivy a carrier. Didn't you say your sisters and brothers are finally on board?"

Eden followed him into the house. "Deb felt it best if we knew all the kids' results first. And now we do. Lexi said Chance is negative, too. I'm sure she was relieved to learn that, even though Fletcher isn't his biological dad."

Hale set the box of extra holly garlands on the floor. "Good. Ivy bent my ear yesterday about when we were going to eat 'Grandma's Christmas food.' And Kenny seconded her, which has to be a first. Usually she follows his lead. Our little girl seems to be coming into her own these days."

"Probably because she's in kindergarten. Growing up, Hale. Your baby girl is growing up." Eden sighed. "I'm glad it was your dad's turn for us to spend Thanksgiving with him. I'll call Deb and find out if this coming Sunday we'll tell Mom and Dad who's positive, who's negative, and that Logan should be tested. Them, too."

"Shouldn't Fletcher take the lead? As the oldest kid?"

"Who happens to be negative," Eden replied. "Wish we were as lucky."

"We still could be, hon. Our status doesn't mean the new baby has CF."

"I hope we're having a girl. You saw those research studies, the ones where boys with CF often are sterile."

Hale squeezed Eden's shoulder when she walked past him. "Maybe we should have gone ahead with the amnio. Then we'd know the sex, too. Want me to ask Dr. Ortiz to reschedule it?"

"No way." She faux-shuddered.

"Okay, okay." He took the last box of Christmas decorations out of her hands, set it on a nearby chair and hugged her. "Hey! I just got kicked. This kid is strong. Feels like a fighter to me."

Eden eased herself out of his arms and pointed to his suit coat pocket. "Your phone just buzzed."

He glanced at his phone, and his heart flip-flopped in his chest. *Attorney's office? Maybe they found the thief! Or the money.* Such a result would make Sunday dinner easier. Nathan was likely to ask him about progress on that score.

"I have to take this." He stepped back outside onto the porch and took a seat on the steps.

"Hello?"

"I have Reggie here with me," the attorney intoned.

"They found the money? And who took it?"

"Are you still in your office?"

"No. Just got home. Want me to come back? I can be there in ten minutes."

"That would be helpful."

Hale trotted into the house. "Edie, I have to go back to the office."

"Will you be back in time for dinner?" she asked. "You've been late so many days lately."

"I'll text you." He kissed her, reversed direction and waved as Kenny and Ivory walked into the yard. "Hey, kids. Just in time to help your mother put some of these decorations in the windows." He pointed to a box on the dining room table.

He turned toward Eden as he picked up the box he'd brought in from the porch. "You want this stuff in the attic, hon?"

"Yes. On the wall opposite the Halloween decorations, please."

"I'll take care of it as soon as I'm back."

~ ~ ~

Hale parked in his usual spot behind the building and sprinted up the back stairs to his office.

He'd barely caught his breath and taken a seat when Helen opened his door and solemnly announced, "The college attorney is here with, uh, some other people. May I show them in?"

"Of course." Hale smiled at her, eager to hear what the man had to say, what that IT kid had uncovered. Maybe he was just passing on what the hacking experts had found. It was past time for some good news. And right before the Christmas break for students, right before final exams, a week when his work usually slowed down. He'd enjoy sharing good news with Eden's father. Hale rubbed his palms together and stood up when James Abernathy entered.

The attorney stepped aside to allow Reginald Shepherd to take a seat. Behind him stood a college security officer, who shrugged out of a large backpack. He placed it on the floor, shut the door and then leaned against it, his arms crossed over his chest.

With a gun on one hip and a taser on the other, the presence of the security officer lent something of an ominous air to his office. Hale willed his pulse to stop galloping. "So, what did you find? Is the guilty party local? In a house just off campus? Or has he been using a public place, like a coffee shop? When are you going to arrest the thief? Tell me this is good news!"

Reggie frowned, his brow furrowed so tightly that his thick eyebrows resembled an unkempt bushy shrub shading his dark eyes. "Here."

"Not a house? You mean the college?" Hale glanced at the attorney.

"He means this office," the attorney clarified.

"But we know they got in via my laptop. Remotely. Which now has all kinds of security features that it didn't have before. Are you saying they managed to get in again?"

Mr. Abernathy leaned forward. "Those outside experts have identified *when* the hacker was using your equipment. Except for that one time when you were at my office and we observed him in action, it occurs whenever you're *not* here."

"When you leave your office, do you lock the door?" the security officer asked.

"Of course! And, if I have work that needs completion over the weekend, I take my laptop home." Hale's pulse galloped, as if it might push his heart through his chest.

"Are you saying someone uses my office when I'm elsewhere in the building? Talking to Helen or in the men's room? But wouldn't that mean it's an inside job? I thought we ruled out our employees."

James waved him quiet. "All true, and we've seen no activity since Reggie here followed instructions from the pros and put all those security features on your machine and every other computer in this office. Even Helen's equipment."

Hale scanned the three men staring back at him.

"So you always lock your office," the security officer countered. "Even when you go to lunch, have a meeting elsewhere in the building or in another campus building?"

"Maybe not then, but Helen knows not to give anyone access. And I'm at the end of the hallway. Where it's quieter. Why would someone come in here, knowing the only way out is past the other offices and Helen's desk?"

"Where is your immediate supervisor, Mr. Brinker?" the attorney asked.

"Anderson? I haven't seen him since early last week. Helen said something the other day about him taking some vacation days. Because we're not so busy this time of year. I told him I would hold down the fort, so to speak, and he knows I've been working with you to get to the bottom of the thefts. Something he prefers that I do. Want me to ask Helen if she knows where Andy is?" He reached for the landline on his desk.

"I'll get her," the security officer said.

Hale waited for what seemed like several minutes, though it was probably less than thirty seconds before he heard the rapid click of Helen's heels in the hallway.

"Yes, Mr. Brinker?"

"Did Andy come in today?" he asked.

"He was in earlier, but then he left. Mentioned something about meeting with his son's counselor." She glanced at her watch. "But he probably went home after that. I haven't seen him since. Would you like me to call his home before I leave?"

Hale turned his gaze from the secretary to the lawyer, who nodded and said, "That would be helpful,"

"Certainly." Helen left and came back moments later. "His wife said Andy took his son and they went up to their cabin near Mount Baker for some father-son time. But there's no phone service there."

"Did she say when she expects them back?" the attorney asked.

"She did not. But, she offered to get him a message. She has the number of the little store where the people with nearby places go to buy food, firewood, that sort of thing. Even the skiers who stay at the resort go in there to leave messages. It maintains a kind of community message-board for the people who go to the mountain to recreate."

"Please call Mrs. Randolph back, and ask her to have her husband get in touch with me," Mr. Abernathy requested, handing her his business card. "The sooner the better."

"Of course."

When Helen departed, Hale slowly took a seat. "I gather we may be here for a while. Mind if I let my wife know that I might be late for dinner?"

"Go ahead." The attorney motioned for the security guard to take a seat.

Hale thumbed a quick text to Eden. *Not sure how late I'll be. Start dinner without me.*

He straightened in his seat and began to answer more questions of the security guard and the lawyer.

Minutes later, he asked, "I'm free to go now?"

Without a smile, the lawyer stood up. "I think it would be best if you stay home until we can get this all sorted out. Whoever made off with the scholarship monies is still trying to break into the system. Unsuccessfully thus far. With you out of the office, the thief may try again. Directly. That is, from your office. And, if you're not here, he might actually pay a visit. Which would enable us to catch him."

"I can't believe those hacker pros haven't caught him yet." Hale looked over at Reggie. "Your boss seemed to think they could do what her office doesn't have the skills for."

The young man shrugged. "They're still working at their end, probably trying to track the money and that fake account."

Right. That and the invisible student it supposedly went to. Hale let out a long breath, unaware until then that he'd been holding his breath. He pulled his keyring from his pocket and removed the office key. Then he reached for the laptop. He'd continue his duties from home.

"No. Leave it, too," the attorney said. "It's best if it remains available for whomever might try to use it. Other than you, of course." A thin smile broke across his face for the first time since he'd entered the room.

Hale nodded. "But how am I to get my work done?"

"For now, consider yourself on paid vacation."

"But with Andy out of the office—?"

"I've already cleared it with the administration. The other people in the office should be able to manage most of the issues that arise at this time of year."

Certain that his reluctance was evident, Hale said, "If you tell Helen, she'll know which employees handle which questions."

"Thank you for that suggestion. I'll be in touch with you as soon as we learn more."

Hale reached for his coat. "We're done for now?"

"Yes. I trust that you will remain in town, available should we need to see you again."

"Of course." Hale watched as Reggie approached the desk, reached for the laptop and opened the back of the machine. After several seconds, he closed the laptop and returned it to its previous position on the desk.

"Are you going to change the locks on my door, too?"

"Not at this time. Because the thefts have been perpetrated remotely, locked doors don't matter. But Security here is going to set up cameras—in the reception area, along the hallway, in here, too. To capture anyone coming into your office, in case they try that since they haven't been successful from a distance. We're hoping he'll be frustrated that he's been stopped and might try to get into the office to 'fix' things." He air-quoted.

"Interesting thought. Does Helen know about all this?" He waved in the direction of the equipment the security office had set down.

The lawyer shook his head. "But she'll know soon enough."

"Won't the thief spot the cameras? You know, those glowing red eyes that show when the camera's on?"

The security officer scoffed. "No one's going to spot our gear." He allowed a hand to slide down to rest on his gun holster. "And as soon as you leave, we'll get started." He leaned down and began to rummage through the backpack.

Message received loud and clear. He wants me gone. Hale nodded. As he departed, he asked Helen to make sure that his office was locked after the attorney and security officer left.

~ ~ ~

Hale barely touched his dinner when he arrived home. When Eden asked him what was wrong, he waved her off, saying only that they'd talk after the children were in bed. He used the children's baths and story times to force his focus onto something enjoyable. But after they were in bed, he escaped to the living room. When Eden joined him on the couch, he told her what the lawyer had said, that the security officer had installed cameras, probably motion-activated. Maybe they even had the ability to detect intrusion in the dark. As he mused about what he should do next, the phone rang. He went into the kitchen and plucked the phone off the wall.

"Fletch. How're things?"

"Just following orders. Lexi's elbow-deep in a big wedding order at the bakery. She asked me to call and remind Eden that we have the extra test kits for Mom and Dad and Logan and that she reached everyone earlier today. We're all in agreement for presenting a united front on Sunday and that we don't need a planning session. You guys do plan to come, don't you? All four of you?"

Hale glanced in Eden's direction, shared Fletcher's message and received a thumbs-up response. "We'll be there. Got a minute?"

"Sure."

"Didn't Todd used to be a criminal prosecutor?"

"Yes, but he does defense work now. And you know we manage mostly civil matters, since he joined the firm. We usually hand off criminal cases to other firms."

"Right. Think he would mind if I call him at home?"

Hale listened to the weighted silence that seemed to zing along the phone lines.

"Are you in some kind of trouble?" Fletcher asked. "If it's family related, you know I'm the designated rep for the family."

"You can't be on my side in this issue, since it may put me at odds with the Lambert Family Foundation, which will likely require representation. Nathan is certain to want you in that role."

"Talk to Todd. You know the number."

Hale turned back to Eden. "You never told me everything's set for a Sunday dinner that's likely to include major fireworks."

"I was getting ready to." She pursed her lips in a minifrown. "I was more worried about what you refused to talk about when you came home. Have you been accused of something that I *know* you would never do?"

"No, but I'm now on official paid vacation, and they've wired up my office with hidden cameras. Apparently those hacker pros have detected efforts to continue to break through all the new security steps that were installed. They seem to think whoever's behind this may now try to break in to my office." He scoffed. "If the latest and greatest techy remote thieving isn't working, maybe they'll revert to old-fashioned B and E. Never figured they'd resort to that when that IT kid told me how slickly people can do their dirty work from afar these days. They even asked me to leave my laptop in the office."

"And now you need a lawyer? But Hale, how could they possibly think you had anything to do with this?"

"Not sure they do. But it looks like the Lambert Foundation is what has really been targeted—it and some of the students receiving aid from it. Since I'm part of the family, as an in-law, maybe the crook figured no one would suspect me and that's why he targeted my office." He ran his fingers through his hair in frustration. "I just wish they'd catch whoever's doing this."

Eden pushed Hale's hand away and began to knead his neck muscles. "I don't even want to think about you going to jail for something you didn't do."

"I doubt that'll happen. I just want to talk to Todd in case things get worse. But he might say he can't represent me since he's a partner with Fletch, who just happens to be the foundation's lawyer."

"That shouldn't matter. Maybe Todd won't charge us. I mean, we're *family* since he married Deb. Your very own brother-in-law!"

Hale chuckled. "One of three, Edie. Chris is, too. And Fletch."

"But Todd is *my* brother-in-law, too! Shouldn't that also count? Why don't you talk to him while I take a shower? I know you're not likely to sleep tonight if you don't. Maybe he can set your mind at ease about what you're up against."

"You know me well, babe." Hale reached over and pecked Eden's cheek. He dug for his phone and punched in Todd's home number.

~ ~ ~

Hale followed Kenny and Ivory up the steps of his in-laws' spacious Southern Colonial all decked out in seasonal greens. From the sounds of things, everyone else had arrived, confirming Eden's conclusion when she'd pointed out the cars in the driveway.

"Even Chris is here already," she said as she opened the passenger slider into the backseat and helped Ivory unbuckle her safety harness.

"Okay, kids. Go find Chance. We'll call you when it's time to eat," Hale said. He watched Kenny and Ivory scamper around the side of the house. Then he reached for Eden's hand and gave it a squeeze. She looked nervous, her eyes wide, one hand brushing her blouse near her baby bump.

"Are you going to talk to Todd again?" she asked.

"No need for that. He said he'd be in touch after he talks to the college attorney. Today's about getting Logan tested."

Eden nodded. "And more questions about my job. Mom doesn't think I should keep working now that I'm pregnant."

"If you focus her attention on the grandbaby news, maybe she'll chill about the job. She loves her grandchildren and, knowing two more are on the way, is bound to put her in a good mood."

"I'd prefer to focus on getting Logan tested."

"One thing at a time, hon." He grinned at Debra, who stood at the door. "I take it we're the last to arrive?"

His sister-in-law smiled. "Yes. Can't remember the last time Chris was here before the rest of us. Probably Teddy's doing. She said Yancy's due home in two weeks. Which means she and Chris will probably announce that they're getting married on New Year's Eve. Too late in the game for Mom to butt in, though she may try. Oh, and Teddy asked if you could stop in at the dress shop and pick up your dress," Deb laughed. "With all of us picking different colors, it's going to be a rainbow of shades surrounding the bride and groom, with the men in their black tuxes mixed in."

Hale breathed out a chuckle. "Except for your mention of the monkey suits, more good news. Right, Edie?"

"Where's Mom?" Eden asked.

"In the kitchen lording it over Elaine and Lexi. Wow, you seem to have blossomed since the last time I saw you. And I like that outfit." Deb walked with Eden in the direction of the kitchen. "Teddy's there, too?"

"No. She went out back with Fletcher to watch over the kids. Or maybe to fill him in on Yance and how long he'll be on leave."

"I'll join the other men," Hale announced. "Where are they?"

"Downstairs, and if they're still talking politics," Deb announced over her shoulder, "you'd better be wearing asbestos underwear."

"Very funny." Hale went downstairs. Although the talk was boisterous, it seemed to be focused on the relative merits of Chris's latest shot at the pool table. "Hey, there."

"You can take on the winner, Hale. Which would be me," Chris exclaimed. He straightened up after sending two balls into the far left pocket. "Just ran the table," he crowed with a grin.

"How many have you won today? So I know how much you should handicap me," as Nathan handed Hale a cue and tromped upstairs.

Chris held up three fingers. "Two over Dad and one over Todd."

"My loss was just dumb luck, Chris," Todd countered with a chuckle. "Your dad brushed up against me at just the wrong moment."

"So Chris cheated again?" Hale grinned. "Aren't lawyers officers of the court, bro? He could call the cops to haul you in."

"Not after I upgraded his guest bath and only charged him for supplies," Chris countered.

Hale nodded before changing the subject. "I hear Yancy's coming home soon."

Chris grinned. "Yep, and you know what that means." Under his breath, he hummed a bar or two of something that badly resembled Mendelssohn's "*Wedding March.*"

"Which means it's finally going to happen. A week after Christmas. You ready?"

Before Chris could reply in the midst of Todd's and Hale's laughter, Nathan's voice ordered them upstairs. "Dinner's on. Upstairs, now!"

Everyone found their seats. While the younger set chattered excitedly about all the presents under the grandparents' tree in the family room, Hale slid a hand up to the back of Eden's nape and rubbed it. She sat stiffly, making him wonder if she'd already endured a tongue-lashing from her mother.

After the food had been passed and quiet descended, Hale glanced around the table. Eden wasn't the only one who seemed tense.

Nathan clapped his hands to claim everyone's attention. "Time for the news. Probably overdue, given how few of you have been around lately. Fletcher, why don't you start?"

"Lexi and I are *still* pregnant. Eden? Your turn." He smiled in her direction.

"Yes, well, we are, too, but that's old news."

Hale gazed at her, aware that her jerky words reflected the nerves she'd been displaying since they'd arrived.

"Which we're thrilled about," he added. "Right, kids?"

"I want a brother," Kenyon declared.

"And I want a sister," Ivory shot back, before sticking out her tongue at her brother.

"Behave yourselves, you two," Hale said, although he suspected Eden knew he really didn't want to stifle enthusiasm. Then, angling his face toward the man sitting to his left, he said, "You're up, Chris."

"Nothing to say yet."

"Hey! Yes, you do," Elaine interrupted.

"What he meant was, Yancy will be home next week. Not sure which day," Teddy corrected her fiancé. "We'll have other news later." Her cheeks turned fiery red.

Skipping over Teddy's comments, Iona said, "That's nice, Eden. I, for one, love the idea of more grandchildren. Perhaps we'll have one of each variety." She smiled at Lexi and looked appraisingly at Eden. "Even if my eldest daughter insists on keeping that job of hers."

Nathan looked around the table. "That's it? No more news?"

All three children began to talk before they were shushed by Fletcher.

"Actually, yes. Todd, want to explain?"

He rose from the table and retrieved the kits Debra had brought in. Todd passed them to Nathan and proceeded to tell the elder Lamberts about the DNA testing and the results.

"When we shared our information with Fletch and the other brothers and sisters, we wondered if your parents, Nathan, might have passed the illness on to their children. Is it possible that your siblings, the ones who died so young, might have had cystic fibrosis?"

Nathan shrugged. "I suppose it's possible. The only sib I really grew up with was my sister, Annoria, and I don't recall hearing why the children born between us died."

"Which isn't surprising, since CF wasn't identified until the 1940s," Debra added.

Todd continued. "After we did some research, we felt it wise for the rest of Deb's family to be tested, to see if anyone else was a carrier."

"Surely you don't think the new babies have the disease?" Iona asked, staring worriedly at Lexi and then Eden.

"Our baby is in the clear," Fletcher said. "I'm negative and so is Lexi."

Hale cleared his throat. "Kenny is negative, but Ivory is a carrier. Like Eden and I. We don't know yet about the new baby."

"But, there's only a twenty-five percent chance of her, er, him, whatever, having it."

"Why is that?" Iona demanded. "I can't believe that anything at all would be wrong with the Lambert genes. Or mine, for that matter. Surely, you're mistaken."

"I'm a carrier," Elaine chimed in.

"Me, too," Chris declared, "but not Teddy. And since she's in the clear, way into the future," —to laughter from around the table and more blushing from Teddy— "our kids have nothing to worry about."

"Fletcher is the only one in the clear?" Nathan asked.

Todd nodded. "We got you these kits. You're likely to be a carrier, too, Nathan, since it's passed from parent to child. We don't know about Logan, so we thought you might want to have him tested. Since he shows no signs of the illness, it's likely that he's either negative or only a carrier. This third kit is for Iona."

As if she'll agree to be tested, Hale thought, anticipating what the rest of the Lambert clan were probably thinking.

"You should do the spit test, too, Mom, for the sake of completeness," Chris urged, a slight smirk spoiling the sincerity of his words.

"That's—why it's just impossible! The Lamberts have been an upstanding family for generations! There is just no way this could be happening." Iona shook her head, looking distastefully at the boxes stacked next to Nathan on the table.

"But if it isn't Dad, it has to be you, Mom," Logan said. "I want a box. All I have to do is spit into it?"

Todd nodded.

"Cool," the youngest Lambert child said with a grin. "Kind of like a science project."

"Just follow the directions and mail it in," Todd added. "A few weeks from now, you'll know your status. You can ask for other results, too. All you have to do is ask." He beamed in Logan's direction. "Maybe you'd like to use your results in a school report on DNA testing."

Iona pushed her chair back from the table. "Disgusting, that's what it is. I have *no intention* of spitting into a tube. So unsanitary." She reached for the remaining boxes, but Nathan clutched them to his chest.

He gazed at his son-in-law, the lawyer. "You're right, Todd. I'll take the test. I agree. Logan should be tested, too. Maybe he'll be negative, like Fletcher. Or a carrier, like Chris and his sisters. Only one way to find out and that's to follow the directions and send in the kits."

Conversation burst out around the table after Nathan's declaration. Only Iona remained silent. She scanned the family members and then left the table.

Debra shared a worried glance with Eden after their mother stomped upstairs. "Let her go, sis. No matter what you say, she's not going to listen."

"But what about our other news?" Teddy asked in a stage-whisper to Chris.

He stood up. "I'll get Mom. She might as well hear this now. Two weeks from now will be a little late," he smirked.

Minutes later, Chris preceded Iona back down the stairs. He seated her at her end of the table. "We have more news. Go ahead, Teddy."

After she sipped some water, Teddy reached for Chris's hand, her diamond sparkling in the light from the dining room chandelier. "We're getting married!"

All but Iona clapped and cheered.

Ivory stood up next to her chair. With a flounce of her dress, she announced, "And *I* get to be Teddy's flower girl!"

"The Saturday after Christmas, New Year's Eve. At three o'clock, in the upstairs room at The Bluff," Chris added.

"That soon?" Nathan asked.

"When Yancy's home. So he can walk me down the aisle," Teddy explained. "We had to schedule it for when he'd be here."

"Of course." Nathan rose and leaned over to buss Teddy's cheek. "I'm glad." He grabbed Chris's hand and shook it before pulling him into a hug. "Congratulations, son." When he resumed his seat, he said, "I gather everything's all planned?"

Hale detected a twinkle in his father-in-law's eyes. The man knew his wife's penchant for wanting to control things, especially wedding-related details.

"Yep. All you have to do is show up," Chris declared, smiling at his father then directing a look at his mother that was unmistakable in its warning that she should not object.

"An afternoon ceremony?" Iona asked.

Teddy nodded. "The reception will be right after and if you want to stay for dinner, you can do that downstairs from where … the ceremony …" Her voice trailed off.

Deb clapped her hands. "Well, if that's all the news, then I think we'll head home." She turned to Eden as they walked over to the coat closet for their winter garb.

"Are you unhappy that Todd and I set all this in motion when we shared what we found out?"

Eden shook her head. "Not really. At first I was upset, mostly because this pregnancy was … unexpected."

"We wondered about that. Since you didn't mention it for the longest time. Kept us guessing why your shape was changing."

Eden nodded. "You were smart to check your genetics ahead of time. I just wish I'd thought of it before we started having children. But it never occurred to us."

"No matter what, your baby will be loved—by all of us. You know that." Deb hugged her older sister.

When Eden glanced at Hale, tears welled in her dark eyes, stinging her lids. "Will you hurry up the kids? Tell them their presents under Grandma's tree have to wait until Christmas morning. Only a week away."

He nodded.

"Let me help you get some dessert to take home for the kids," Lexi offered. She bumped into Eden's belly as both turned in the direction of the kitchen.

Eden grinned. "Guess we introduced them, didn't we? The littlest Lambert babies?"

"That we did."

Eden carried the covered plate to the car while Hale opened the door so that the children could pile into their SUV.

~ ~ ~

That evening, Eden said what she'd been thinking.

"I don't think Mom's done talking about all this. The DNA tests, I mean. At least she has something else to focus on besides my job."

"Think your dad can convince her?"

Eden sighed. "I've decided I'm not going to worry about it. If Dad and Logan are tested, we'll know more than we know now. Maybe that's enough."

Thirteen

Weeks later, Eden looked up when her mother entered her office. She shut the door, the sound mimicking the thud of Eden's heart as it slammed against her lungs, temporarily halting her ability to speak. She sucked in a quick breath.

"Mom. What are you doing here?"

"I wanted to see where you work, now that I know this is where you've been hiding all these months since Ivory started kindergarten. You didn't even pop over before you drove to Hale's father's home for Thanksgiving with that poor man."

Ever the guilt-giver. Have you been saving up to dump that on me after we spent so much of our Christmas vacation with you? "We weren't hiding, Mom. It was his turn for Thanksgiving. He was eager to see the children, and he doesn't get many opportunities, now that he's volunteering at the senior center."

"But you didn't feel you could come over until right before the Christmas holidays?" Iona sniffed and seemed to look down her nose as she appraised Eden.

You don't like what I'm wearing, Mom?

"You're really showing, Eden. Are you sure you're not having twins?"

"The doctor says it's one baby, not two." *Thank God.* Eden sat back in her seat, wondering how best to get her mother to leave without sounding ungracious. "I really need to get back to finishing what I'm in the middle of. Why, exactly, did you stop here instead of coming to the house?"

Iona ignored the question. She pointed at the stack of contracts on Eden's desk. "Are you sure you can get home today before the children arrive? With those big piles there?"

"Yes." Eden could stay as long as necessary, now that Hale was still on his paid vacation. Not that Eden wanted her mother to know. Such an admission was sure to result in uncomfortable questions about Hale. Had he lost his job? Why was he *not* supporting his family by doing his part? Yada yada yada.

Iona pursed her lips and frowned. "I just came from the post office. Your father and Logan insisted on taking those kits you all brought over."

"I'm glad. What about you, Mom? Did you take the test, too?"

Iona's lips turned downward and she hissed out a breath. "Your father insisted. Spitting into those tubes was so … distasteful," she sneered. "Not that it's likely to reveal anything. I simply can't imagine that he or I passed on any bad genes. That disease must have skipped a generation, probably from your grandmother Lambert's side of the family. The Oleson side. That lowly Scandinavian fisherman's family."

She chose to ignore her mother's disparagement of the woman Eden remembered as being gracious to everyone, even her unpleasant daughter-in-law. "I don't think the CF recessive trait skips generations, but maybe you're right. Remember what Fletcher said? It takes *both* parents to pass on the gene that results in the illness."

Eden recalled that Aunt Annoria was a spinster, a well-educated one. She'd become a doctor, maintaining a thriving practice somewhere in the Midwest. Was the early death of all but one of her siblings the reason her aunt had insisted on studying medicine? So few women back then did that. Eden recalled meeting her only a couple of times. Iona had not been all that welcoming the last time her husband's sister had shown up in Pacific Knoll following her attendance at a medical convention in Seattle.

Iona continued to stare at Eden. "So, you don't know if that baby you're carrying is sick?"

"No."

"You should have done that test sooner."

"The spit test?"

"No, what Deb mentioned after you left. Where they stick a needle in your belly." Iona shuddered. "Although the very thought makes me cringe. I can't *imagine* doing that myself, but if it meant I'd know if my baby was sick, I'd insist on it."

"Yes, well, I wasn't interested." Eden pushed her chair back, intent on sending her mother home if the conversation was going to remain on what Eden should or shouldn't have done about the baby she'd never expected to have. A baby whose due date was less than sixteen weeks away.

"Mom, I really have to get back to work. Mr. McCue isn't paying me to talk to you. He's paying me to keep track of the money his agents are bringing in. And I'm surprised Opal didn't announce you."

"Who?"

"Our receptionist."

"If she was supposed to be at that desk out front, she isn't at her post." Iona huffed, but seemed to get the message. She stood up, clutching her purse to her side. "A third baby is going to mean lots of expenses, Eden. Is that why you went back to work, even though you said you always liked being at home, like me, making a traditional home?"

"No, Mom. I *always* intended to go back to work after Ivory started school. Being pregnant didn't change my mind."

"Hmmph," Iona muttered. "Well, I expect to see you at our Sunday dinners again, now that you've broken the news to your father and me. About those tests, I mean. And your new work. I do miss seeing Kenny and Ivy."

"They're busier now, Mom. With school and afterward, too. Kenny's enjoying after-school soccer this year, and Ivy likes her dance lessons, might even try ballet."

"She's much too young for that kind of disciplined activity," Iona declared, her voice rising. "Why, she's barely out of diapers!"

"She's five and a half, Mom. Please don't discourage her. Two of her best friends at school are in her tap class, and Hale and I are totally okay with her sticking with it through this school year."

"Yes, well …"

Iona left Eden's office, her stiff back attesting to her decision to hold any further comments about Eden's fitness as a mother until a later time, perhaps next week's Sunday dinner.

Quincy McCue's quick smile and engaging voice never felt more welcome to Eden than when he thanked Iona for coming in and enthusiastically declared after being introduced how much he and the entire office appreciated Eden's skills.

She retreated to her office after sending him a grateful smile. She pulled out her cell phone and dialed the house.

"Brinker residence, Hale speaking," sounding official, much like when he answered his office phone.

"Mom was just here. I have a feeling she may stop by the house. Better be prepared to explain why you're home already," Eden said in a rush.

"She doesn't know I've been banished from the office?" he asked.

"She didn't mention it. I can't imagine Dad not sharing that news with her unless he doesn't know. I just wish there was more action on catching whoever took all that money."

"According to Reggie, there haven't been any more thefts. Which probably means all the extra security measures are doing their job."

"Good for the IT department. Are they still working with those pros you told me about?"

"I'm assuming so, although I'm out of the loop at the moment." He blew out a breath.

"Are the kids home yet?"

"I expect them any minute." Hale paused. "There they are, about half a block away."

"If Mom says anything about Ivy not taking dance class, will you ask her to back off? She seems to think I'm not capable—we're not capable—of knowing what's best for our daughter."

"You know I will. By the way, I just picked up two tax time clients—both with new businesses. They want to get off on the right foot regarding their IRS responsibilities. Money we'll add to the kids' college fund."

"Good for you. I'm a little behind on what I wanted to finish today because Mom showed up, so I may be later than usual."

"Take your time. I know you like having gone fulltime and being able to do all your work at the office."

Eden's heart swelled. "You are the best husband, Hale. I was so lucky to find you, to fall in love with you. I'd never be happy if I hadn't married you."

He laughed and smacked her a kiss through the phone. "I'm the lucky one, hon. See you when you get here."

She heard him welcome the kids before the phone connection was broken.

~ ~ ~

Eden cleared her desk of the paperwork that had clogged her in-box all day. She was tired, eager to get home and put her feet up. Was it her mother's impromptu visit, or the additional contracts that had suddenly appeared minutes after Iona left? Maybe it was the work ethic of the two new agents who had joined the McCue team.

Eden was about to reach for her coat when her door opened and Elaine breezed in.

"I'm *so* glad you're still here. We *have* to talk."

"About what?" Eden reclaimed her seat. Her feet ached.

"Chris and Teddy's wedding photos. Have you seen them?" Elaine slung her coat over the back of a chair before leaning forward to stare back at her older sister. "They are *so* cute. Teddy sent me a link, said she and Chris are putting together a book of the best photos. Each of us will get a copy. I never dreamed how they were going to turn everything upside-down and how cute it would be with us women wearing dresses in our favorite colors and all the guys wearing cumberbunds in deep purple. Same hue as those long thin ribbons that decorated her dress and Ivy's. Check these out." Elaine thrust her cell phone at Eden.

She grinned. "Nice. The photographer even caught Mom smiling. I thought she was going to stroke out when the guys from Chris's company preceded Teddy down the aisle after the two women workers. But she seemed to relax after the kids were seated with her and Dad."

"Yeah, she held it together pretty well. Probably because Logan and Fletcher took their places first next to Chris. But when the rest of us Lambert sisters joined them, she must have realized things weren't going to be *normal*."

"Yes, well, Mom may never divest herself of her views about what's *right* for us, what's *wrong*," Eden air-quoted. "One thing she should know by this time: Chris does his own thing and Teddy's the woman for him. Always has been. And they'll never change. Kind of like Mom. I call that tit for tat."

"By the way, who alerted the press? If Dad hadn't been next to Mom, I think she would have blown a gasket when they started taking pictures of the wedding party after Lexi and Chris walked into the reception."

"I think that was just dumb luck. I heard one of the servers say something about a news photographers group having an end-of-year party downstairs. At least Mom admitted to me that she liked Teddy's dress. Said it was 'creative,'" Eden added. "I thought it was beautiful."

"And Teddy was, too. I love it when she wears her hair down. From the looks of him in this picture," Elaine pointed, "so does Chris."

"And there's Yance in his uniform. What is it about men in uniform? They always look so handsome." She stopped staring at the pictures Eden was thumbing through and gazed around the room. "Did he say where the army was sending him?"

"South Korea. Teddy said he texted her from the airport right before he boarded the plane. Said he'll be staring down the North Koreans for two years. As long as those guys at the DMZ don't end up shooting one another, he should be safe there."

"Of course he will." Eden stood up, approached the door and motioned for her sister to precede her.

Elaine placed a restraining arm on Eden. "Before I go, tell me. There's a hot guy out there talking to the receptionist. Who is he?"

"Probably a client." She gave Elaine a searching glance. "You're dating again? I thought you said you'd sworn off men."

Elaine shook her head. "Hey, I can look, can't I?"

"I suppose. Describe him. Maybe he's one of our agents."

"Kind of light brown hair. And he has the most gorgeous eyes, kind of gray. Reminded me of that soft wool coat Dad's had for ages."

Eden pursed her lips. "That would be Mr. McCue, my boss. And he's divorced. Not that long ago, either and it wasn't pleasant, from what Opal said. Don't even *think* of going out with him."

"Hey, I was just asking. How old is he?"

"If I had to guess, I'd say mid to late thirties." She began to turn the knob. "Which means he's too old for you. Besides, he's my boss. If you get involved with him and it doesn't work out, it could get messy for me and I want to keep this job."

Elaine scowled. "Who says I want to get *involved?* I was just thinking he might be interesting to get to know." Her cheeks pinked slightly. "Besides, I may need an agent if I decide to buy a house ... or something."

"Since when are you interested in real estate? You had to be convinced to even look at that condo you and Norm were thinking of buying. Which you're still renting."

"Maybe I'm tired of renting. Weren't you one of the many who kept saying I was throwing money away not *owning* something?"

"Maybe, but it's a good thing you didn't buy. Getting Norm's name off the deed would have made your nonengagement mess even messier."

Eden led Elaine into the reception area and introduced her to Opal, Quincy, and Dan O'Mara, who'd just come into the office, a contract in hand.

"Just put it in my in-box, Dan. I'll get to it first thing in the morning," Eden urged.

As they walked to Elaine's car, Eden said, "Dan's the guy you should date. Unmarried, closer to your age. A nice guy and not on the rebound. And I doubt you'd be able to push him around, like you did with Norm. Until he pushed back." She grinned at her sister, whose cheeks had turned a burnished red, and probably not from the early February breezes blowing the leaves around. "Just think. If you marry him, that'll make two red-headed spouses for us Lamberts."

Elaine laughed and punched the key lock. "I'd rather go for a bad boy and that boss of yours looks like he might be one."

"Oh, please, Ellie. Be smarter this time."

~ ~ ~

Three weeks later, Chance beamed as he opened the door for Eden when she entered her older brother's home.

"Hey, there, buddy. How are you? All ready to welcome a new baby brother or sister?"

"I guess." He sighed. "Dad says I'll have to keep my door closed if I want to protect my stuff when the baby starts walking. But when babies are little, all they do is sleep and eat and poop."

Eden smiled. "That's about it, all right. Where is your mother?"

Fletcher approached from the back hall. "Lexi's lying down. I promised I'd serve up the goodies so she doesn't have to." He kissed Eden on the cheek then pointed to her baby bump. "How are you doing?"

"So far, so good. But why did she want us here? We should have put this off for another day."

Fletcher scoffed. "As if Lexi would let you do that. She's been planning this birthday party for Deb since the day after her and Todd's anniversary." He turned and opened the front door for Chris and Teddy. "Where's Hale?"

"He's coming. The kids said they had to show him something in your yard."

Fletcher laughed. "Let me guess. Chance's four-legged Christmas present."

Eden nodded. "You realize you've created a monster, right? It's all my two have talked about since Christmas. How lucky Chance is to get a dog. Now they want one."

"Be warned. I've already lost my newest pair of shoes to that teething pup. Which is why he's in the doghouse this afternoon. Literally." He grinned.

"Is Elaine coming?"

Fletcher nodded. "She said something about a problem at the mall that she had to take care of, and that we should start without her."

Eden rubbed her hands together. "Then I'll help you set things up—or, oh! You already have." She glanced at the laden dining room table. "Wow! Lexi outdid herself. That cake is just like the one she made for Todd and Deb's wedding."

"Yes, but this one doesn't have a chocolate center." Fletcher chuckled. "And I'm sworn to secrecy about what it holds. Let me take your coat."

Eden handed it over and followed Teddy into the kitchen, where they began filling glasses with lemonade for the children and coffee in some cups, reserving two for tea.

Hale brought the children inside, their cheeks rosy from the February chill right before Todd and Debra arrived, smiling.

After Lexi came out of the bedroom, Eden helped her set up the children's table in the kitchen.

"Aren't Mom and Dad coming?" Deb asked.

Fletcher shook his head. "Dad's got a cold, so Mom said she would stay home with him. And Logan has a science project he's working on with a friend."

When everyone was seated and the food had been passed, Fletcher stood and pointed to the filled champagne flutes in front of the adults' places. "A toast to the birthday girl, my middle sister."

He waited until everyone held up their glasses. "Deb, you're always helping others." He leaned closer to her and sotto voce murmured, "Today you relax and let us do whatever you ask."

Everyone laughed.

Fletcher looked over his shoulder when the front door opened and Elaine entered.

"Am I late?"

"We just sat down," Lexi declared. "I saved a place for you, right next to Deb."

"It's a good thing you rescued this old table and Chris refinished it," Elaine said after she was seated.

"It has two more leaves, too, should we need them. Everything's good at the mall?" Fletcher asked.

Elaine sighed. "Finally."

"Good." Fletcher grinned as he looked around the table. "So, anybody have news we should know about?"

"I love my job," Eden declared. "But that's nothing new." She gazed in Hale's direction, but he just shook his head.

"Mom told me Logan's negative for CF," Elaine said. "Dad's a carrier, like we suspected."

"What about Mom?" Chris asked.

"She wouldn't say," Deb replied. "Not that it makes a lot of difference, now that we know Logan isn't even a carrier."

"Pass the salmon plate, will you, Fletcher?" Teddy requested.

Fourteen

After weeks at home, Hale returned to his office, pleased that he'd been summoned back to resume his duties. He glanced over the data confirming that no new hacks had occurred since he'd been forced to take an inadvertent staycation. He hoped the absence of new thefts was one reason he'd been called back, although he suspected that his father-in-law's oh-so-casual remark when Hale had helped him plant several shrubs in Iona's garden also had something to do with the college attorney's call bringing him out of exile.

"Number One man in the finance office seems to be over his head with work, Hale. Know why that might be the case?" Nathan's brown eyes had sparkled with amusement.

"Probably because he's doing his job and mine, something he foisted off onto me fall quarter. Maybe he doesn't like doing two jobs, though he didn't seem to mind me doing them." He'd glanced at his father-in-law before shaking his head. "Sorry, Nathan. I didn't mean to sound bitter. It's just that—"

"No need to explain. You've always taken your job seriously, which put a lot of pressure on you, what with those thefts and upset parents and all. Anderson is probably getting a taste of what you experienced, and he doesn't like it. Wants his second-in-command back to help shoulder the responsibility."

Remembering, Hale leaned back in his chair, surprised that Andy wasn't in the office to welcome him. Not that it mattered that much. But his fervent wish that the hackers had been identified lingered like a bad dream capable of coming to life at any moment.

A knock sounded on his door.

"Enter." Hale glanced at his appointment calendar. Helen had penned in no notice of any appointments for him. His brother-in-law entered, unsmiling.

"Todd." Hale stood up. "Did I forget we had a meeting? From the looks of you, I must be in trouble."

Before Todd could reply, James Abernathy entered, followed by Anderson Randolph, who closed the door.

The college attorney began. "Hale, I understand you received a promotion last March, nearly a year ago."

"Correct."

"And, after a delay, your salary was adjusted accordingly."

Hale turned his gaze toward Andy, who had remained standing and looked like he'd swallowed a lemon.

"Yes."

"And you're still blaming me for that," Andy demanded, his voice rising.

Hale stared at his boss. "What are you talking about?"

Todd stepped closer to the side of Hale's desk. "Let me handle this, Hale."

"If you're accusing my client, you need proof of that accusation."

Hale stared at Anderson Randolph, whose face was mottled with high color that extended from his cheeks and onto his fiery red ears.

"Here." He thrust a paper at Todd, who smoothed it out, then showed it to Hale.

He read the letter before looking up at the two lawyers and Anderson Randolph. "This says— never mind what it says. I would never disparage Anderson's work with a letter like this. And what's important is, that's not my signature."

"Not your signature?" Mr. Ackerman acknowledged. "Then it appears we have yet another problem. This is your first day back?"

Hale nodded. "After the call from your secretary." He turned to face his boss. "I'm not so petty that I would have accused you like that, Andy. Besides, the problem of my delayed raise was resolved by President Ingraham. Why would I raise it now? Or the other stuff in that letter?"

Hale ran a hand across his brow. "This tells me the hackers are at it again. Trying to sow discord." He gazed at the college attorney. "Don't you agree?" He glanced at Todd, who nodded.

Andy backed up and stopped when his backside encountered the door. "Then who sent it? Why are they trying to get me in trouble? See? This went to the president."

He stepped forward, closer to Hale's desk.

"You weren't happy about staying home," Andy insisted. "Helen said so. You must have got someone to send that letter to get back at me for making you the one responsible for clearing up this hacking mess."

Hale shook his head. "I'll admit I wasn't thrilled that I was doing the heavy lifting, but at least our online processes are secure, now that the IT office has finished with everything. Isn't that right?" Hale recalled Helen's remarks keeping him appraised of progress, leaving him tidbits of news on his home phone at times when he suspected she was at lunch.

"Enough with the accusations," Todd said, pointedly directing his remarks at Andy. "Unless you plan to ask Mr. Abernathy here to charge my client, these accusations need to stop. Now." He looked at the college attorney, one brow raised.

"Show me your signature, Hale," Abernathy said. After comparing Hale's scrawl on the copy of a letter to a parent with the signature on the damning letter, he nodded.

"I agree. We should move on." He took the letter in question. "I'll make a copy of this and return the original to President Ingraham."

Todd nodded. "I'd like a copy as well."

"Certainly. Why don't you follow me to my office?"

Hale stared at his brother-in-law. "So we're done here?"

Todd smiled and pointed to the letter in the college attorney's hand. "With that, anyway. You probably want to get to work, now that you're back in the saddle. I'll come talk to you after I have a word with Mr. Abernathy."

Minutes later, Todd returned and took a seat in front of Hale's desk.

Hale heard a door slam and concluded that Andy had finally retreated to his office after claiming he had to speak with Helen. "Did you know Andy was going to accuse me like that?"

"I suspected it when Abernathy gave me a heads up. Said you might want me here." Todd took a seat and drily noted, "Your boss seems on edge."

"He's been like that for months now. Helen thinks it's because he's having trouble with his oldest kid. Whatever it is, it's obviously interfering with his work. I've noticed. Helen has, too. Don't know if the higher-ups are aware."

"Well, now Abernathy knows, though he was careful not to say anything to me."

"He believes me?"

"He saw your signature, made the comparison. Wasn't that hard to figure out something wasn't right about that letter, either the part about your raise or the other elements mentioned, like you doing the work but being denied the title and so on." Todd rubbed his ear and added, "I told him I appreciated that he called me when this little nastiness occurred." He grinned and crossed one leg over his other knee. "So, what are you going to concentrate on, now that you're back at work?"

"I'm due to schedule meetings with all the students whose financial aid was messed with last term, to make sure all is well this term, and to confirm there are no problems moving forward with awards for the next academic year."

"Your boss doesn't do any of that?"

Hale shook his head. "He turned that over to me a couple years back. Prefers to run the other chores we take care of. Although last fall, he had me meeting with department heads, too, reviewing budgetary needs. That sort of thing." Hale grinned.

"Come to think of it, I was handling almost everything last term, before I was kicked home."

"Is Randolph always so sensitive about what he takes as a personal affront? Like that letter? Seems to me he could have handled that by simply asking why you wrote it."

"He's increasingly hard to talk to. Flies off the handle at every little thing, according to Helen." Hale rubbed the nape of his neck. "What gets me is why whoever sent that letter is trying to make me out to be the bad guy, and that Andy isn't doing his job. Think someone wants me fired?"

"There's a thought. Are you up against it with any of those higher-ups you mentioned?" Todd asked.

"The big guns administratively are the chancellor, the president, and members of the Board of Regents. But I'm not aware any of them are out for my blood."

Todd pointed to the email with attachment that suddenly clicked onto Hale's computer screen. "Open that. I asked Abernathy to send you a copy of that letter."

"Here it is." Hale hit the button and both men watched the printer go into action.

"Back to your boss," Todd said. "Is he nearing retirement?"

"I wish. He's at least five years away, maybe longer. Why?"

"Do you have any reason to think he might need extra money?"

Hale rubbed a hand along the back of his neck. "Wouldn't know, but his son has been in and out of trouble. At least he was last year. And Andy took time off right before the Christmas break. Helen mentioned something about him taking his kid up to the mountains for a personal retreat. I figured he conducted one of those 'Come to Jesus' talks between fathers and sons. You know, in a place where the kid couldn't hide behind his cell phone. There's no service in the woods."

Todd grinned. "I can't imagine you ever having to worry about your kids getting into drugs."

Hale's pulse spiked for an instant before settling down again. "I certainly hope not. But it happens in all kinds of families, Todd. Remember what Iona did? What Yancy saw and copped to that day we were all at Fletch's house to celebrate Chris's engagement? Time flies, doesn't it? That was more than a year ago."

Todd nodded. "I remember. Not a good day."

"The Queen Bee of the Lambert Tribe— what Eden calls her mother in the privacy of our home —would never have admitted her abuse of prescription drugs if she hadn't been outed by Yancy. Almost ruined Chris and Teddy getting together. I'm betting none of her bridge-playing friends has a clue that she was addicted and buying stuff on the sly. For sure, Nathan had no clue."

"Point taken." Todd pointed to the paperwork sitting on Hale's desk. "Back to this. Here's what I want you to do every day before you head home." He briefly outlined his plan.

~ ~ ~

Hale leaned back in his chair and stretched out his legs. Todd and Deb had agreed to watch the kids so he could take Eden out. The reservation for a special St. Patrick's Day dinner complete with a fancy chocolate dessert was in the works. So also was the delivery of two dozen red roses at Eden's job. *Good things are finally happening,* he thought. He glanced at the clock. *Time to go home and get this show on the road.*

He'd noticed that Eden seemed finally to be enjoying this pregnancy, which Hale knew would be their last. *A bonus baby, that's what we're having.* Even if it had cystic fibrosis. "We'll deal with it," he'd told her more than once. No matter the cost.

When Hale arrived home, he helped buckle the kids into their car seats, and went around the front of the car to open Eden's door. He kissed her on both cheeks before focusing on her lips. "Love that scent you're wearing. You smell good, taste good, too."

"That's because I'm wearing your favorite perfume," she murmured after settling in her seat. "The kids are getting antsy. Let's get them over to Deb's."

Hale grinned. "You read my mind."

After dropping off Kenny and Ivory, Hale headed for the restaurant.

"You really impressed Opal with those beautiful flowers, hon. She said I'm a lucky woman to have a husband like you." She reached over and stroked his cheek.

"I'm the lucky one," he replied, "even if I'm not Irish."

"Now that you're back at work and things have settled down, can you talk about it?"

"Nothing much to tell yet, but I'm confident we'll find the hacker. That IT guy, Reggie, showed me some computer hieroglyphics that I didn't understand, but which he claims are a clue. I told him the sooner he calls me with news he's identified the perpetrator, the better."

"If it's a student, what are you going to do, hon? Turn him over to the chancellor? The disciplinary board?"

"A bridge I don't want to think about. Frankly, I'm hoping it's someone unrelated to the college. Not even a former student with a grudge."

Hale brushed Eden's hair off her cheek. "You still like what you're doing at the realty office? No need for late days or evenings like right after the first of the year when I was home to pick up the slack?"

She smiled. "Not at the moment, but I agreed to handle the tax forms for the office. Opal was thrilled when I told her I would take care of them. She claims she was worried they were going to get audited last year because she wasn't sure how to handle everything, especially after Mr. McCue's ex-wife dumped the forms on her desk unfinished only two days before the deadline. Quincy had to scramble to secure an extension. I guess his divorce happened right about the time his ex-wife was supposed to be working on the taxes." Eden chuckled. "I'm not sure if it was her hatred of tax work that precipitated the divorce or if the divorce made everything else untenable."

"You're a whiz at that. Doing them will show your boss your real talents. Not that you haven't been doing a bang-up job as their bookkeeper."

Eden nodded. "Jonnie and Dan and the two new people—Usher and Winter—asked me to do their personal taxes, too."

"You are charging them, aren't you?"

"Of course. I estimated what their bills could be. If it takes me more than eight hours on each of their forms, we'll renegotiate."

"Good thinking. Did anyone argue?"

"No. But Dan gave me two big garbage bags of receipts and stuff. I told him after his taxes are done, I'll help him figure out how to collect what I need for next year so that he doesn't do that again."

Hale chuckled. "He should give you a bonus for that kind of help."

"I like him, which is why I'm giving him the benefit of the doubt this time. The questions he asks makes me feel like his surrogate mother. His mom died when he was only ten, and from what Opal has said, Dan could use some mothering." She grinned.

Hale scoffed. "You've already got two kids, and another on the way. No need to adopt someone else, especially one who's already grown. How old is this Dan character, anyway?"

"In his late twenties, I think. A good Realtor, the best in the office, I think, if the number of his deals is any indication."

"What about the owner? I'd think he'd be pretty good,.."

"Oh, he is. But Quincy only handles high-end properties and spends more time running the office than selling. Dan's clients tend to be first-time buyers, so he's more likely to handle properties a lot less pricey. Kind of like Elaine's condo."

"How is Ellie these days? She hasn't been at your mom's much since Chris and Teddy's wedding."

"Who knows? At least she's stopped coming into my office to flirt with Quincy. I tried to shoo her away from him. He's too old for her. She deserves more than a rebound relationship."

"I take it that means she's dating again?"

"Maybe. Last time we all got together, all she talked about was a couple of issues at the mall that were giving her fits. My guess is work is her number one priority right now. At least I hope so."

They enjoyed a quiet dinner, their conversation mostly focusing on the children, despite Hale's determination that this was a date with his wife, something they hadn't engaged in often enough. It was a situation he was glad he'd rectified, and the new pattern was one he intended to continue.

After they picked up the children and returned home, Hale tap-tap-tapped on Eden's baby bump, his usual hello to the little creature. He grinned when he felt the baby move under his fingers. "She's pretty active today. Have you talked to your boss about taking time off after the birth?"

She nodded. "He says I can take all the time I need. I know Opal won't be happy about doing my work, but since I've reorganized how deals are now recorded, she shouldn't have any problems. I'll talk to her again when the time gets closer." Eden grinned. "Besides, I'll have finished all the tax stuff by then, so Opal will owe me."

She waggled a hand. "Help me up, hon. I want a shower. Will you check on Kenny? I heard noises from his room. Maybe he's playing with one of his Christmas toys."

"Consider it done." Hale stood up then pulled Eden to her feet and gave her a grin.

"Don't say it," she warned, the corners of her mouth slanting upward.

"How do you know what I'm going to say?" he countered.

"You were thinking it, that I'm at the hoist-and-derrick stage, and I still have more than two months to go. Maybe the doctor's wrong and I really am carrying twins. Either that or a sumo wrestler." She rubbed the small of her back as she headed for the master bathroom. "I'm almost as big as Lexi and she's about ready to pop."

"Are you two sharing belly measurements?"

"When I went to the bakery to pick up cupcakes for Ivory's birthday-for-everybody party at school, Monet had us comparing bumps. She declared that this particular Lambert baby-making race is a tie, in the how-big-is-the-mother race."

"How'd that make you feel?"

Eden laughed. "I wanted to slug her."

"Lexi's taller than you, hon. Probably why she doesn't show quite as much."

"Thank you for that explanation. I'll meet you in bed." She kissed him and walked down the hall, humming a tune Hale had heard many times before.

~ ~ ~

"What's up, Todd? You have news?" Hale asked, as he entered the attorney's office.

Todd held up a hand, then pressed a button on the office intercom. "Hold that thought for a sec. You need to hear what Fletcher has to say."

Hale took a seat, his heart slamming into his lungs. Any louder thumps from his chest and both of his brothers-in-law would hear it. But when Fletcher beamed at him from the doorway, Hale relaxed his stiff spine against the back of the chair.

"You first, Fletch," Todd encouraged.

"You recall that money that was removed from the Lambert Foundation?"

"The equivalent of two full-ride scholarships for a year," Hale replied. "I remember."

"Well, we think we know where some of that money went," Fletcher announced.

"Supporting students, I hope?" Hale mentally crossed his fingers that the thief had only wanted to help deserving students, that he was a latter day Robin Hood.

"In one case, possibly. A new student, undocumented. She's living in sanctuary at the Catholic church in town. One Maria Santiago Cortez."

"Are you saying the thief has a heart?"

"You're giving him too much credit, if you ask me," Fletcher replied. "One more thing. Are you aware that your boss's son is currently at a rehab clinic in Colorado?"

Hale tugged on his left ear. "Didn't know that, but that news is better than he's still on the street shooting up." He glanced first at Fletcher and then at Todd. "I guess that means Andy was successful getting his kid to accept help. He tried that before, the rehab route, which didn't work. Maybe it will this time." He loosened his tie. "What are you saying?"

"We're thinking that Andy might be the guilty party," Todd said.

"What?!" Hale's heart seemed to slam into his lungs. "You've got to be kidding."

"No," Todd continued, "but we're not sure. Which is why you're here. Based on information from the two hacking experts and the guy at your IT office who's working with them, we think the support for Ms. Santiago is part of the Lambert Foundation money. But they still don't have a handle on who stole it. We want to see if you can find out."

"How am I supposed to do that?" Hale's mind whirled at this latest twist in the mystery of the missing scholarship money. "Wait a sec. Do the police know what you just told me? And if they do, why aren't they here, asking me to wear a wire—like they do on those TV shows Eden loves so much?"

Todd again raised his hand. "You're a couple steps ahead of us. We haven't alerted the police. Not yet anyway. We don't want the cops or the college to get into hot water after the rents refused last year to cooperate with the ICE folks. And we don't want to jeopardize Maria's safety. She blends in on campus easily enough, but we didn't want to take a chance the cops might try to talk to her, and ICE is then called."

"How often is she on campus?" Hale asked.

Todd glanced at his laptop. "Two days a week, according to Reggie. I asked him to check. Registrar clustered all her classes on those days. Oh, and she's taking another one online. A heavy load, twenty hours."

"Under her own name?"

"Yes," Fletcher grinned. "But here's what we want to know. Besides yourself, and we know you didn't set up the funds for her college education, who else might have registered her in a way that minimized her risk? The Lambert Foundation is private, so the law that prevents an undocumented student from receiving federal funds isn't relevant."

"And Andy would know that, has done it before." Hale ran a hand across his nape. You think he might have used some of the Lambert money to fund his son's rehab, too?"

"Maybe. But there's no way to trace it. It's the timing of the Santiago scholarship that makes us think he might have had something to do with it."

"And his son needing rehab would explain Andy's behavior over the last several months."

Todd nodded. "It's possible whoever he's working with chose to test the system, to see how easy it might be to hack into those other files, before he focused on the Lambert Foundation. But you said Randolph knows next to nothing about the internet. Why he turned the improvement in security issues over to you."

Hale nodded. "Maybe the hacker decided to see if taking small amounts wouldn't be noticed. Trouble is, he did so right before the affected students registered for fall quarter, which meant that the students might not have noticed, but the registration helpers certainly did. Probably why he waited before he went after the Lambert Foundation funds."

"And, if Andy's involved," Fletch mused, "he knew the thefts would place you under the gun, personally as well as professionally. Which could be why he accused you of writing that letter, to make people look at you instead of him."

Hale winced. "Could be."

Fletch leaned forward and patted Hale on the shoulder. "We know you're honest. And we're here to protect *you*. Just so we're clear, I spoke to Nathan. He insisted that I convey to you that the foundation board is not accusing you. They know you're doing whatever you can to protect current and future Lambert scholars."

"Why didn't Eden tell me this?"

"The Board members insisted that it come from me, as the Foundation's legal rep. An *official* statement. Not that your wife's assurances of your honesty, your innocence in all this, isn't meaningful. She kept saying that you would *never, ever* take scholarship money from students. Her words, Hale. Multiple utterances." He smiled. "And Eden's feelings are shared by the rest of the family. Surely you know that."

"The last few months have been tough, wanting to find out who the bad guys are, hoping to catch them."

Todd leaned forward. "Are you willing to see what you can find out? Maybe get Anderson to talk to you?"

"I've tried numerous times. Not sure I'll be any more successful now."

Fletcher broke in. "We have some ideas about what to let slip that might get him to see that it's better if he owns up to what he did— or didn't do —or maybe give up what he might know. We think it's likely he was behind supporting the undocumented student, although why he didn't go a regular route and simply award her a scholarship. I spoke with your admin person about Santiago. She happened to mention other such students have received private scholarships, that Mr. Randolph was enthusiastic about providing them an opportunity to go to college."

Hale breathed out noisily. "You're right. He's always approved such funds. But I think the fund set aside for special situations was depleted by the end of the fall term. You think that is why he might have diverted Lambert funds?"

Todd continued. "Possibly."

Fletcher added. "But he's not into tech stuff, would need help to secure those funds and why, if he's in financial trouble because of his son, he might have considered doing what he did."

"Doesn't make sense that he would take money from some students to give to another." Hale shook his head. *A sign Andy was losing it?*

He glanced from one brother-in-law to the other. "So you want me to secretly record our meetings? Even if that kind of evidence couldn't be used in court?"

"You're right, but we want you to raise the issue again, perhaps when Helen's in the room." Todd leaned down and placed a plastic bag on his desk. "Sophia's equipment. You know she was a P.I. while going to law school? Use this. It looks like a tie pin, will pick up sounds up to a hundred feet away. And it's a camera, too. All you have to do is wear this and engage the man in conversation."

"Okay." Hale reached for the baggie and stuffed it into a pocket. "When do you want me to start?"

"Tomorrow, if possible."

Todd handed a paper to Hale. "Check out this list of topics Fletcher and I would like you to drop into conversations around the office. Think of them as bait."

Hale looked over the list and handed the paper back to Todd. "What about Helen? She speaks with Andy more often than I do. I doubt he'd think she was trying to get him to admit anything. He might suspect me, but he would never suspect her."

Todd and Fletcher seemed to send subliminal messages as they looked at each other.

Fletcher nodded. "Use your own judgement about what to say to Helen, maybe that you heard about Maria and want Helen to tell you if there's a problem like someone trying to talk to her, see her, say you want to protect her. Do this when Anderson's in the office. Mentioning Maria might make him react, give himself away."

"But am I even supposed to know about her?"

"Tell Helen you heard about her from someone else. Maybe the priest."

"As if I see him on a regular basis," Hale scoffed. "Okay, I'll think of something. But Helen has an excellent lie-meter. I'll have to come up with something she doesn't suspect."

Todd chuckled. "Good to know. Maybe she's picked up information that'll make it easier for you to trip up Anderson. If you're right about Helen having her fingers in every pie, it's very likely she knows all about that student. Probably helped set up her registration for the current term."

"Okay." Hale patted his pocket. "Do I have to worry about charging this thing when I get home?"

"Sophia claims it can be used for several days before needing a charge. Whatever it picks up, video and audio, is connected remotely to my computer. You're good to go," Todd assured him. "I suggest you create a reminder at home to plug it every few days. We figured since you're always in a coat and tie, this will be easy for you. You'll probably even forget you have it on."

Fletcher nodded. "But if you think Andy's on to you, let Todd or me know. We don't want you in danger."

Hale's pulse jumped. "You're not saying he'd get violent? Andy?" He couldn't imagine the soft-bellied man who avoided exercise of any kind threatening him, other than verbally.

"Hey, he's already accused you. You never know what someone might do if he thinks he's been caught. Talk to him when other people are within shouting distance," Fletcher warned.

"Okay." Hale rose from his seat. "I guess I'll go back to the office now and check in with Helen about what's on tap for tomorrow."

Fletcher raised his hand. "Let's try this out before you go."

Hale took off his tie bar and replaced it with the device. "Hmm. Looks normal, similar to what I usually wear."

Todd grinned. "The whole point."

"Okay. Go into the hall then knock on the door and come back in," Fletcher ordered.

Hale did so.

Todd flipped his laptop around so that Fletcher could see the screen. He hit a key and all three listened to Todd and Fletcher talking while Hale was in the hall and then what he said when he joined them.

"It caught every word. Picture's not bad, either," Hale noted, as he stared at the computer screen.

Fletcher nodded. "Sophia said it was expensive."

"She still uses it?" Hale asked.

Todd laughed. "Not unless she's doing undercover work we don't know about."

"Okay. I'll see if I can get Andy to talk to me about that student." He gazed back at his two brothers-in-law. "Part of me hopes Andy isn't your man."

"So noted," Todd said. "You've worked with him a long time."

Fletcher nodded sympathetically.

Fifteen

Eden sat in her car and stared straight ahead. Early April winds had piled up the winter-killed leaves and deposited them against the wall of the building, giving the parking lot next to the real estate office an unkempt look. To the left of her car sat Quincy's sporty ride, its vanity license plate declaring him to be Realtor #1. To the right, nearest the front door, was a car she didn't recognize. *Probably one of Quincy's clients*, she thought. The silver-gray Mercedes screamed old money.

She glanced up when Dan O'Mara wheeled into the lot behind her. She opened her door and ungracefully slid out from behind the wheel.

Dan slung the strap of his laptop case over his shoulder and strode in her direction. "Eden! So glad I caught you. Thank you for finishing up my taxes. Never thought you'd be able to wade through all my stuff so fast. And on time, too."

Eden chuckled. "Next year I'm going to charge you double if you hand me your records in garbage bags."

"No worries. I've already put your suggestions to work. Spent the weekend going through all my expenses for the first two months of this year, putting them in spreadsheets, like you said."

"Good. What about last month?"

"I'm giving myself next weekend to do that." Dan opened the door and ushered Eden inside.

"As long as you stick to that plan, getting your taxes done next year will be a piece of cake. Cheaper, too." Eden nodded in Opal's direction. "Morning, Opal."

"Good morning to you, too," she replied and followed Eden into her office. "Guess who's in talking to Quincy right now?"

"A high roller? The owner of that fancy car in the parking lot?"

"Nope. That old man's in talking to Jonny. A relative, I think she said."

"Oh. Well, let's hope she signs him up for something to sell or something to buy, or both." Eden pulled off her black coat sweater and pushed up the sleeves of her blouse. "Is it hot in here, or are my pregnancy hormones working overtime?"

"Probably your hormones. The wind this morning blew me in the door and was downright nasty cold," Opal replied. "'Course, I run colder than you these days. You're going to come back after the baby's here, aren't you? Just can't imagine you not being here to make sure our deals are recorded right. Quincy's tickled pink that you handled the office tax returns. Never seen him so happy." She plucked a withered leaf off the bouquet of flowers Eden had received two days previously, another gift from Hale. When she asked why he had them delivered, he'd said, "I thought you'd like to enjoy them all day. Not just at home." She loved that he'd taken to having flowers or the small plants that decorated her window sill delivered to her almost weekly since their fancy St. Patrick's dinner.

"Wanna guess again who's in with Quincy?" Opal's bright eyes reminded Eden of Chance's overeager Labrador puppy when the children prepared to throw him a stick.

"I'm all out of guesses. Go ahead and tell me."

"Your sister. Such a pretty girl! And such a great job at the mall," Opal chortled. "If I worked there, I'd be broke in a week. So many things to buy."

Eden stopped straightening the papers on her desk that had slid out of her In-box and looked up at Opal. "Elaine? Did she say why she wanted to talk to Quincy?"

"No. She just waltzed in on the dot of eight, asking to speak to the boss."

Opal turned on her heel. "Which reminds me to get back out front so you can do your work and I can do mine!" Opal left Eden's office, shutting the door behind her.

Ten long minutes later, Elaine knocked and popped her head around the door. "Hey, there, sis!"

"Curiosity requires that I ask why you wanted to see Quincy." Eden straightened in her seat when Elaine entered, clad in a figure-hugging sweater set in shades of mauve and pink, a dark gray raincoat draped over her left arm.

"I've decided to buy a house," Elaine declared, her voice overly bright.

"Really." Eden cocked her head and appraised her sister. "Why, when you've been renting for years?"

Elaine's gaze slid downward, conveniently avoiding Eden's steady stare. "Change is good, Edie. Don't you agree?"

"And you asked Quincy to help you. What makes you think he'd even give you the time of day? What you can afford isn't what he sells."

Elaine's lower lip pushed outward in an almost pout. "My money's as good as anyone's."

"Not arguing that point. What exactly are you looking for?"

Elaine adjusted her gaze upward and settled for a moment on Eden's face before skittering away again. "I was thinking a condo."

"Like what you were renting with Norm, what you're still living in? Doesn't sound like much of a change."

"A different neighborhood. More upscale," Elaine insisted. "One with a view more exciting than a busy street or the building next door."

Elaine took a seat and stared past Eden's shoulder. "What do you think about me putting color streaks in my hair? Green, maybe?"

Eden felt as though she had just taken a sudden left turn as she tried to follow Elaine's change of topic.

"Green streaks? Why not purple? Wouldn't that color go better with that outfit you're wearing? Is it new?"

Elaine glanced down at her mauve pencil skirt. "As of last week. Like I said—"

"I heard you. You're into change." Eden took in Elaine's pensive expression. "I'd stick to buying a condo and nix coloring your hair."

"You don't have to get nasty."

"Hey, I'm your oldest sister. It's my *job* to steer you away from stupid ideas, and streaking your hair green is really *dumb*, Ellie." Eden leaned back in her chair and forced her lips into a half smile. "But if you're really serious about buying a condo, work with Dan. He knows the condo market upside-down and inside-out. Lists and sells lots of them. Way more than Quincy. He handles homes with a water view, four-car garages, tons of bedrooms and baths, and lots of the latest expensive extras. Think of Mom's and Dad's house, only updated. Way out of your price range."

Eden stared at her sister, whose gaze again began to wander, before settling on the picture on the wall to the right of Eden's desk, then the window nearby, the windowsill decorated with Hale's gifts of greenery, the table under that window, and Hale's most recent bouquet of spring flowers.

Determined to steer her sister away from the owner of the real estate office, Eden added, "Quincy's too old for you. Didn't I already tell you that?"

Elaine blushed.

Bingo! She's angling for a date. As if pretending to look at condos is her excuse for getting Quincy to notice her. Which he will in that getup she's wearing. "Ellie, listen to me. You've just come off a long-term engagement that Norm ran away from. I know you're still hurting from what he did, what he said. Please don't go after Quincy. He isn't right for—"

Elaine jerked out of her seat, her hands on her hips, her chin jutting out and her eyes seeming to shoot sparks of anger.

"How do you know who's right for me? I can pick my own boyfriends, my own dates!"

"Please sit back down and lower your voice." Eden had almost asked her sister to use her inside voice, as if she was Ivory. Would she be having a similar conversation with her daughter in not-so-many years to come? The thought sent shivers down her spine and forced her to suck in a quick breath before she started over.

She waved a hand at Elaine. "You're right. I'm sorry. You're perfectly capable to picking your own boyfriends. And dates."

"Besides, I'm not looking for anything permanent," Elaine vowed, her cheeks red.

"Fine. Then pick someone who's *not* coming off a nasty divorce."

"Please don't say that I'm too young for him. What do you know about his divorce?"

"Opal filled me in on the details. Trust me. Quincy is *not* for you. And I don't want you hurt. Again." Eden pushed herself out of her seat and approached her youngest sister, motioning for her to stand up.

Eden put her arms around her sister, getting as close as her baby bump would allow. She murmured quietly, "You deserve a nice man, a good man, one who will treat you like you should be treated. That's all I'm saying, Ellie. And I don't think Mr. McCue is that man. Besides, he's married to his work. One of the reasons he's divorced." She kissed her sister's cheek. "If you're serious about finding a condo, talk to Dan. He'll find you one with a snap of his fingers. He deals with lots of younger buyers, singles as well as couples. And he won't expect a date out of it, either," hoping that last comment was convincing. "Although he'd be a better choice for you," she added.

Elaine eased out of Eden's hug. "Maybe you're right. But I'm not going to rule out coloring my hair." She patted her sleek pageboy.

"Whatever." Eden reached into her corner desk drawer and pulled out a business card. "Dan's card. I don't know if he's free to see you right now. He just got here, and he usually has appointments scheduled every morning. But you could call him. Or ask Opal to tell him to call you. Tell him what you're looking for and how much you want to spend. He'll take good care of you. Or, if you prefer, I'll ask him to text you."

"I'll take care of it myself." A faux-pout reappeared for an instant.

"Can I help it if I want to help you find what you're looking for—in men as well as a place to live?" Eden was relieved when Elaine finally deigned to smile.

"You and Deb are two peas in a pod, always trying to take care of me," Elaine said.

"It's what big sisters do. Comes with that T-shirt of Ivory's that you got her on Valentine's Day, the one that says, 'I'm a big sister.'" She giggled. "She insisted on wearing it every day the week you brought it over. I was only able to get it into the wash after she spilled chocolate sauce on it."

Elaine chuckled. "Give her a hug for me."

"You could come over and give her one yourself. Maybe after you find the condo you're looking for and invite us to come over to ooh and ah."

"I have to get to work." Elaine held up her hand and Eden high-fived it.

"Yes, you do." Eden watched as her sister left her office.

She walked over to Quincy's office and knocked. "Got a minute?"

"For you, even two," he replied with a grin. "What's on your mind?"

"I understand my little sister asked for help finding a condo," she said, deciding to cut to the chase.

"That she did. I'll have to check with Dan to see what he recommends. Don't do much business in that market these days."

"Why don't you turn her over to Dan? I already told her that's not where you focus your efforts."

Her boss gave her a speculative glance. "You trying to tell me something, Eden? Like maybe you don't trust me with your sister?"

Eden felt her cheeks warm, that Quincy was onto her. "I just don't want you wasting your time when you have much bigger fish to fry. Like landing the listing for that big fancy building downtown. The one with the million-dollar units." She crossed her fingers behind her back and hoped he'd buy her reasoning.

"Uh-huh," he said, sounding unconvinced. "Your sister's safe with me. I'd date her in a New York minute if you didn't work here. But combining business with my personal life — even if it's your sister and not you— didn't work with my first wife. I doubt it'll work any better now." He waved a dismissive hand in Eden's direction. "Stop worrying about Elaine." He paused and chuckled. "I have a better idea. Stop worrying about *me* and who I date. Since you're not *my* sister."

She wasn't sure Quincy's last statement was for her or for himself. No matter. He was right on both counts.

~ ~ ~

"Eden. Glad I caught you." Fletcher's voice seemed to catch in midsentence.

"You sound upset. Is Chance sick? You want me to pick him up from school? I was just on my way home. It's no trouble for me to swing by—"

"No. Chance is fine. Deb just picked him up. I'm at the hospital. With Lexi. We're in labor. Could you let the rest of the family know?"

"Of course. But I'm guessing you don't want us all descending on her right about now." She imagined how her older brother must be feeling, worried about Lexi and the new baby, maybe thinking back to the first time Lexi had gone to the hospital, after losing their first baby.

"Isn't she a bit early? I thought she wasn't due until the end of the month."

"Two weeks away. Seems like our daughter doesn't want to wait any longer."

"Your daughter? You know the sex?"

"I'm trying on the idea, even though Chance is still hoping for a boy." Fletcher chuckled.

"You're okay with this, if it's a girl, I mean?"

"Totally. A healthy baby is what we want. Though we might need your help getting Chance to go along if he doesn't get his brother."

Eden nodded. "I'm sure he'll be fine with whatever he gets. But you have to call me right away. With height, weight, hair color. All the usual details. I'll tell everyone to stay away until you say we can show up."

"Thanks, Edie."

"Give Lexi my love." But Fletch had already hung up. *Oh, my.* Eden rubbed her baby bump as she drove home.

She waited until Kenny and Ivory entered through the kitchen door, each asking for something to eat. Eden dished up small dishes of the peach cobbler Hale had made the night before.

"Guess what, kids? You're going to have a new cousin pretty soon. Maybe tonight or tomorrow." Would Ivory be happy, or Kenny?

Kenny looked at her, a question in his expression.

She nodded. "Your uncle Fletcher just called to say they're at the hospital."

"Is Chance there, too?"

"No. He's at Aunt Debra's house."

"Can we go see the new baby?" Ivory asked, spilling a slice of peach down the front of her dress.

Eden handed her a napkin and pointed to the stain. "The baby isn't here yet. We have to wait until Uncle Fletcher calls to tell us it's okay to visit. While we wait, we should wrap up the baby gifts, don't you think?"

"Yeah! Let's do that!" Ivory clapped as she slid out of her chair and trotted in the direction of the master bedroom. "I'll get them!"

While Ivory wrapped and unwrapped then wrapped again the tiny green onesie she'd picked out for Lexi's new baby, Eden's mind raced, recalling how Lexi had confided that she'd lived in fear the first three months of her pregnancy, afraid she'd lose this baby, too.

Eden rubbed her baby bump. She had a feeling this baby might be a girl, but when she'd refused the amnio, she'd also eliminated her chances of finding out. *As it should be,* she reminded herself. Hale had said he wanted to be surprised, that they should stick with that decision. But it wasn't the baby's gender that Eden really wanted to know.

She tried to imagine how she might feel if this active little one had cystic fibrosis. The doctor had been reassuring when she'd complained about how busy the baby was, its daily movements suggesting an acrobat swinging from one side to the other before doing a two-step on Eden's bladder, especially after she climbed into bed to snuggle with Hale.

Her middle-of-the-night dreams too often devolved into nightmares, leaving her sweating and breathing hard, near-constant reminders of her fears that she might not be the best mother for this new baby. She'd wanted to read all the articles Hale had brought home, but halfway through most of them, she set them aside, unable to see herself monitoring her child's breathing, or practicing those back-pounding exercises designed to loosen the phlegm in her child's lungs.

"There, Mommy! Look what I did." Ivory held up the gift, its wrapping paper gaping along one side. "See! I even printed the baby's name on the front."

Eden stared down at the letters her almost-six-year-old had written: B-A-B-Y. "Very nice, Ivy. After the baby is born, we'll know the real name, won't we? A girl's name—" *oops*— "or a boy's name."

"Uh-huh," her daughter nodded. "Kenny! You should wrap your present. Want me to do it for you?" Ivory trotted off to retrieve the gift Kenny had insisted was perfect for the baby, a small soccer ball with blue and red stripes standing out against the white.

"Let's leave Kenny's gift in the box," Eden urged. "It will be easier to wrap that way."

"Okay. When Daddy comes home, I'm going to show him what a good wrapper I am," Ivory declared.

~ ~ ~

Eden led the way to Fletcher's front door.

He stood aside, beaming as she entered. "Welcome to our mad house! Deb and Elaine and Teddy are all in with Mom and Lexi. Why don't you join them?"

He hugged his sister and shook Hale's hand before addressing Kenny and Ivory. "Hey, kids. Want to go out back and play with Chance and Racer?"

Kenny nodded, and headed for the kitchen door. Ivory continued inside, behind her mother. "I want to see baby Megan," she declared.

Fletcher followed Hale into the house. "Then I guess we might as well all say hello."

The cry of a newborn sounded from the master bedroom.

"That's my page," Fletcher said with a laugh. He entered the room and took the tiny bundle from Iona's arms. "Hey, now, kiddo. What's the problem? Oh. Food. Okay." He turned on his heel and approached the bed where Lexi was propped.

Eden thought her sister-in-law looked tired, but happy beyond her wildest dreams when Fletcher handed the baby to her.

"Lunch time for the little munchkin," he announced before depositing a quick kiss on Lexi's forehead.

Eden caught his arm as he moved closer to the door. "You look beat. How are you holding up, Fletch?"

"We're great. I actually got three straight hours last night." He chuckled. "I'd forgotten how babies are." He ran a hand through his hair, leaving it spiked on one side.

"You're happy about—"

Fletcher seemed to have guessed what Eden was thinking. "If you're worried that I wanted a boy, don't. Like I said, I wanted a healthy baby. Which is what we got." Lowering his voice, he added, "A beautiful little girl." He glanced over his shoulder at Lexi and the baby, whose shock of thick dark hair was visible in his wife's arms. "Lexi was right. Not knowing ahead of time meant we focused on what was important. Not the past."

Eden grinned. "How'd Chance react to having a sister after insisting he wanted a brother?"

"He fell in love with her about two seconds after I did. Last night when she started to fuss and Lexi was taking a shower, he insisted I pick her up *now* so she would stop crying. Told me it wasn't good for babies to cry, that she should be happy *all* the time, like he is." Fletcher's eyes took on an obvious sheen. "But I'm glad we got him a dog. He's already signed up for obedience classes." He chuckled. "Lexi and I have bets on who will benefit more, Chance or Racer."

"You won the lottery when you and Lexi got together."

"No argument from me."

"And Chance is the perfect son for you—smart, caring, and now a big brother. Something you can teach him all about." Eden wiped a tear off her cheek. "Lexi hinted that you might expand your family further."

Fletcher's left brow rose. "Hey, Meggie's only four days old. We're going to have to wait a while before having another child."

Eden patted his arm. "I didn't say I expected it would happen right away, but I'm glad for you. All of you." She slid her phone back in her handbag after snapping several pictures of the family. "Hale has something in the trunk for Megan. She won't be able to use it right away, but we thought you'd like to have it on hand before she's ready to try it out."

"What is it?"

Eden laughed. "One of those jumping swings. Both Kenny and Ivory loved to exercise their leg muscles while watching me cook."

"Always thinking ahead. Thanks, sis." He grinned. "You want it back for your new one when the time is right?"

"No need. We still have ours. One of the few things I didn't sell when we were getting rid of baby stuff."

Eden grabbed Ivory's hand and pulled her away from Lexi, with whom she'd been chattering while the baby nursed. "Come on, everyone. Let's let the new mom and baby rest while we see about food for ourselves."

"Good idea, Eden," Deb seconded the effort and walked with her mother, Elaine and Teddy toward the kitchen.

"With all that dark hair, Megan looks just like Fletcher," Teddy exclaimed. "Do you think it will lighten up later?"

Deb shrugged. "We'll have to wait and see. I think her eyes may turn, too."

"What do you mean? They're such a pretty blue color," Teddy objected.

"Yes, but most fair-skinned babies' eyes are blue to start with. Some become brown or green later. Time will tell if she keeps her baby blues," Deb said.

Teddy nodded. "Hmm. Didn't know that."

The women joined the men, who were chatting in the living room while nibbling on the crackers and cheese that had been set out. Eden overheard words that drew her closer to Hale, who was talking with Todd about his still unsuccessful efforts to learn who was responsible for the stolen scholarship funds. His frowning countenance told her they hadn't made much progress. She'd agreed not to ask him for details, as it just put him in a bad mood, but she knew that scholarship announcements would be going out soon to the high school seniors who had applied. When she'd been part of his team in the finance office, he'd turned what he called puzzles over to her when problems remained that others hadn't been able to solve. She'd always loved solving puzzles. Maybe it was time for her to offer to help him. If only she knew how.

Sixteen

Eden glanced in the direction of the stage, aware of the commotion occurring behind the closed curtain. Ivory's kindergarten class was putting on a play to celebrate May Day. The night before, Hale had watched Ivory act her part, a takeoff on a favorite Dr. Seuss story, after telling his daughter that he had to go to Olympia and would miss seeing her on the big stage.

Happily, Ivory offered to give him a preview after insisting that Eden go in the other room so she wouldn't see her ahead of time. Eden acquiesced by going to the grocery store. When she returned home, Hale was clapping, signaling the end of the performance.

"Oh! I see you made it," Eden said when Elaine slid into the seat Eden was holding for her in the auditorium. "I told Ivy I wasn't sure if you could get off work in time to see her today."

Elaine grinned. "Wouldn't miss it, and I brought my camera to get all the action. But, it was touch-and-go in the parking lot. Total madness out there."

"No one was directing traffic? I saw the principal doing that when I arrived."

Elaine shook her head. "He must have gone inside already. I think I got the last spot on the near side of the building." She pointed toward the stage. "Who's that really tall guy?"

"Ivy's teacher. Mr. Wyecliff."

"Wow. He towers over everyone. I'll bet the kids think he's a giant."

Eden chuckled under her breath. "Ivy said he told the class his nickname in high school was 'Redwood.' Deb told me he played semipro basketball before he started teaching. And, according to Ivy, Mr. Cliff can do no wrong."

"Really." Elaine placed her camera in her lap. "Like my hair, Edie?" She flipped one side of her shoulder-length chestnut hair, festooned on one side by two streaks of red.

Eden stared at her sister's do. Usually she wore it in a classic chignon at work or captured on the top with a squeeze clip. "So you went ahead and streaked it. At least it's not green."

"And no one's said a word," she added pertly, as if to imply that Eden's worry about unprofessionalism was unwarranted.

"Ssh! The curtain just opened." Eden straightened her shoulders and looked for Ivory among the smallest group of children on stage. "There she is—left side, front row," she whispered.

Elaine waved at Ivory, who enthusiastically waved back and poked her neighbor with her elbow.

"Elaine, stop it!" Eden shushed. "You're setting a bad example."

Her sister stuck her tongue out at her from behind a hand. "Chill, Eden. Don't be a spoilsport. I'm having fun with my favorite niece."

"You mean your favorite talking niece," Eden retorted.

"Right," Elaine whispered as the lights came down and the audience settled into their seats.

The play began, provoking laughter and other sounds of appreciation throughout the forty-minute program. When it was concluded, thunderous applause filled the auditorium. The children on stage bowed when motioned to do so and began clapping and giggling as they jumped around excitedly.

Elaine pulled on Eden's arm. "You're headed home? Not going out for a special treat?"

"I have to pick up Ivy at her room. It's a new rule the kindergarten teachers instituted after one little guy got lost and ended up on the wrong bus. They want each child accounted for, so everyone has to have a ride home or tell the teacher who they're walking home with."

"What about Kenny?"

"He has soccer practice this afternoon. Fletcher said he'd pick up Kenny and Chance."

"Then I'll walk with you, so I can congratulate Ivy. I thought she was an especially endearing cat in that huge hat."

Eden grinned, her heart swelling with love. "She was, wasn't she? Last night she insisted on doing her part for Hale, since he couldn't be here. He doesn't know there were fifteen different cats taking turns saying their lines, wearing the hat."

Eden angled past several clusters of parents in the hallway before entering Ivory's classroom. Mr. Wyecliff was already there, notebook in hand, and checking off students as they departed.

"Ms. Brinker, hello. Did you enjoy the play?" Walker Wyecliff welcomed her. "Ivory should be along any minute now." His gaze rested on Elaine, shifted to Eden, and then back to Elaine. "You must be a family member. You two look a lot alike."

"I'm her youngest sister," Elaine replied and offered her hand. "Elaine Lambert. And you must be Redwood." She grinned. "Without the leaves."

The teacher laughed as he rubbed his bald head. "You've been talking to Ivory." He leaned down when the little girl pulled on his hand.

"I'm here, Mr. Cliff. Can I go now?"

He high-fived Ivory. "Are you walking with your brother today?"

"Nuh-uh. Mommy and Aunt Elaine are taking me home 'cause Kenny has soccer practice." She wiggled her fingers and grinned at Eden and Elaine.

"Got it." He made a show of checking off her name in his notebook. "Then I'll see you tomorrow. Good job today!"

His gaze turned back to Elaine. "I'm sure your niece was glad that you were here to see her performance. You're visiting from out of town?"

"Actually, I'm local. A manager at the mall."

"Good to know. Perhaps I'll see you around." He shook Elaine's hand again, holding it an instant longer than Eden expected.

She squinted at her sister, whose cheeks now resembled the red streaks in her hair. "Come on, Ellie. Ivy just scooted out the door. Don't want to lose her in this crowd." As an afterthought, she said, "Good-bye, Mr. Wyecliff."

He nodded, his eyes seeming to follow Elaine as she headed for the door.

"You had to call him Redwood? And without the leaves?" Eden asked. "Kind of presumptuous, don't you think?"

"Hey, you were the one who told me his high school nickname. But you never mentioned he was bald. How old is he?"

"I have no idea. You'll have to ask Deb. Or just Google him." Eden stared at her sister. "Are you thinking of dating him?"

"Of course not. You know I'm off men. But I can still rate them, can't I? I mean, I'm not dead, sis. Or married." She huffed out a short laugh.

"Being married doesn't mean a woman is dead," Eden retorted. But at her stage of pregnancy, making love required more agility than usual and lately, she was too tired to suggest it. The missing scholarship money hadn't helped in the spousal lovemaking department. Hale was too often preoccupied or staying up late to muse about what to do to protect future scholarship awardees. Which reminded her to ask him how she might help him identify the guilty party. She had a feeling someone in the finance office was involved, even if that person wasn't the actual thief.

She'd worked in that office and knew some of the many ways used to keep track of money, incoming as well as outgoing. At least she had before all those new security measures had been put into effect. She recalled a part-time secretary, years earlier, who had squirreled away the coffee money one summer until she, Eden, had discovered the depleted coffee fund and who had taken it.

Eden knew no one would suspect her if she snooped around, talked to people in the office. After all, she'd been a trusted colleague years earlier, and was now Hale's wife. Everybody in the office looked up to him. Everyone except Andy, probably because he suspected Hale was better at his job than he was, or that Hale was angling for Andy's job. Which he wasn't. But Eden knew he'd be good at it, much better than Andy was. Hale was a natural-born administrator, a leader by example as well as encouragement. Unlike Andy, Hale never resorted to scare tactics when an employee's work needed improvement.

Eden reached the car, unlocked the doors and helped Ivory into her car seat.

"Are you coming home with us, Aunt Elaine?" Ivory asked.

"No, darlin', I have to go back to work. But I'll see you on Sunday."

"Does Mom know about your, uh … new hair color?" Eden fluffed her own hair to make the point.

"She will on Sunday," Elaine remarked with a chuckle.

~ ~ ~

Eden climbed into bed and sighed as she stretched her legs. She ran her hands over her belly, aware of the baby squirming inside, as if he or she, too, was seeking comfort after a long day of work. First, at the office, then an afternoon spent preparing for the new baby. Which meant three loads of laundry, lots of bending and stretching, folding clothes and putting them into the small dresser she'd found at a neighborhood garage sale and asked Hale to haul home and place in the corner of their bedroom until they rearranged things in Kenny's or Ivory's room.

"You look tired, hon." Hale pulled back the covers and climbed in next to her.

"You smell so good," she replied and rolled in his direction, still rubbing her belly. "Love that sandalwood shower gel."

Hale kissed her then nuzzled her nose. "Is he jumping around tonight?"

"Feel for yourself." She reached for Hale's hand and placed it on the highest point of her protruding abdomen. "I think that's a heel or maybe an elbow."

"Kid doesn't have much room anymore." He rubbed her belly then did his usual tap-tap-tapping hello to the baby.

Eden arched her back and then relaxed into the mattress. "My dad was right, hon. You're so good to me."

"I accept your compliment, but what brought this on?" Hale kissed her.

"Just thinking about last fall when I was so unhappy, scared I wouldn't find a job, wanting one so badly and then finding out I was pregnant. You never gave up on me, even when I was in a foul mood. You stood by me, encouraged me, said we'd deal with whatever came our way—like a cystic fibrosis diagnosis." She slid a hand up to his chin and cupped his face, the better to look into his eyes. "You never doubted everything would work out." She sucked in a long breath. "And it has. At least with *my* job. I wish things weren't so difficult for you these days."

"I'm your husband, hon. Of course, I stand by you. I love you," he declared.

"And I'm your wife and I should worry less, trust more." She kissed him. "Even if worry seems to be my M.O."

"The doctor says the baby is growing right on schedule." Hale rubbed her baby bump.

Eden nodded. "Getting bigger every day. I have a feeling this kid's going to be bigger than Kenny or Ivory when he finally pops out."

He grinned back at her. "Could be. As long as she's healthy. You know that's all I care about."

"Right. Even though that's still a big question mark."

Hale eased closer to her and resumed tap-tap-tapping a message to the baby. "I have a feeling everything will work out fine. Just like Fletcher and Lexi's new daughter. *Our* baby will be healthy, too, and just as cute as their new little one." He kissed her cheek. "Wonder if he'll look like Kenny, or Ivory. Or you. What do you think, honey?"

"Maybe she'll look like you. Meggie looks so much like her daddy. I never thought Fletcher would be happier than that day he married Lexi and then adopted Chance, but seeing him with Megan? He's totally besotted with her."

Hale smiled. "Of course he is. Listen, are you going to be okay with me being gone overnight Tuesday and Wednesday? What'll you do if you go into labor and I'm not here?"

"I'm still a month away, Hale. And I was late the last two times. I seriously doubt I'll be early with this one. If I am, I've got three brothers I can call. Fletcher or Chris or Todd. Probably Chris, since he lives closer. Come to think of it, definitely not Fletcher." She giggled. "He's not getting a lot of sleep these days. Not sure I'd trust him to drive me to the hospital and not fall asleep en route."

"What about Elaine? You didn't mention her."

Eden scoffed. "I think all her talk about swearing off men was just that. Talk. You should have seen her eyeing Ivy's teacher. She and Mr. Cliff would look so silly together. He's six feet six or seven and she's only five feet three. But they were giving each other the once-over when we went to pick up Ivy."

"As long as you know who to call. So I won't worry. Andy's coming with me to Vancouver for that conference on private college finance issues. I was surprised he said I should come, too. These days, all he asks about is why we're making so little progress finding the person who hacked into the scholarship accounts."

"How is that going?"

"Slowly, maybe even turning cold. As far as I know, nothing's been seen on those hidden cameras Security set up in my office. Helen wants them removed. Says she feels like she's being spied on."

"You agree with her?"

"I don't know. The cameras haven't yielded anything of value any more than my meager attempts to get Andy to tell me something incriminating. I was shocked that he was suspected.

Maybe he'll talk more on our way to Vancouver or back." He chuckled. "About the only thing being picked up by my hidden tie tack is the sound of me blowing my nose now that it's spring allergy season."

Eden snuggled closer. "I've been thinking, hon. Maybe I could help you find the thief."

"Huh?" He stopped stroking her belly and stared at her.

"No one would suspect me if I asked questions. They know me, love me. And you. And I know the systems you use."

"But we've added all kinds of features you're not familiar with."

"I know, but you can show me. Bring your laptop home on Friday and show me what's new. I could wander around the office and talk to people. Helen hasn't seen me since I got pregnant. My showing so much now is a perfect reason for people to talk to me, the women anyway. Aren't most of your employees women?"

"You're right about that. But, if Helen mentions that you came to the office, Andy is sure to suspect something. He suspects everyone," Hale countered bleakly.

"I thought you said his mood has improved."

"It did, but lately he's turned sour again. Which is why I was surprised he wanted to attend the conference. Maybe he just wants to get away from issues at home. His son may be out of rehab and using again."

"Then this is the perfect time for me to talk to Helen, tell her how much I miss my old job. Think she'll buy it?"

"Probably. And Helen probably doesn't know when you're due. Can't remember if I told her." He stroked her cheek, brushing a strand of hair behind her ear.

"Then Tuesday and maybe even Wednesday would be the perfect time for me to go to the office. When I was at the park with the children, I had one of those 'aha' moments. I'm thinking there's a reason why most of those hacked student accounts had something to do with the family foundation.

"You know I was good at looking for patterns when problems showed up. Patterns no one else saw or spotted. I want to see if I'm right, but it means I need to go to your office and look at those locked-up files again. So far, you've focused on the students whose accounts have already been hacked. I'm wondering if I shouldn't look for students who might become *future* victims."

Hale frowned, as if still unconvinced.

"If everyone knows that both you and Andy will be out of the office for at least two days, maybe the thief— if he works there —will slip up and give himself away. Even if he doesn't, maybe I'll spot something you and those hacking pros could use." Eden slid a hand across Hale's chest before angling her fingers downward toward his waist. "What do you think, honey? Give me your key so I can look at those records?"

Hale looked at her, his gaze heating as her fingers changed position. "Hmm. Maybe you're right about looking at things differently. What can it hurt, to have another brain working the problem?"

Hale sucked in a breath and one corner of his mouth quirked upward. "Are you trying to tease me into saying yes?" His gaze followed Eden's hand as it trailed still lower.

"I'm your wife, Hale, and I love you. Love making you happy, love making love to you—even in my advanced state of gestation." She rested her hand just below the waistband of his pajama bottoms, aware that her strokes were having the desired effect. "I'll go in tomorrow afternoon."

"What about the kids?"

"I'll ask Lexi if she'll watch them for an hour or so. She's home with Megan. Chance and Kenny play well together. And Ivy would love to see Megan again. It's all she talks about, having a baby of her own, just like Auntie Lexi." She mimicked her daughter's voice.

"Think she'll be disappointed if our baby turns out to be a boy?"

"She'll just have to adjust."

Hale nodded. "I wondered about Fletcher having another girl. I think the baby looking so much like him, not being blond like Lexi and Chance made it easier for him to separate his memories of Raffie from his love for Meggie."

"I know, and I'm glad." Eden slid her fingers inside Hale's pajama pants. "Tell me you're okay with me visiting your office while you're gone."

"You have a way of making me see things … your way," he said and sucked in a breath when she began to stroke him. He shifted slightly to give her better purchase and slid his hands under her nightgown.

"So glad you see it my way," Eden murmured right before she focused on how he began pleasuring her, how they turned her seductive teasing into mutual enjoyment.

Seventeen

Eden pulled into Hale's usual parking spot, now graced with a sign reserving it for Mr. Brinker, Vice Chair, Finance. She smiled to herself. When had that sign been erected? She'd have to ask Hale when he returned from his conference.

She climbed out of the car, aware that her baby bump was now scraping against the steering wheel. *Time to move the seat back again.* She reached into the back seat for her personal laptop and the soft-sided bag that contained Hale's notes about the new office security measures. She straightened her shoulders in her black maternity dress, the gold epaulets matching her determination to find something Hale might have missed in his search for clues leading to the hacker. Even though her obvious baby bump gave a different impression, she imagined herself going to war to not only clear away any vestiges of suspicion clinging to her husband's reputation, but also to find the missing money.

As she stepped around the front of the car, laughter from a pair of students cutting through the parking lot to the nearby lecture hall abruptly stopped, replaced by silence when they saw her.

"Good afternoon," Eden cheerily called out. She was still grinning when she pulled open the door and nearly bumped into Chancellor Middleton.

"Whoops! Malcolm. How are you?"

"Eden Brinker, as I live and breathe. Hale mentioned you were pregnant, but I don't recall he said it was imminent. Next week, perhaps?"

Eden grinned. "In about a month, although some days I feel like it should be sooner."

"Is this number three or four?"

"Number three."

"If you're here to see Hale, isn't he attending that big conference of private colleges this week? Or am I confused?"

"You're right, of course. I came right from work for something Hale left in his office. He promised to bring it home and in the rush to get ready ..." She felt her cheeks heat at the little white lie she and Hale had agreed she'd use if anyone asked why she'd come to his office.

"Fathers-to-be can be forgetful," the chancellor intoned. He held the door for Eden before ambling outside.

Eden walked slowly up the stairs, arriving more winded than she'd expected when she finally approached the finance office. She adjusted her shoulder strap and pushed open the door.

"Hello? Anybody here?" Eden asked, surprised that the reception area was empty of the usually-smiling Helen.

In the silence that followed, a young woman Eden didn't recognize ambled around the corner.

"Oh, hello. You are?" she asked, looking unsure what to do.

"I'm Mr. Brinker's wife. Where's Helen?"

Madison appeared out of her office. "Oh, hello, Ms. Brinker. Can I help you? Helen went home early. She wasn't feeling well."

"Sorry to hear that." The other young woman moved out of sight. At Madison's questioning look, Eden added, "I stopped by to get something from Hale's office. And to work on some files he asked me to update. On his laptop, so he'll have it as soon as he gets back from the conference."

Madison frowned. "I suppose he told you all about the cameras and other security stuff here?"

Eden nodded and waved his office key in the air. "He was very clear about that. And he gave me his key. I'll be sure to lock up again when I leave. Would you like me to leave Helen a note that I was here?"

Madison smiled. "No need for that. The cameras will take your picture." She glanced over her shoulder. "That student you saw will be leaving soon, and I'll be gone in the next half hour. Will you be done by then?"

"I'm not sure. But if you set the lock on the outer door when you leave, I'll double-check it when I depart. I recall doing that when I worked here."

Madison nodded. "Oh, that's right. A former employee. Sure, I can do that. And I'll shut out the reception lights when I leave. That way, you'll know we're all gone."

"Good. I'll tell Hale how helpful you were." Relieved that Madison didn't question her further, Eden walked down the main hall, unlocked Hale's door and flicked on his overhead light. After closing the door, she opened the file cabinet, grabbed the student files, and spread them out on Hale's desk. She jotted each name on a post-it note, and ordered them first by the last names of the students. Then she placed them in a pile representing each of the sources from which the funds had been stolen. She set aside the two names representing students who had received money from a source other than the Lambert Foundation, and those first stolen by dates. Only thirteen remaining names, all of them Lambert Scholars.

There had to be a pattern. But what was it? Why these particular students, when the Foundation had funded nearly fifty students for the previous academic year? Eden closed her eyes. She set out more Post-its, this time with the first initial of each Lambert Scholar. She moved them around, at first randomly, and then more deliberately. Was this it? *It has to be.* She glanced at her watch. Forty-five minutes gone already? But she wasn't done yet.

Eden then scanned the last name initials of the same students. But there appeared to be no pattern there. She returned to the first name initials, by which she was able to spell out Lambert Family. On a hunch, she added the date of each theft to its correct student name. After checking the first three names, her pulse began to race.

I was right! The first name initial of the first Lambert scholar whose money had been taken began with an L. The first name of the following student by date began with an A. The third name that began with an M confirmed it. She'd found a pattern, one that continued through all thirteen names. Whoever had stolen the monies had selected students whose first initials spelled out Lambert Family.

If the thefts continued to occur, in spite of all those security efforts in place, would it be from a student whose first name began with an F for Foundation? If so, watching out for Lambert Scholars with such a first name might enable the IT experts to catch the thief in the act. But how many such students were there?

To save time, Eden took pictures of the Post-it notes as they sat on Hale's desk. Why hadn't he seen this, or those professionals who were supposed to be so bright? Maybe because they'd ignored the victims' names, focusing only on the money that had been taken.

Whoever it is has something against the Lambert Foundation, Eden concluded. But why? Because it was the biggest funder of student aid? But that wasn't right. For years, two federal grants had provided the largest scholarships. Because the Lambert Foundation was the *oldest* private funder? Maybe. Or because it was a local source? Another possibility.

Eden looked again at the student names that didn't fit the pattern she'd discovered. Those two thefts had occurred at the very beginning of the fall term. Hale had speculated that the thief might have been trying out how to get into the subfiles to remove money. But maybe the thief had a personal vendetta against those students, something other than what had prompted him to steal from the Lambert Foundation.

She looked again at the summary sheet Hale had provided. Excepting those not receiving monies from other sources, thirteen students, all Lambert scholars, their monies taken during the fall term. Would the thief attack again, going after another ten students, whose first names spelled out Foundation? During the current spring term? Or would he wait until right before the next fall term, thinking that no one would be watching after so much time had elapsed since the last thefts?

Eden grabbed the Post-it notes off Hale's desk and tossed them in the nearby trash can. She opened the door and leaned out. Shadows at the end of the hall told her Madison must have shut off the lights. From the other offices, she heard no conversation or the sound of printers or other equipment that the employees used. She stepped outside Hale's office, walked down the hall and confirmed that she was alone.

Eden returned to Hale's office, opened his laptop and pulled up all the names of the Lambert Family Foundation scholars for the current academic year. She began by selecting the students who first names coincided with the ten letters in question. She then ordered them by first letter: F, O, U, N, D, A, T, I, O, N—the subfiles that needed to be flagged for special attention. Eden's excitement grew. If their monies had not yet been stolen, could the professionals do something to protect them from attack? She hoped so.

She keyboarded a lengthy email describing what she had discovered, and attached the list of students who might now be in the crosshairs of the thief. She then noted in each year those students who'd received financial aid from the foundation, clumping the masters candidates, fifth- and sixth-year students, into a single batch. Added to the freshman through senior undergrads, that made five categories. Most such clusters included no more than ten names, some as few as three. Only the freshman students were more numerous, totaling twelve.

Finally, out of a sense of completeness, she saved the names of those who had received financial assistance from other sources into a separate file. She hit Save and then Send, and hoped that when Hale took an after-dinner break at the conference, he would check his email and get back to her. He'd be able to read what she'd found on his cell phone, but would he be able to do so without Andy looking over his shoulder?

She glanced at the wall clock. *Nearly six!* Eden gathered up Hale's paperwork, placed the files she'd been studying back into the cabinet and locked it. She then tucked her laptop into her shoulder bag, locked his office and pulled the outer doors closed, checking twice to make sure the latch had caught.

As Eden drove home, she pondered what to do next. Would Hale agree with her, would he contact the students whose scholarship funds might be in jeopardy, even if they hadn't yet been hacked? Would he alert the hacking experts to the names of the students she suspected might become future victims? Or would they simply wait until the thief struck again before taking action? Was it even possible to mark the student files she'd identified as probable victims in such a way as to catch the thief? If only she knew more about the anti-hacking process.

When Eden pulled up and parked, Lexi was sitting on the porch nursing the baby and looking like a benign Madonna as she watched over the other children playing with Racer in the side yard.

Eden plopped down next to her sister-in-law and gazed at the baby. "She looks busy."

Lexi giggled. "That she is. I'll let you hold her when she's done."

"Was it really crazy with all the children here?"

"No. I had the boys work on their homework right after you left. Ivory insisted that I read her favorite story. She said Meggie would like it, too."

"Which one was that?"

"*Green Eggs and Ham.*"

Eden laughed. "I should have guessed. She asked Hale to make her green eggs last Saturday."

"Did you get all your work done?"

Eden nodded. "I did. And I think I was right."

"About what?"

"For a long time, I've had this feeling that there had to be a link connecting the students whose money was taken. Hale and those hacker experts he's been working with seemed to pooh-pooh the idea. I wanted to look for myself and I think I found it. But I'm not sure what anyone can do with the information."

"What was the link?"

"Their first initials. When I put the first letters of their names in order from first theft to the most recent, I was able to spell out Lambert Family, as in Lambert Family Foundation. Only a few other students had their financial aid tampered with."

"Really?" Lexi's eyes widened. She shifted the baby onto her shoulder and began to pat her back. "But how does that get you any closer to finding who took the money?"

"I'm not sure. But it suggests to me someone with a grudge against the family or the foundation. I'm just glad my hunch panned out, that there was a pattern, even if it doesn't hold for all of the students who were affected."

"What are you going to do now—besides tell Hale?"

"I listed every student who received any level of financial help from the family foundation, no matter the amount, whose first initials complete spelling out F O U N D A T I O N. And there were only three names beginning with the letter F. If I'm right, they could be possible future targets if the thief is able to break in again."

"Not too many to alert beforehand?"

"No, but I'm not sure Hale would say something to the students. However, maybe he could get with the IT people and they could watch those accounts for any untoward activity." Eden help up her hands and Lexi handed over the snoozing baby.

"Oh, she's so cuddly," Eden exclaimed when Megan's head snuggled next to her neck and one tiny hand slid under her chin. Eden shifted her weight slightly then relaxed against the back of the porch seat. "She feels heavier than last week. She's gaining well?"

Lexi chuckled. "Two pounds already. At least on our home scale. Fletcher stepped on it alone, then had me hand her over and weighed himself again."

"Which explains why I see rolls on her arms." Eden lifted the baby's arm and kissed it.

"You look like you're going to enjoy doing that with your baby," Lexi remarked. "Or are you still worried about a CF diagnosis?"

"I'm trying not to focus on that. Hale keeps saying this baby will be fine and I hope he's right." She chuckled. "There's only one way to know, and that's to birth this basketball that's getting bigger every day. I felt like an overstuffed whale climbing the stairs to Hale's office."

Lexi smiled. "I remember. But look what I got as a reward."

"A beautiful baby girl. Hale said Chance doesn't seem to mind having a sister."

"No. But I expect he'll say he'd prefer a brother about the time she starts getting into his toys. Having Racer is a nice distraction. That dog seems to think he has to watch out for both of them. He usually sleeps on his bed under Chance's window. But the other night after he was asleep, Racer wandered into our room and lay down under Meggie's cradle."

"Ahh. I can't imagine how you manage with a new baby and that puppy, too."

"Racer has a typically sweet lab disposition and so far, this baby is pretty easy. Eats, sleeps, fills her pants. Rinse and repeat," she laughed.

"I suppose." Eden shifted the baby onto the top of her baby bump, the better to gaze at her. "Mom's right. She looks just like Fletcher when he was her age. Same color hair and lots of it, which Mom says he never lost. Think she'll end up becoming a lawyer, like her dad?" she asked with a grin.

"Whatever she wants," Lexi replied.

Eden sniffed. "I smell baked goods. Did you make cookies for the kids?"

"Monet brought them over. They're some of the ones we occasionally make for the younger set. We add a hidden ingredient in the cookies and label them 'Today's secret batch.' We tell them if they find the secret, we'll give them an extra cookie."

"I've seen that sign. What do you usually add?"

"Usually an extra-large white chocolate kiss. We don't add nuts to those cookies because so many children have nut allergies."

"And you hang a sign as an alert to the parents?"

Lexi nodded.

"A great idea. I wonder if Hale and those hacking pros could make some kind of announcement that the thief— assuming he's local —might see that would entice him to try to strike again." Eden grinned at Lexi. "I'll tell him I got the idea from you. If they decide to try it and it works, you'll be famous. I can see the headline now. 'The baker who caught the scholarship thief.'"

Megan began to stir, stretched her arms and yawned.

Lexi stood up. "Want me to take her?"

"I'm happy holding her as long as she's happy letting me."

"Then I guess that's a sign I should take advantage and get dinner on the table. You and your kids will stay and eat with us, won't you?"

"Sure. But there shouldn't be much to do. Didn't Kenny show you my note about the casserole? All you had to do was pop it in the oven."

"Which I did, and it smells like it will be ready soon. I'll just get the salad fixings if you'll call the kids in to get washed up. Fletcher should be here any minute."

Eden stood up, her niece cradled in her arms, the baby in her belly doing a jig on her bladder. Again. She waved at the boys who were taking turns with Ivory on the swing set. "Come on in, kids. Time to wash your hands. Racer can stay outside until we're done eating."

~ ~ ~

The next evening, Eden welcomed Hale home with a quiet smile and waited for the children, in their excitement, to finish their stories about what they had done in his absence.

After dinner, he asked, "How were your two days without me?" His kissed her once, twice, and pulled her down to sit with him on the couch. "Did our two ragamuffins wear you out?"

He glanced in the direction of Kenny's room, where both children were watching a new DVD.

"Not really. Yesterday, Lexi and I spent a lovely evening sharing Megan. The boys played outside and then collapsed on Kenny's bed. And the dog, too. Ivory insisted on a story as usual before she went to bed, her second of the day. Lexi read her one while I was at your office." She grinned. "Did you take a look at my email on your phone? The long one?"

"About the scholarship money? I did, although I didn't get a chance to really study the attachments. From what I did scan when Andy wasn't around, it looks like you're on to something."

"I'm glad you think so. It was all I could do not to call you and interrupt all those sessions you said you'd be attending to ask if you thought I might be right."

"I'll talk to the IT chief tomorrow."

"You're a good man, Hale Brinker," Eden declared.

"Oh? Why's that?" He smirked right before leaning forward and kissing her.

"You listen to your wife."

"Of course I do. Dad told me that's what smart men do."

Eden kissed Hale back. "Next time we see your dad, I'll tell him you learned that lesson well."

"Keep telling me that, I like hearing I'm appreciated."

"How was Andy on the drive down and back? Somehow, I doubt he was the most pleasant of passengers. Maybe you shouldn't have offered to drive. The train might have been easier."

Hale leaned back and closed his eyes. "I'd have still been stuck with him bending my ear about all the things that are wrong with the world. If it weren't for our health insurance and how much we need to take advantage of it this year, I'd look for another job. Not that your father would be all that happy if I quit. He seems to think I should be heading up the office, but that's not likely unless Andy leaves or resigns."

"I'm sure he'd understand, and I know Dad doesn't blame you for what happened."

"No, but in our last conversation I got the impression he thinks I'm somehow remiss for not having found the thief yet. He wants that criminal found and convicted."

Eden nodded. "My father, a law-and-order guy. But, Hale, if you create a reason for the hacker to strike again, you're sure to catch him with all that security apparatus in place."

"From your mouth to God's ears, hon. Come on, let's get the kids into bed."

~ ~ ~

After the children were tucked in and sleeping, Eden spread several papers on the dining room table and reviewed her detailed findings with Hale.

"Here's the list of students who also received Lambert money, some large, some small, and a couple of these—the ones with asterisks by their names—with full rides. I personally think they are at higher risk than the others."

"Only thirty-two names. From what you were saying, I thought there might be more."

"But these are the only ones the Lambert Foundation helped. Since that first set of names are linked as I showed you, I concluded these students' monies are still at risk. You just have to figure out a way to get the thief to strike again."

Hale stared at the names before raising his gaze to his wife's face. "Remind me again."

"Those IT professionals should attach something to each of those files, a kind of electronic buzzer that will alert you and them, or maybe just them, if anyone other than you goes into the file. You could call it the 'cookie caper.'" She grinned.

"Because?"

"Because it's what Lexi and Monet sometimes do. They add a surprise to certain batches of cookies. Any child who buys one and gets the surprise is entitled to a free cookie. In the case of these scholarship students, the surprise would be an electronic signal that the thief is at work *while* he's in there. So you can catch him in the act—you or Reggie or one of those outside experts."

"Interesting thought. Okay. I'll talk to Reggie first and ask if he can come up with an instruction that will alert us. If he can't do it, I'll see what the outside pros have to say about your idea."

"Good. Lexi and I decided we want to see the following headline in the college paper: 'Pacific Knoll Baker and Real Estate Office Bookkeeper Solve College Scholarship Caper.'"

She waved her arms in the air and twirled in a circle before plopping back down on the couch.

Hale chuckled. "How exactly do you plan to celebrate?"

"We'll come up with something. Maybe a daddy's day taking care of all the kiddies while Lexi and I indulge in a girls-only facial and mani-pedi day."

Hale hauled her back onto her feet and kissed her. "If your idea works, I'm happy to oblige. And I'm sure Fletch will support the cause."

Eighteen

Eden slid her legs over the side of the bed and pushed to her feet. Another Braxton-Hicks contraction, one of several that had wakened her through the night. She glanced at Hale, feeling his gaze on her as she breathed through another squeeze of her uterus.

"They're just practice ones, hon. I'm still more than a week away."

"Doesn't mean you won't go early this time," he countered, as he climbed out of bed.

"Not going to happen, since I didn't with the other two. My body practiced forever with Kenny and he was two weeks late. So was Ivory." She sighed, rubbed her right hip and pressed upward against her abdomen. "Although I wouldn't mind getting it over with. This baby—so active, and now these contractions. It's like my body needs more practice to push him out."

"Are you sure you want to go out to dinner tonight? We could stay home, maybe order in."

"It's your birthday, Hale. The kids want to make it special. They're the ones who said we should take you out to your favorite restaurant."

"As if I need to be reminded I'm a year older." He pressed his front to her back, his hands cupping her breasts. "Best present would be making you more comfortable. Next best would be getting that guy who stole the scholarship money." He breathed deeply, slid his hands down her sides and then stretched his arms toward the ceiling.

"He's sure to bite sooner or later. I thought it was a neat trick, you doing that interview on the campus station about how you were certain no one would ever be able to hack into any of the departments now that the new security is in place. Goading the thief to prove you wrong. Think it'll work?"

Hale chuckled. "I hope so, since those anonymous letters to the editor that we know weren't really anonymous didn't result in any action."

"Patience, honey. I'm sure your interview will do the trick." She waved him into the bathroom for his morning shower.

Eden fed the children and finished brushing Ivory's hair, affixing two barrettes to her ponytails.

After breakfast, Hale took a final sip of his coffee and headed for the door, laptop case in hand. "You'll meet me at the office this afternoon?"

She nodded. "We'll pick you up. Follow your father, kids. Time to go to school."

Tomorrow Hale planned to send out letters announcing the scholarships awarded for the next academic year. Eden hoped none of those students' accounts would be attacked. Hale had asked Reggie to pay particular attention to the students already receiving Lambert Foundation support. And, Hale had said he would add the new Lambert Scholars' names to the list of students Reggie had electronically targeted. If any of the alerts were activated between now and the fall term, Eden suspected the thief probably worked on campus, or knew someone who did.

She hated to think that the thief was someone Hale worked with. When he'd posed that possibility, she'd said, "I just want the person caught, whoever it is. Then everyone can relax, the students and their parents won't have to worry, and your name will be cleared. I still can't believe anyone would think you were behind all this."

~ ~ ~

That afternoon, Eden leaned against the railing to catch her breath after climbing the stairs to the hallway that led to Hale's office. In front of her, Ivory and Kenny had skipped up the steps, eager to see their father. She rubbed her right hip and waited until she wasn't breathing so hard, then opened the door to the finance office and waved the children in ahead of her.

Helen beamed on seeing them. "Hello, you two. Did you come to see your dad?"

Ivory trotted over to Helen's desk. "It's his birthday and we're taking him to dinner. Kenny and I got him something special. But my gift's specialer," she declared with a conspiratorial grin.

"I'm sure it is. Tell me about it." Helen stage-whispered as she leaned close to the little girl.

"No, I can't. It's a secret. Until Daddy opens it. 'Sides, Mommy has our gifts in the car."

Eden waved the children forward, and they headed for Hale's office.

Just before they arrived, he opened the door. "I thought I heard elephants gallumping down the hall."

Ivory giggled. "No elephants, Daddy. Just us." She jumped into his arms.

Hale set his daughter on her feet and said, "Kenny, you said you wanted to see what all those computer people do. I have to check in with one of the workers. Want to come with me? And, after that, I have a quick meeting with the president that shouldn't last more than ten minutes. But you'll have to be quiet as a mouse if you come along. Want to?"

Kenny beamed. "I'll be quiet."

"Are you sure the kids should come with you?" Eden asked.

"I doubt either meeting will be long, hon. President Ingraham just wants me to nail down something having to do with the June Convocation and the students whose special awards I'll be announcing."

Hale turned to Ivory. "What about you, babycakes? Want to come with me to see the computer lab and the president?"

"No. I'm going to draw you a picture."

"Then you stay with Mommy. Kenny and I won't be long."

Hale glanced at her as she rubbed her right side again. "More contractions?"

She nodded. "But not as strong. I wish this baby would settle down. He's been more active than yesterday."

"Probably doesn't like being squeezed," Hale replied.

She yawned and pointed to the old couch Hale had retained from his college days. Even with a new cover, it could stand to be replaced. "Maybe I'll lie down while you're in your meetings."

Hale kissed Eden, motioned for Kenny to follow him, and father and son left for the computer lab.

Eden leaned against the arm of the couch and took a deep breath.

"Okay, Ivy. Look in the bottom drawer of Daddy's desk for your coloring book and crayons. Can you get them?"

"I see them. He's a good daddy."

"Yes, he is. How about you sit in his big chair?"

"Yeah. I'll draw a quick picture, so it's all done when he comes back," she declared.

"Wonderful." Eden walked slowly out to the reception area. "How long do you plan to be here, Helen?"

The department secretary beamed. "I'm meeting with my daughter in a few minutes for some much-needed retail therapy, but if you want me to wait until Hale gets back, I could delay my departure. You look tired. I'll bet you can't wait to push that baby out."

Eden nodded. "I'm going to take a quick nap until Hale comes back. If Ivy wanders out here, could you chase her back to Hale's office? Right now, she's coloring, and…"

"No worries, Eden. Go rest. If Hale isn't back before I leave and you're asleep, I'll remind Ivory to stay with you."

"Is anyone else here? The office seems quieter than usual."

"I sent the interns home after lunch today. And Madison picked up the cold I was brewing earlier this month. Thank goodness, it's been slow this whole week, what with exams coming up. No sense keeping my workers here with nothing much to do."

"Then if no one else is here, I guess it won't matter if Ivory plays in the hall."

Helen glanced at her appointments calendar. "Did Hale tell you we have a pool going, some of us secretaries in the building, about what you're going to have and when?"

Eden snorted.

"I've got my money on next Tuesday, a boy, eight pounds on the nose, with brown hair like his daddy." Helen grinned. "There's more than twenty bucks in the kitty as of yesterday. And I have my eyes on a pair of sandals I'd love to buy."

Eden chuckled. "Please don't tell Ivory you're betting it's a boy. She wants a baby sister." She walked slowly back to Hale's office and closed the door.

"Ivy, I'm going to take a nap. Please stay in here with me, even if you finish your picture before your father comes back."

"Are you tired, Mommy?" Ivory didn't bother looking up as she busily scribbled a yellow cloud into the sky of her picture.

"Yes."

"Have a nice nap."

Same words I've used so many times. Eden stretched out on the couch. She pulled the afghan her mother had made over her shoulders, listened to Ivory's quiet murmurs and slowly drifted off.

~ ~ ~

Eden opened her eyes and looked around, at first confused about where she was. *Oh, right. Hale's office.* She listened for Helen's voice. Nothing. And where was Ivory?

Eden slid her feet onto the floor, pushed herself into a standing position, and sat back down when a contraction began a slide over her abdomen. Her bladder urged her onto her feet again. She padded into the hall and around Helen's desk in the direction of the women's room at the end of the other hallway.

A flushing toilet told her she'd found Ivory. The little girl stood on her tiptoes, trying to reach the faucet to rinse her hands.

"Let me help." Eden turned on the water then headed for a stall, but a contraction stopped her in mid-stride and she leaned against the wall until it passed. She emptied her bladder and rejoined Ivory at the sinks, aware of another building contraction.

"I think we better call your father, sweets. These pains mean business. Are you about done?"

"I need a paper towel."

Eden washed and dried her hands, pushed two towels into Ivory's grasp and began a slow waddle out the door, down the hall. She counted to ten and then twenty, determined to make it before being slowed by another contraction.

She took advantage of the secretary's absence to sit in Helen's chair for a long moment. If the contractions continued, she imagined they'd be delaying their dinner reservation for a trip to the hospital.

Ivory pushed open Hale's door and Eden followed her inside. But before she could retrieve her purse and rummage for her phone, she was shocked to see a young man bent over Hale's laptop.

When he realized he was no longer alone, he brushed past her and slammed the door, shutting the three of them in the room. "Damn! No one was supposed to be here!"

Eden stared at the young man as she tried to recall where she'd seen him before, when she'd seen him. His dirty-blond hair lay in unruly dreadlocks, and his face was pockmarked with acne scars. His red-rimmed eyes suggested he hadn't slept well or recently, and he was dressed in that casual unkempt look so many students effected.

A kick to Eden's bladder momentarily distracted her. "Who are you?" she asked as she gaped at him. *Andy's son? His eyes—he's high on something,* she concluded, as his fingers pounded the laptop keyboard even as another contraction began to build.

Then Ivory demanded, "Did you ask my Daddy if you can use his stuff? He says people have to ask first. He'll be mad if you didn't."

Eden reached for her purse, found her cell phone and quickly texted Hale. *Man in your office. Come back!* Before she could act on her decision to leave Hale's office, Eden groaned as a deep squeezing contraction nearly doubled her over. She forced herself into a standing position and reached for Ivy's hand. "Come on, hon. Let's go find Daddy," she whispered.

"But I didn't finish my picture." Ivory pressed her head into Eden's side.

"You can make him another one." Eden felt another contraction. She grabbed for the door handle, breathed through the pain and pulled the door open.

But her words must have registered with the stranger. Dreadlocks Guy seemed to realize he wasn't alone and his keyboarding stopped. He stepped close enough to grab her arm with his tattooed fingers and pulled her away from the door. "No! You can't leave! Not yet!"

Ivory slapped at the man's hand on Eden's arm and tried to push him away. "You let my Mommy go!"

At Ivory's shout, the young man Eden now felt certain was Anderson Randolph's drug-addicted son jerked her arm a second time and she fell heavily onto the couch. Another contraction moved up and over her uterus. She gasped at the intensity of the pain.

The laptop pinged, and Piers Randolph turned and hit three keys in response. When a second ping sounded, he muttered half under his breath, "Done. You stupid techie dweebs. Thought you were smarter'n me? That'll show you."

Eden struggled to stand again just as she felt a gush of warm fluid. She couldn't see her feet, but the rivulets of water sliding down her legs and onto the floor were unmistakable.

Ivory pointed to the floor. "Mommy, you had an accident!"

"No, sweets. Looks like the baby is on his way."

"But I want a sister," Ivory wailed.

Andy's son stared at her for a long moment, and chose to bolt. But as he pulled open the door, he collided with Hale.

"Stop him! He's—" Eden gasped out in the middle of another contraction. "I think he's An—" She waited for what felt like an eternity. "-dy's son. Who would have guessed," she murmured through a tight jaw.

Ivory released her lock on Eden's right thigh and aimed a kick at the young man in her shiny Mary Janes that she'd insisted on wearing to her father's birthday dinner. "You're a bad bad man!"

"Ivy, stop." Eden reached forward to pull her daughter away from Andy's son. His body odor made her want to retch, but she suddenly slipped in the puddle she'd created, fell backward, bumped against the couch and slid onto the floor.

Hale ducked to avoid the young man's fist. He lost his balance and rammed his shoulder into the wall before bouncing off Piers Randolph. Both men fell onto the hallway floor. Hale straddled Andy's son, then grabbed his arms and pulled them around to his back.

"Get off me!" Piers demanded.

"Nothing doing." Hale glanced up in time to avoid being hit a glancing blow by one of Ivory's arms as she yelled at the man who'd grabbed her mother and aimed another kick at his nearest leg.

"Ivory Maris Brinker!" Her father's command halted Ivory's attack in midkick. "Go sit on the couch! Now!"

"But, Daddy—"

Lowering his voice only slightly, he repeated, "Sit! And stop yelling." He spotted Kenny, wide-eyed, standing near the doorway. In a more controlled tone, he ordered, "Kenny, reach into my pocket, and grab my phone."

Kenny did so. He held the device out for his father.

"Dial 911 for me."

Kenny nodded. "The lady wants to know our emergency," and held the phone out again.

"Tell her we have a burglar. In the finance office. At Lambert-Knoll College. Ask her to send the police, and to call campus security."

Excitedly, Kenny relayed the message. He again pointed the phone at his father. "She says they're coming. But she wants to talk to you."

"Okay. Give me a sec." He released one the intruder's arms, pulled out a handkerchief and tied the man's wrists as his captive again tried to buck him off.

"You're not helping your case, kid. Lie still or I'll sic my daughter on you." For the first time since his arrival at the office, Hale glanced over his shoulder at Eden. "You okay, hon?" When she didn't reply, he twisted his body toward her, for the first time taking in her wet slacks and her uneven breathing.

He paled. "Jesus, Eden. Are you in labor?"

She nodded and tried to smile through the end of another waning contraction. "When it rains, it pours."

"Hang on, babe." He grabbed the phone from Kenny and spoke to the dispatcher. "Send an ambulance, too. My wife's in labor." He looked again at Eden. "She wants to talk to you."

But Eden shook her head and began breathing through another contraction.

"She can't talk right now! Hurry up with that ambulance, will you?" He listened to the dispatcher for a moment. "Okay."

After a prolonged silence during which Hale nodded, Kenny scooted past his mother and over to Ivory, who remained on Hale's couch, aiming death stares at the man on the floor.

Hale said, "Kenny. Go stand by the outside door. Hold it open so the police know to come in here."

Ivory slid off the couch and started to follow her brother.

"What did I tell you, Ivory?"

"But, I want to help like Kenny," she objected.

"Not now. Stay where you are."

Eden beckoned Ivory to her side. "Why don't you go to Helen's desk and bring me her box of tissues? That would be a big help."

Eden watched as Ivory nodded, squared her shoulders, and glared at her father as she sidled past him.

Had Eden not been in the midst of yet another contraction, she would have laughed out loud. "Oh, my. Here comes another big one."

Hale glanced her way as Ivory scampered out of the room to do her mother's bidding.

Commotion in the hall announced the arrival of a pair of city police officers, two college Security personnel and, right behind them, a pair of EMTs hauling a gurney. "Are you going to take him to jail, that man my dad's sitting on?" Kenny asked.

The police officers motioned for Hale to step away from Piers, who remained sprawled on the floor. An officer leaned down, cuffed the young man and removed Hale's handkerchief from around his wrists.

Hale bent over Eden. After a nod from her, he pulled her to her feet. "He's the one in your text?"

"Yes. You should tell Reggie."

He nodded. "I'll get with him later."

Eden leaned against Hale. "We were planning a nice dinner for you. But, I guess we'll be having a baby instead." Another contraction hit. Three minutes later, she slowly breathed out a cleansing breath and added, "Happy birthday, hon."

"Those contractions are coming fast." Hale motioned to the EMTs who entered. "Come on, kids. Stand back so they can help your mother. Over here, Kenny." He reached for his son and grabbed Ivory's hand to pull her out of the way.

The two police officers left, with Andy's son sandwiched between them.

Hale nodded at the campus security guards. "You might want to get with Reginald Shepherd in the IT office. He might still be there. I saw him about a half-hour ago. Even if he's left, call him. Tell him to check all the student files he's been following. If you don't mind, I'll give you a statement after I see to my wife. If you need it right away, you'll have to follow me to the hospital."

"We can wait," one of them said.

Hale leaned over the gurney on which Eden now lay. He kissed her. "I'll call Dr. Ortiz. Tell him we're bringing you in."

She nodded. "I never thought it would be Andy's son."

Hale followed the EMTs as they headed in the direction of the elevator. "I'm right behind you, hon. Just gotta lock up the office. Come on, kids. We're about to have a baby."

Eden waved at Hale and the children before the EMTs angled the gurney into the elevator. She closed her eyes and counted through the contractions that now seemed to come one on top of the other. Would she even make it to the hospital?

Nineteen

Hale tiptoed out of Eden's room, aware that it was almost midnight. After a labor that lasted less than four hours, she'd given birth to a baby boy, whose size helped explain some of Eden's pregnancy girth. Kenny and Ivory had each weighed in at what Hale had thought at the time was a healthy seven pounds. Looking back on it, his first two babies as newborns seemed kind of puny after checking out this kid, who was a hefty nine pounds ten ounces and twenty-three inches long! The baby reminded Hale of a tiny sumo wrestler. He wondered if this boy might grow up to be taller than him. Maybe from Eden's Lambert genes. After all, Fletcher was six-three.

The on-call pediatrician had reminded them that the routine blood draw included screening for CF, but that they shouldn't stop there. Their family doctor would order another blood draw at around ten days. And, the sweat test Eden asked about would be done sometime after two weeks. Dr. Shelby reminded Hale that newborns didn't sweat enough for the test to be reliable earlier than that.

But he was already hopeful. Relieved, too. Both the on-call pediatrician and Dr. Shelby, the Brinkers' family doctor, were confident that the blood tests would be negative after the baby passed a huge meconium stool an hour after his first nursing. Dr. Shelby reminded Eden that babies with CF often had difficulty passing that sticky first stool. Baby Garrett had had no problem filling his diaper.

As optimistic as the doctors were, Hale knew Eden wasn't likely to set her worries aside until all the tests came back negative.

Shortly after she gave birth and the baby had his first nursing, everyone arrived to see the newest Brinker and his proud parents. Within minutes, the birth center room was festooned with flowers, balloons and congratulatory cards. Lexi and Deb thoughtfully brought big brother-big sister gifts for Kenny and Ivory, too.

The children ate cafeteria snacks in Eden's room after everyone but Elaine left. Elaine, bless her, insisted on assuming babysitting duties at the Brinker household an hour after seeing the new baby. She motioned for the children to come with her after declaring that she didn't have to be at work until ten the next day. She would get the kids off to school, too. "Don't you worry about a thing, Hale. Stay as long as you like. I'll leave the porch light on for you."

Hale kissed the children good night and Kenny followed Elaine out of the room, but Ivory stood resolutely next to Eden's bed.

Hale pointed at the door. "Better get a move on, Ivy. Aunt Elaine's eager to get you and your brother home. It's way past your bedtime."

"I can't." She shrugged a shoulder in her mother's direction, who was cradling Garrett.

"Why is that?"

"He's still holding my hand. Real tight."

Hale confirmed her declaration with a nod. "I see."

Then she surprised Hale after all her talk about wanting a baby sister. "Can he sleep in my room when he comes home?"

"No, babycakes. His cradle will be in the big bedroom with me and Mommy. After he gets bigger, he'll sleep in the boys' room, with Kenny. You'll have your own room." *I need to get busy on whether we can expand into the attic.*

Her hopeful smile turned downward at the corners. "What if Kenny doesn't want to share his room?"

"He told you that?"

"Nooooo." She pursed her lips in a tiny pout. "But he might if you ask him."

Hale loosened Garrett's fingers from around Ivy's, patted her on the butt and held the door for her. "Go with Aunt Elaine. We'll talk about this later."

When the door closed and Ivory's chatter disappeared down the hall, Hale leaned over the bed and bussed Eden's forehead. "That daughter of ours. I have a feeling she's going to be a handful as a teenager."

Eden smiled tiredly. "As if she isn't already. See how he's wiggling? I think he wants to nurse again."

He tucked the baby's hand under the receiving blanket. "Did you hear the doctor? If you'd waited until your due date, this little guy probably would have weighed more than ten pounds."

Eden chuckled. "It was hard enough as it was, even though this birth was so much faster than the others." She glanced up at him. "You're okay that he's our last?"

Hale nodded. "Totally. Look at him—he's perfect. And half grown already!" He stroked the newborn's satiny skin as his arm rested next to Eden's cleavage.

"But what if—"

"Don't say it, hon. I have a good feeling about this. You heard what the doctor said. Garrett's eating well, has nursed how many times already? Three? Four?"

She yawned. "And with a really strong suck."

"To go with his size."

"Right. Go home, Hale. It's late." She shifted the baby to the other breast as the baby let out a series of complaining squeaks. "*Ssh* now," she murmured. "Just give me a minute."

"Impatient little bugger, isn't he?" Hale leaned down and kissed the top of the baby's head. "He's blond, like Ivory. Think he'll lose it?"

"Maybe." She closed her eyes. "Kenny did."

"Want me to ask the nurse to put him in the isolette for you?"

"No. I want him next to me for a while. Maybe you could put up the sides so I can tuck a pillow against them."

He did so then leaned over her again. He kissed her once, twice. "You did great, Eden. I'm so glad the birth is over. And I'm laying in a new supply of condoms. No more accidents. Or maybe I should get snipped." But he imagined his balls shriveling out of sight at the thought.

She grinned. "We have plenty of time to decide. I'll see you in the morning. And please drive carefully. It's been a long day—for all of us."

He nodded and left her room. The night air was bracing as he wandered the parking lot, looking for the car. He spotted it crookedly taking up a portion of three spaces, climbed in and sat for a moment, reliving the excitement of the baby's birth after an intense labor he knew he couldn't have endured. Hale turned the ignition key and headed home.

Five minutes later, a police siren shocked him into sitting up straighter behind the wheel. When the police car didn't pass him, he eased into the slow lane and stopped on the grassy shoulder.

"License and registration, please." The words may have been polite enough, but their tone suggested the officer was all business.

"Of course." Hale squinted out the window at the officer.

"Know why we pulled you over?"

"Uh, no. Don't think I was speeding."

"You were weaving all over the road. How about you climb out and show us you're sober," the second officer ordered.

Hale chuckled. "Only drink I've had tonight is coffee. Hospital sludge, actually." Todd had brought him a second cup before the family left Eden's room.

"Show me you can stand on one foot," the officer ordered. "You a doctor?"

Hale balanced on his left foot. "No. We just had a baby. Bigger than our other two. Almost ten pounds. My wife was awesome. So's he." He beamed at the officer.

His words brought an answering grin and a nod. "Huh. Well, you'd better take it easy or you won't be making it home to take care of your kids. Maybe we should follow you."

"No need." Hale said. "I'll be careful." He stared down the road, blessedly empty of cars. He continued on his way, aware that the police car remained behind him for several blocks before turning onto a side street shortly before he took a sharp left then a gradual right into his neighborhood.

The house was quiet when he entered. Elaine's note on the kitchen counter read, "Welcome home. Kids crashed around nine-thirty. If you're looking for a snack, don't touch your birthday cake, or you'll have to answer to Ivory. I'm on the couch. Please don't wake me. ☺"

Hale tossed the note into the trash and checked out the slightly lopsided cake with wobbly red letters spelling out "For Daddy!" on the chocolate icing. He looked in on the children. Kenny was buried in his covers, his pillow on the floor. Ivory was spread-eagled on her bed, one arm clutching her Winnie the Pooh stuffed bear, the covers in a lump at the bottom of her bed. Hale covered her up and entered the master bedroom.

He pulled off his clothes and lay down, tears sliding down his cheeks as he recalled the emergence of his newest son from Eden's body. A miracle it was. As special as when he'd been present for Kenny's and then Ivory's birth. The last miracle he would help create. Now, if only all those tests came back negative. Then he would feel doubly blessed.

~ ~ ~

In his pajamas the next morning, Hale kissed the children good-bye and watched as Elaine drove them to school.

When she returned several minutes later, she joined him at the kitchen table. "I see you ate the last waffle."

"There's some batter left. Want me to fix you one?" he offered.

"No. I'm fine." She gave him a sidelong glance. "What's going on at your office? Shortly after we got home, a detective showed up, wanting to talk to you and Eden. I told him you were at the hospital and not to bother you. Then Ivory told him it was a boy."

"Leave it to Ivy," Hale snorted. "What else did she say?"

"When he mentioned your office, she said a bad man grabbed Eden and wouldn't let them leave your office. Oh, and that you sat on his back until the police came."

Hale chuckled. "That's about right. Did the detective leave a card? I'll call him, tell him he can get a statement from Eden and me today."

"Here." Elaine handed him a business card. "Think he'll wait until Eden's home?"

"He'd probably prefer to talk to her as soon as possible."

"What do you know about that guy Ivy mentioned?"

"Eden said he's Andy's son, but I was sure he was in drug rehab. Last time I saw him, he had short hair, home-made tattoos and a really bad attitude. His attitude was still bad, but now he has long dreads."

Eden nodded, departed for the guest bathroom and shortly thereafter, Hale heard the shower.

He picked up his phone. "Detective Walsh, my name is Hale Brinker. I understand you came to the house last night to speak with me and my wife."

"Yes, Mr. Brinker. Congratulations on the new baby. Your daughter filled me in with some particulars." His voice contained hints of humor.

Hale smiled. "I'll bet she did. Eden's not home yet, and I'll be at the hospital within the hour. You could get both our statements there. My wife probably knows more than I do, since I came in toward the end of all the excitement."

"I'll see you there."

~ ~ ~

Hale entered Eden's room in the midst of what sounded like a heated exchange between her and his mother-in-law.

What I hate most, running interference between Edie and her mother, he thought. Aloud, he said, "Iona. Morning. Any chance you could lower the volume? So everyone in the hall can't hear you?"

Iona frowned, but complied. "I was just making a point."

Eden brushed a tear away. "And I'm done talking about it. Time for you to leave, Mom."

"But I haven't even held my newest grandson," she protested.

"Because you've upset him and me!" Eden's voice rose again. She looked Hale's way, pleading in her gaze, as she tried to settle her wailing baby.

He opened the door and motioned for Iona to leave. "You'll have plenty of opportunities to hold him after we get home."

Iona must have sensed Hale wasn't going to change his mind. She left Eden's room with a quiet huff.

Hale leaned over the bed and kissed Eden. "What was that all about? And why do you let her upset you like that?" He handed her a tissue.

Eden sniffed. "Can you believe it? She actually hinted that we should leave Garrett in the hospital until all the tests are done. As if that would make things easier." Her sniffs turned to a full-blown sob. "How dare she ask to hold him after saying that!"

Hale took the baby from her, soothed him with several pats of the baby's back, and tucked him into the isolette, still complaining, though at a lower volume than before. He pulled a chair closer to Eden's bed, the better to pull her upright and into his arms. "Hey, hey. Forget about what your mom said. She was thoughtless, as usual. And look. He's settling down already. Just needs to sleep off what his grandmother said. I'll bet the little guy was just trying to tell her she was nuts, that he wants to go home so he can hold Ivy's hand again. Maybe even punch his big brother in the shoulder. Like your brothers do."

"Oh, Hale," Eden cried. She blew her nose and wiped her eyes a second time before reaching out for a hug, which he was happy to provide.

"How'd you two do last night? Get any sleep? Not that I expect him to do much of that when we get him home." He grinned at her.

"He mostly nursed and slept and slept and nursed. And gave me another big dump this morning. The nurse cleaned him up while I took a shower. I'm keeping my fingers crossed that it's a good sign. A sign that he's normal."

"Of course he is, as much as a baby wrestler can be normal," Hale huffed out with a laugh. "At the rate he's nursing, he'll be twenty pounds by next week!"

"Oh, Hale," she repeated, hugging him tighter before she laughed against his chest. "You are the best possible medicine."

He glanced at the baby who was waving an arm as if to gain his parents' attention. "Looks like he's decided he wants breakfast now. Or is it again?"

Hale slipped his arm under the swaddled baby and lifted him out of the isolette and into Eden's arms. "You up to talking to a detective about what happened yesterday?"

"I suppose." She settled the baby at her breast. "I'm not going anywhere. Dr. Shelby's already been here. He wants me to stay until tomorrow."

Hale stroked her arm. "I told the detective who called the house last night that he could get both our statements if he comes here. You'll have to fill me in on what happened while I was with President Ingraham."

"He was Andy's son, like I thought? I'm so hoping he wasn't a student. The way he talked I'm hoping he wasn't. But he used the same weird words you said Andy used after those early meetings with those campus IT people. 'Techie dweeb' is what I remember." She paused, reached for her water glass and sipped.

A knock sounded.

Hale opened the door. A man with dark auburn hair, a detective's badge in hand, entered.

"Detective Walsh?" Hale asked.

"Mr. and Mrs. Brinker. Thank you for seeing me." He turned toward the bed where Eden had covered up. "Congratulations on the new baby." He glanced at the bundle in her arms.

"Thank you," Eden replied.

"Have a seat, Detective," Hale offered, standing away from the only chair in the room. "Who do you want to talk to first? Want me to leave?"

"No need. I'll start with Mrs. Brinker, if you don't mind. I already heard from your daughter." He smiled. "Just to be clear, we don't interrogate children without parental permission. Her aunt was present. And your daughter volunteered her impressions of everything that happened."

Eden grinned. "I'm sure she did. What do you want to know?"

The detective pulled out a notebook and sat down. He walked Eden through the events of the preceding day, asking her to start with when she arrived at Hale's office, why she and Ivory were there and what she heard and saw.

He then turned to Hale and asked him similar questions.

"Have you talked to the campus security people?" Hale asked. "We've been trying to find out who's been hacking into our offices for months. The IT people concluded it was all being done remotely, using what they call intercept software. They set up hidden cameras, too."

"I spoke with" —Walsh flipped back several pages in his notebook— "a Mr. Reginald Shepherd. Said he was meeting today with some other people experienced in remote hacking. That they were able to halt the tampering going on yesterday. He was actually at his terminal when it all went down. And he's eager to talk with you." The detective nodded and stood up. "Oh, and he said that your wife was right about the next student who might be hacked. Someone whose first name began with an F."

Eden beamed broadly. "Yes!" she said under her breath.

"So he'll be charged with grand theft?" Hale asked.

Walsh nodded. "You could also charge him with assault, since your daughter claims he threatened her and your wife."

Hale gave him a rueful smile. "Given that Ivory tried to kick him, I think we'll leave her out of this." He glanced first at Eden then returned his gaze to the detective. "Which means she won't have to testify. Right? She's only five."

Detective Walsh laughed. "You've got a real pistol there, Mr. Brinker. Grand theft—based on the amount Mr. Shepherd claims to have evidence of him attempting to divert—should be sufficient to send him to jail for a long time."

"We'll talk with Ivory about keeping her mouth shut."

"Good luck with that," Detective Walsh deadpanned. "I have a daughter, too. She just turned ten. Keeping her mouth shut isn't exactly one of her strong suits, either."

Eden giggled.

"If I have any other questions, I'll be in touch." Detective Walsh gave them a casual salute and left.

Twenty

Eden burst into tears. "You're absolutely sure?"

"Both blood test results were negative. The sweat test, too." Dr. Shelby smiled. "If you want us to repeat the sweat test, we can do that, but I don't feel it's necessary."

"Eden, look at me," Hale said. "You can stop worrying now. Garrett's doing great. And didn't you hear what Dr. Shelby said? At four weeks, he's gaining every day, is only two ounces from twelve pounds. Kenny wasn't that big until he was almost four months old."

She nodded and wiped her eyes before cuddling baby Garrett against her chest. She lifted him higher in her arms. He snuggled his head into her neck and sighed.

The doctor patted the baby's back. "We can all relax that he doesn't have a single sign of Cystic Fibrosis. You can still run that DNA test on him like you did for the older kids. He could be a carrier like Ivory. But I say, enjoy him. The way he's eating, it's no wonder you're back to your prepregnancy weight already."

Dr. Shelby beamed at Hale and headed for the door. "Eden, be sure to make an appointment for his first set of shots when he's two months old."

Hale slid his arm around Eden as she redressed Garrett in a blue-and-white striped onesie with a pair of baseball bats decorating the chest. He recalled that Kenny had worn it, too. "He's healthy, Edie. Totally. Growing like a weed, and you're shrinking just as fast. Come on. Let's grab some fixings at the bakery and celebrate with a picnic lunch. Didn't Lexi say she and Monet have expanded their sandwich menu? A perfect excuse to eat in the park over by the kids' school."

"I thought you had to get back to work." She slid her purse into the diaper bag and watched as Hale picked up Garrett in his carrier.

"I'll text Helen that I've been unavoidably delayed." He grinned. "If we eat slowly, we could pick up the kids and then go back to my office. Helen's been asking when you'd bring the baby for her to admire. Even though she missed winning the pot because he was so much bigger than she thought."

"Who did win?"

He shook his head. "Don't recall. Might have been Madison."

"Okay. First the bakery for lunch stuff, then the kids, and then your office to show off Garrett."

Minutes after leaving the doctor's office, Eden and Hale walked into the bakery. Lexi, her baby daughter in a backpack and peeking over her shoulder, was chatting with a grandmotherly type at the register. She waved. "Be right with you."

"Take your time," Hale said as he scanned the sandwich menu. "Edie, I'm inclined to grab one of those salmon po'boys. What's your pleasure?"

"Make it two, and how about four of those double chocolate brownies? Two for us, one each for the kids." She took a seat next to the window and watched Lexi fill several orders.

He nodded, grabbed a pair of water bottles from the refrigerator and gave his order to Lexi. "Looks like Megan enjoys working with you, Lexi."

She laughed. "She's good in the mornings, but she tends to turn grouchy after lunch. That's when I leave her with a sitter."

"At home?"

She shook her head. "No, Maira comes here after her one o'clock class and watches Meggie upstairs in our old apartment. Monet decided it makes sense to use it as babysitting central, at least until Meggie's weaned and I don't have to take nursing breaks. When Chance doesn't have soccer practice, he comes here, too. He can play games with Maira or do homework. She's teaching him chess on an old board her grandfather carved. She brought it with her when her family fled Syria."

Eden nodded. "Maybe we could share babysitters after I go back to work? I'm still not sure if I want to ask Quincy if I can work at home, or just go in a couple hours a day I'm no longer on maternity leave."

"I'm sure Maira won't mind. She's really good with my two," Lexi replied.

Hale picked up the sandwiches Lexi had wrapped and placed in the bag along with the brownies. "Sounds like a great arrangement."

"My acknowledgement that I can't do it all every day." Lexi waved at them. "Enjoy your lunch, you three," she said. "Will we see you at your mom's on Sunday?"

"We'll be there," Eden replied. *With good news about Garrett. Finally.* She glanced at Hale and smiled.

~ ~ ~

Eden followed Hale and the children into the office.

"Helen," she announced. "We're here to show off the baby after his four-week check-up."

"Oh, my! And look at you, Eden. A regular Skinny Minnie, you are. Let me guess. You must be feeding that baby every hour on the hour." She pulled away the blanket draped over a sleeping Garrett. "Wow! Hale said he was big at birth. Think he'll be ready to join the freshman class this fall?" She laughed.

Ivory nodded. "He's big 'cause he nurses *all* the time! Even more than Kenny and me when we were babies." She beamed up at Helen.

"Want to hold him?" Eden offered. "He's a lot heavier than you think."

"Such a pretty baby, too. All that blond hair! Where does he get that, Eden?" Helen exclaimed.

"Hale's parents, where Ivory got hers," she chuckled. "Both his parents were blonds as children. Hale, too. Then it darkened to brown. We'll have to see if Garrett's does that, too."

Hale handed Kenny his office key. "Go ahead and open my office door. Ivy, you go with your brother. We'll be there in a sec."

Eden watched as the children trotted down the hall. She leaned closer to Helen. "Hale said Andy's on sabbatical."

Hale picked up the baby blanket as it slid out of Helen's arms and onto the floor.

"Which reminds me." Helen turned toward her desk, picked up an envelope and handed it to Hale. "President Ingraham's secretary brought this up right before lunch. He'd like you to stop by his office. I was going to call you, but then you said you'd be in to show off the baby."

"Thank you, Helen." Hale opened the envelope and motioned for Eden to follow him. "Let's see what the kids are getting into."

Eden looked at Helen as she rocked the sleeping baby. "As long as you're okay holding him for a couple minutes, I'll go with Hale. But if he starts to fuss, let me know you need rescuing."

She caught up with Hale as he entered his office. "What's the letter say?"

He handed it to her, looking dazed.

Eden scanned the letter quickly, her pulse jumping at certain words. She then reread it slowly before handing it back to her husband. "Oh, my. He wants you to tell him what you prefer." She gripped Hale's hand, which felt unaccountably cooler than usual. Was he in shock?

Hale gazed at Eden, his green eyes taking on a sheen. For a moment, he glanced at the children. Ivory was busily coloring, having taken over one corner of Hale's desk, against which she leaned. Kenny sat in Hale's big chair, slowly swiveling in a circle. "Kids," he said. "Your mother and I will be right outside. You stay here."

Kenny nodded.

"Ivy, did you hear me?" Hale asked.

She looked up and nodded. "Okay, Daddy."

Hale grasped Eden's elbow and backed out of the room, shutting the door behind him. His voice low, he said, "You know I was thinking of finding another job, one that pays better. After all the difficulties we've had this year, and Andy acting so weird. It seemed I'd never really be able to be my own man here. You know, run the department like I think it should be run." He gulped. "But now?" He shook his head and waved the letter.

"Why don't we talk to Roger? You can ask him what he has in mind. Certain parts of his letter … I'm not sure what he means." She pointed to the paper dangling between Hale's fingers.

He nodded.

Together they walked back to Helen's desk in time to hear Garrett starting to tune up.

"Perfect timing," Eden said, gathering him up and propping him against her shoulder. "You showed him off to everyone, Helen?"

She beamed. "Oh, yes. We're all just amazed that you grew such a big child, Eden."

"He wasn't this big at birth."

"Almost," Hale countered with a chuckle. "Helen, the kids are in my office. Will you chase them back in there if they come out looking for us? We won't be long, but we need to talk to President Ingraham."

"Of course. Don't worry about a thing. Madison brought in some cookies that her mother made. Is it okay if I give the kids one? Don't want to spoil their dinner."

Eden nodded. "They'll like having a treat. But only one. Ivory is certain to ask for more."

Eden and Hale walked downstairs to the president's office. When they were ushered into the large corner office, she took a seat on the couch near the windows and let the baby suck on one of her fingers.

Hale remained standing, looking down at the letter.

When Roger Ingraham closed his door, smiling, he said, "I was hoping you'd make time to see me today." He glanced at Hale's letter. "I chose to be deliberately vague, knowing you'd feel the need for clarification."

Hale nodded.

Eden's pulse picked up. Was her husband going to turn the man down? She knew he'd been unhappy for months, frustrated really, especially because it had taken so long to identify the thief who'd stolen all that scholarship money, only some of which was recovered. And only because Reggie had been alerted to what Andy's son was doing the day she went into labor. At least those monies hadn't been diverted from their rightful recipient.

She leaned back and settled Garrett at her breast, glad that the blouse she'd worn today allowed for easy access while still covering key portions of her anatomy. She glanced down at the baby as he began to gulp, each exhale ending in a tiny squeak.

When she looked up, the president was smiling at her. His attention returned to focus on Hale as he sat next to Eden.

"I gather you knew I was looking around," Hale said.

Roger Ingraham nodded. "I wasn't surprised. Being asked discreetly for my opinion as to your accomplishments here, and your work ethic, wasn't something I wanted to provide if it meant you wouldn't remain an important part of the administration. But, of course, I answered their questions fully."

Hale's brows rose. "But I never got around to making any official applications. May I ask who approached you?"

"Doesn't matter unless you're intent on leaving. Face it, Hale. I could name a number of people in several business operations here in Pacific Knoll as well as farther afield who would benefit from your skills, your level of expertise. I'll just say that one was someone you've approached to provide financial aid for our students. The people who approached me were hopeful that you might be looking for a better gig than what you have here. And, much as I hated to encourage them, I provided the information they sought." He paused and folded his hands on his desk.

"At the same time I was clear that I hoped you wouldn't receive an offer from them, even unofficially. At least, not until I had an opportunity to speak with you. What with all the difficulties you were dealing with, I didn't feel I could do so until now.

"Let me be clear. I don't want you to leave. Nor do any of the Board of Regents. As much as you and Andy did your best to keep things under wraps, word got out about the hacking we suffered. As well as how you were dealing with it, the students directly affected and their parents, to say nothing of the aid sources whose money was stolen."

Hale nodded. "Good thing it was only two grantors that were affected."

"Yes, and it was too bad that most of the monies came from your father-in-law's foundation."

"Fortunately, he doesn't hold me responsible," Hale huffed out with a chuckle. "I'm sure Eden had a word or two with him about that when we were in the middle of that mess."

"I didn't have to," Eden interjected quietly from her spot on the couch. "You know Dad trusts you, Hale. Both of you know that," she added, gazing at President Ingraham.

"Yes, well …," Roger began. "So, what are your thoughts about the subject of that letter?"

"I'm interested." He paused and looked over his shoulder at Eden. "But with a growing family …, even after you corrected my delayed promotion money." He glanced back at the president. "I'm sure you understand why I felt the need to look around, to test the waters, if you will."

"Of course, and that's why I was hoping you'd ask me for the details. As you can see from that letter, the Board of Regents has authorized me to offer you the Chair of the finance office. Your salary will, of course, be raised commensurate with your increased responsibilities."

Hale was silent as he stared again at the letter.

Eden sucked in a quick breath. *What Hale's been eager to assume so that he could put into place all those plans he wasn't able to get Andy to agree to.* But would Hale take what the president was offering? Could Hale feel her gaze on the center of his back?

Roger continued. "In addition, in recognition of all your work with the IT people, as well as what you were doing *before* they came on board to improve security campus-wide, but especially in your office, they insisted upon offering you a substantial bonus." Roger reached into the center drawer of his desk and pulled out an envelope. "Mr. Shepherd in the IT office, and the representatives of those people outside the college whom Ms. Bedrossian insisted on hiring, were impressed with Eden's puzzle-solving skills. Another reason the Board members were hoping this will assuage at least some of the angst you were experiencing when Anderson was fighting your efforts, to say nothing of the last several months when you were doing all you could to find the thief."

Roger acknowledged Eden with a wave of his right hand. "And you were right, Eden. Mr. Randolph's son had it in for those other two students. The police informed me he told them why their money was the first to be taken. They threatened to turn him in when he was selling dope to other students."

Eden nodded in acknowledgement. "I've always liked solving puzzles, Roger."

"For which we are extremely grateful."

"Do you know why he went after the Lambert Scholars?" Eden asked.

"I understand Piers Randolph wanted to give the Lambert Family Foundation a black eye in the eyes of the entire academic community. Not that he succeeded, and his father shouldn't have allowed it to continue when he realized what was going on."

Eden gasped. "Andy knew?"

"It's my understanding that he was as much in the dark as anyone in the beginning." Roger Ingraham turned his gaze on Hale. "You're probably aware he's also being investigated by the police. We'll probably learn more about Andy's complicity after his son goes on trial, but it appears that Andy provided at least some assistance. I suspect it had something to do with keys to the office, that sort of thing. Detective Walsh chose not to share the details with me when the police scoured his office. If it's any comfort, his conscience got the better of him toward the end. That's why he used some of the money his son stole from the Lambert Foundation to cover the undocumented student who's in sanctuary at the church. Those professionals who were working with Reggie could probably tell you more about how Piers managed to break into your subfiles.

"Oh, and at my request, Anderson tendered his resignation a week ago Friday, effective that day. I prevailed on Helen not to tell you, to call it a sabbatical until we knew how you might respond to our offer. Knowing you were on parental leave and busy at home with Eden and your new baby, I opted not to bother you with the details."

The president handed the second envelope to Hale. "Feel free to accept this with our thanks. I'd appreciate if you'd get back to me about your decision regarding the Chairmanship by the end of the week. However, if you intend to explore other avenues for your skills, if you decide you need more time, let me know when you feel you can get back to me."

Hale shook his head at the news. "I haven't read a word about Andy's sabbatical. In the local paper or the campus weekly. How'd you pull that off?"

"I referred the detective to the campus newspaper advisor when they caught wind of Anderson stepping down. Don't know how that got out so quickly. And I have no control over what the *Pacific Knoll Daily* prints, so it's anyone's guess why neither paper hasn't moved forward with what I suspect they would consider a scoop." Roger winked. "Maybe the college paper is waiting to print that you have accepted the chairmanship in Andy's place." He beamed.

Hale nodded and took a seat next to Eden. He showed her the check and she gasped, her gaze shifting to President Ingraham. "That much?"

"It seems a small recompense for all the hassles your husband had to put up with, not just lately, but ever since Anderson was promoted to head the finance office. He wouldn't have been my preference, if you must know, but he was selected before I assumed the presidency."

Hale glanced at Roger. "Oh. So, you know about Andy's, um, reluctance to enact my early attempts to expand our financial aid program, to improve our security system? Even though—"

Roger nodded. "Presidents sometimes have to use back channels. I'd never call them spies, but I have my ways," he uttered in a halfhearted attempt at an eastern European accent.

"Should you decide to head up the finance office— and that's my fervent hope —you should be able to move into Andy's office upon giving me your decision."

"If it's all the same with you, I'd prefer to stay in my current office. I like that it's at the end of the hall." Hale grinned.

"So noted." President Ingraham held out his hand and Hale shook it heartily. "I'll wait for your official response to my letter."

Hale nodded. "You'll have it by the end of the week. Maybe sooner. And thank you." He waved the check in the air. "For this, too. It will be my pleasure to send a thank-you to the Board of Regents."

Eden rose and handed the baby off to Hale. She shook Roger's hand and then gave him a quick hug. "I can see why my father was so pleased when you agreed to assume the presidency of Lambert-Knoll College. You do us all proud."

He acknowledged her words with a humble bow, saw them out and retreated into his office.

When Hale and Eden entered the hallway, he said, "Let's take the elevator. Even though it's only one floor up."

They hit the button, entered and he closed the doors, but did not touch the second floor button. Instead, he pulled Eden into his arms, with baby Garrett sandwiched between them on his mother's shoulder, and held her close. His kiss began as a tender, loving caress that slowly turned passionate. "Good news all around, don't you think?" he murmured before nibbling her left ear lobe. "What do you think, hon? Should I accept the chairmanship? It means another raise. And this check, too. Which feels like a new kitchen, and maybe even a renovation of the attic. Should we call Chris over for a chat about making some of those improvements you've been dreaming about for years?"

"That's a wonderful idea." She kissed him once, twice, three times and would have continued, except that someone knocked on the elevator door.

Hale hit the button for the second floor and called out, "Sorry. It'll be back down soon."

"Where were we before we were so rudely interrupted?" he whispered as the elevator slowly rose. After capturing her mouth again, he murmured, "You are my most precious love, Eden Marie Lambert Brinker. My wife, first, last and always. Beloved mother of our children. The woman I'm looking forward to spending the rest of my life with."

"Oh, Hale," she replied, not caring that tears slipped down her cheeks.

They were still in a clinch when the elevator doors opened on the second floor, surprising a flabbergasted Helen, who was holding the hands of the two older Brinker children.

# # #

Thank you for reading this book. My characters reflect the life experiences of people I know. Perhaps also, people you know, or even yourself! A reader's greatest gift to an author is a review. If you enjoyed this story, please post a brief review on Goodreads.com and/or your other favorite social media sites.

Questions for Book Clubs and Reading Groups

1. If you took time off to raise children before returning to the work force, how was your return influenced the your family situation? In what way(s) do Eden's struggles reflect your own and/or other women you know?

2. How does Eden's reaction to her unexpected pregnancy reflect other women in the same situation? Were you in the same situation, would you have reacted similarly? Differently? Why?

3. Hale has his own frustrations at work. He's been promoted, but has yet to receive the increase in pay that was supposed to come to him. What should he have done immediately upon finding that his pay wasn't increased? Should he have waited as long as he did to learn what happened? Why do you suppose he waited?

4. How would you characterize Hale's immediate supervisor? If you were in Hale's shoes, what would you do to keep things moving in a positive direction at work?

5. Debra calls all the adult Lambert sibs over for a family meeting. Was her reason for doing so appropriate? Were you a member of that family, how would you react to the news she offers?

6. If you were in Eden's shoes, would you have insisted on asking the doctor for an amniocentesis? Why or why not?

7. Things go from bad to worse at work and Hale is sent home. Were you in his situation, how would you have handled things?

8. Should Hale have confided in his father-in-law about his troubles at work when they first came to light? Why or why not?

9. When Eden gets her job, she chooses not to share that she's pregnant. Do you agree that this news was no business of her employer?

10. When Eden finally shares her news that she's pregnant, should she have immediately begun negotiations about what she would do after the baby was born?

11. Eden goes to Hale's office and discovers something that she is certain will help the IT experts find out who is stealing the scholarship money. How was it that she made that discovery when neither Hale nor the IT experts did so?

12. When Eden encounters the thief and suddenly realizes who it is, how do you think she feels?

13. Eden goes into labor in the midst of encountering the thief. Is she right that "when it rains, it pours?"

14. What do you know about cystic fibrosis? Do you know any families contending with this disease? How would you react if one of your children was so afflicted?

15. Are the college president's actions following the catching of the thief and Hale's promotion to head of the finance office appropriate? In what ways might his actions keep Hale working at the private college instead of seeking a position with a higher salary?

About the Author

Kate Vale lives in the beautiful fourth corner of north-western Washington state. She enjoys the slower pace of a small city located between Vancouver BC, and Seattle WA. Her stories reflect the many different careers she has experienced and some of the challenges that confront real men and women. Helping her characters get to a happily-ever-after is a continuing goal.

Reviews, a link to her blog and first announcements of new titles appear on her webpage: http://katevale.com. Feel free to visit it.

You can contact Kate at katevale@sent.com,
find her on Facebook at
https://www.facebook.com/kate.vale.127,
tweet her at http://twitter.com/katevalewriter; or,
on Google+ at katevalewriter@gmail.com

www.ingramcontent.com/pod-product-compliance
Lightning Source LLC
Chambersburg PA
CBHW051424170626
46809CB00006B/2302